Praise for Roger Croft

Croft's world of double dealing and treachery, with a suggestion of indifferent, manipulative bureaucrats, confirms the dour observation of a veteran spymaster that loyalty among spies verges on being an oxymoron. Croft's moral wilderness and compilation of treachery ring far truer than the glamour of James Bond. And the clash between romance, personal loyalty and institutional duplicity bears the stamp of one who knows.

Publishers Weekly [Starred Review]

Croft once again intrigues his reader with this fast-paced sequel… Tightly written and laden with dramatic tension, Vaux's quest for truth and freedom is constantly tested, especially when his own friends become less and less trustworthy and his own safety is further compromised. Surprises lurk behind every character in this original storyline fraught with suspense…A suspenseful, behind-the-scenes look at espionage and politics…a web of secrets and betrayal, sure to grab spy novel fans.

Kirkus Reviews

Operation Saladin is an amusing read and may please fans of the spy genre, particularly those who take the professionalism of the secret services with a pinch of salt. One thing Croft does well is character study.

Beirut

D1398602

Our protagonist Michael Vaux is not a career intelligence officer—he's a retired journalist, independent-minded, and seemingly never without a drink in his hand...The plot is elaborate and takes the reader down countless blind alleys. But the reader would be hard-pressed to foresee the final outcome.

Egyptian Gazette, Cairo

Croft's style of writing is perfectly matched to the rhythm of a good spy novel. *The Wayward Spy* takes the best of spy novels from the likes of John Le Carre and kicks it up a notch...Wayward this spy might be but I couldn't put the book down.

San Francisco Book Review

Croft's principal characters fit the story line. This one is not what I would call a page-turner, more Le Carre than Clancy, but there are times when it is nice to have a protagonist with a brain and sentiments. One thing about Croft is that he writes females in a more realistic fashion than many male authors in this genre.

Linda Root, critic and novelist

The love of Vaux's life, Alena, Syrian born and beautiful, returns in this sequel and appears much more complicated than originally thought. Vaux also becomes her prey. *Operation Saladin* is a terrific follow-up to Croft's first spy novel...

Brian Taylor, Portland Book Review

* * *

WAREHOUSE
OF SOULS

* * *

WAREHOUSE OF SOULS

A New Michael Vaux Novel

ROGER CROFT

Cassio Books International
Cover: Concept by Adam McCrum

ISBN: 1547077271
ISBN-13: 9781547077274

To Geordie and Yolotl Rose and newly arrived Evelyn—
for times and places and friendship

* * *

OTHER BOOKS BY ROGER CROFT

The last temptation is the greatest treason:
To do the right deed for the wrong reason.
—T. S. Eliot (1888–1965)

PROLOGUE

Nobody at Vauxhall Cross could recall the first betrayal. But after the sixth gruesome killing of an undercover agent operating in the turbulent political waters of Lebanon, even the cautious mandarins who ran the queen's secret intelligence service finally came to an inevitable consensus: something had to be done.

The decision made, the minions were ordered to act with alacrity and to produce a strategy plan "soonest." Imaginations were set free, conferences behind the securely locked doors of debugged rooms were held, and airtight secrecy was of the utmost importance—code for keep the planning and proposed execution under tight wraps and away from all potential adversaries and, just as important, friendly but curious parties including the ever-present, probing Yanks.

Sir Percival Bolton, director general of the UK's Secret Intelligence Service, usually referred to as the DG or by older hands as C, observed his orders percolate through the labyrinthine channels at MI6's riverside fortress with some equanimity, for he had already worked out the solution to the problem: unilateral action. He would do what his trusty instinct told him would get the job done. In all his years of trudging Whitehall's corridors of power, his basic, off-the-cuff instinct had served him well. And he didn't see the latest crisis as any different from previous panicky alarms and excursions. Damn the special committees, the internal inquiries, the pondering, eternal inquests.

So, as he observed the haze of a warm summer evening begin to lift from the turbid Thames, a resolute Sir Percy picked up his secure phone and punched in the three-number contact code for the head of Department B3, a specialist group of field agents, hived off several years ago from MI6's increasingly over-manned and cumbersome Mideast and North Africa desk.

Chapter 1

HERTFORDSHIRE, ENGLAND
JUNE 2010

The pub's landlady stood behind the long oak bar as she slowly wiped the beer glasses and looked over to the two quiet men who ten minutes earlier had waited impatiently while she struggled with the brass keys to open the three mortise locks of the main door.

She knew one of them well enough all right, but his companion, a tall slim gent in an elegant navy-blue suit and bowler hat, was obviously some City type; she could detect a posh accent, too, even though they had both chosen to sit with their backs to her as they looked through the french windows to the small paved yard. The saloon bar was too long for her to make any sense of the muffled conversation, and she wondered what had prompted her regular customer to break his old habit of not drinking (as he always put it) until sundown.

"You've heard of the government's new austerity drive surely, Vaux. Cameron and his boy toy George want to slash spending by 19 percent all around—including the military and the intelligence services. Sir Nigel's absolutely livid: Vauxhall has decided to freeze B3's budget, and that means that the possibility of the second deputy he's been demanding all these years has now vanished once again—probably for another five years! Me, I'm soldiering on at a frozen salary and as the old man's lone deputy. It's going to be all work and no play for the foreseeable future."

Michael Vaux, the evening drinker, detected an air of false anger, a bit of theater on Craw's part, the masking of an irrepressible feeling of satisfaction at the prospect of not having to compete with any new colleague with equal rank and status. No threats to his fiefdom—probably until his retirement on full pension.

Vaux got up, walked back through the saloon to the bar.

"Another round of the same, Mr. Vaux?" asked the landlady.

"Yes, but make mine a double this time, please...very quiet today."

"It's early yet, love. I'll bring it over. We're out of Cutty Sark—got to go downstairs for another bottle."

* * *

Earlier that morning, Vaux had been woken by three loud bangs on his front door. He looked at the discolored face of his ancient Accurist wristwatch perched on the bedside table and saw that it was 8:30 a.m. He had slept later than usual and the cause was no mystery: he had drunk too many whiskeys, and the dull throbbing at the back of his head demanded an antidote.

He threw on the polka-dot silk dressing gown Anne had given him as a going-away present, a reminder of why he had drunk so much the previous evening: it was to be his first night alone for two years. Anne had left to look after her helpless and ailing father, promising to see Vaux on the odd weekend until, as she put it, nature took its course, and her beloved father departed this world.

Alan Craw, deputy to Sir Nigel Adair, who headed up Department B3, stood before an incredulous Vaux, whose first impulse was to tamp down his untidy hair and show his astonishment by mumbling, "Christ, what brings *you* here this time of the morning?"

Craw took off his bowler, made a modest bow, and said, "We have to talk, Vaux. I thought this was the ideal time of the day, since no one will be around to overhear or intercept...Could I come in?"

Vaux made a brave attempt to shake off the hangover. He opened the door and gestured Craw to enter. He observed a sleek red Ferrari 458 in the driveway. Craw had evidently not lost his taste for fast expensive cars, despite the divorce from his rich wife a few years back.

Craw knew the layout of the bungalow and went straight through to the lounge whose glass doors overlooked the long garden—the overgrown lawn sodden with early morning dew—and beyond, Vaux's beloved rolling fields of Hertfordshire.

"Sit down Vaux. We have something serious to discuss."

"Not before I shower and shave. And then we'll have coffee before leaving for the Pig and Whistle for what I need badly—a hair of the dog. It's only a few minutes—we'll walk. Sit down, Alan. I'll be with you shortly. Oh, and don't worry about eavesdroppers. I have the place debugged once a month."

Craw ignored Vaux's weak attempt at a joke. He could hardly order Vaux about—he wasn't working for them anymore. He sat down with a sigh and grabbed the latest issue of the *Economist* from a low glass-and-chrome coffee table.

* * *

Mrs. Clark put down the scotch along with Craw's bottle of Peroni on the small bistro table. She wondered why the two men sat facing the small patio since the drab view consisted of leaf-strewn flagstones, several straggly potted plants, and a tall brick wall. The few veined marble-topped tables were covered with splotches of bird droppings.

"I can open the doors if you like, but it's a bit chilly this morning, isn't it?" she said.

"No, we're fine," said Vaux.

Craw wanted to drive back to London as soon as the business at hand was completed. He knew from past history that Vaux could be a stubborn bastard when he liked, and he also knew that Vaux's bolshie attitude toward his periodic employers was unchangeable. So he planned to tread lightly.

Vaux suspected Craw's visit had something to do with some previous assignment with the spy outfit. He sipped his scotch and wondered if he shouldn't have asked for a bloody Mary.

"The thing is, Vaux, we have a problem on our hands: the DG, who as you probably know, is a great believer in our department and has defended us and Sir Nigel countless times when the panjandrums at Vauxhall figure we're dispensable and superfluous, has decided to assign B3 a critical role in an imminent major intelligence operation in the Mideast. He has cited B3's record in recent years as justifying his confidence that we can get the job done."

A gentle clink rang around the bar as the two men touched each other's drinking glasses in a toast to Department B3's undoubtedly creditable record. And to the DG's continuing support of the subgroup, whose critics charged that the small team of lone-wolf operatives hardly earned its keep and should be disbanded or at least reabsorbed into the bigger, main body of the Secret Intelligence Service.

Craw looked up at the big round brass-framed clock above the patio's doors and thought he could be back on the road in about half an hour. He would leave Vaux on his own to eat the sandwich he had suggested and ponder his future. He had seen a Hilton on the M1 as he turned off for Watford and thought they probably offered a slap-up Sunday lunch.

"So this is the situation, Vaux. As I told you, we are chronically short staffed. You know the team: Sir Nigel himself, deskbound; Chris Greene, your colleague on Operation Helvetia; and Seb Micklethwait, whom you worked with on that Tangier caper. And yours truly."

"That 'caper,' as you so lightly put it, ended with my being shot and wounded by an Al-Qaeda terrorist and the fatal shooting of a prisoner in our care," said Vaux.

Craw decided to go in another direction. "I know—I visited you in hospital, remember? But you were key in these operations. And Sir Nigel and myself, I might add, were thoroughly impressed with your adroit skills in persuading that Syrian nuclear scientist to defect--"

Vaux ignored this history rewrite. The Syrian scientist had been assassinated by mystery killers while under Vaux's safe-house care and protection. Vaux had always entertained two main suspects: the Syrians, having learned of the scientist's plan to defect, or Mossad, in a targeted killing of a nuclear scientist suspected of aiding its potential Mideast enemies. But the subsequent hush-hush police inquiry found insufficient evidence to charge anybody. And the last thing Whitehall needed at that time was a dust-up with either Israel or the Russian-backed Syrian leader Bashar al-Assad.

"Go on, Alan. Get to the point."

"Very well. I've always liked the way you want to get down to the nitty-gritty." Craw drained the last of the beer. He looked over his shoulder. Mrs. Clark was still shining glasses as she talked to a newly arrived couple at the bar.

"I'll get straight to it. We have a serious security problem in Beirut. Our operation, MI6's operation, is a sieve: leaks right, left, and center. Every time our station people make contact with a key informant and everything seems secure, we lose them. They disappear or are found dead—just as we thought we'd made a breakthrough. Over the last year or so, several key operations were blown—with fatal consequences in some cases. You know what Beirut's like. Talk about a nest of spies. The leaks have got to come from the very top; it's the only feasible explanation. We need someone of your experience to get over there, act as a loner, and worm himself into the whole British diplomatic complex in Lebanon. I'm talking the embassy, the MI6 station, and what we call our M network—*M* is short for *mosque*. You would be expected to operate in deep cover, of course."

Craw paused to check Vaux's reaction.

"But that's a theater where dozens of different religious sects and scores of political parties have been fighting one another for bloody decades. What on earth are we trying to do over there? Arbitrate a miraculous solution to their problems?"

Craw was used to this sort of cynicism from Vaux, and he had prepared himself. "You surprise me, Vaux. You have been on enough jobs with us to realize we work in different channels. We are not interested in the country's current political problems. It's a shambles over there, quite honestly. But it's fertile ground for gleaning vital intelligence on some of the most vicious terrorist and quasi-terrorist groups in the Middle East. I know you read your papers—including *The Economist*. So you hardly need me to tell you there's a veritable cornucopia of political and military intel among all the rival sects, clans, and private militias whose tentacles spread far and wide—to Syria, Israel, Iraq and Turkey, to name a few."

Craw saw a glint of interest and perhaps a nascent excitement in Vaux's red-rimmed blue eyes. "And you want me to find an Englishman with divided loyalties?"

"In a nutshell, yes. Frankly, it has to be one of the home team. Your main assignment is to find who is leaking key information on our projects and exposing the identity of our undercover agents in Beirut and Tripoli. We already have a dossier made up for you: several prime suspects, marginal players, and all that."

"Do I have some help?"

"Chris Greene's already over there, Vaux. But we need a heavy. More to the point, we need you to operate as a freelance. We think Greene's efforts have been somewhat compromised by his relationships with the embassy people. In fact, as things stand now, nobody but nobody on the embassy staff is above suspicion."

Vaux's eyebrows rose to register genuine surprise. "Including the ambassador?"

Craw adopted his well-practiced mute look of deadly seriousness while nodding several times to emphasize his reply in the affirmative.

Vaux seized the opportunity to change the subject. "How is Chris anyway? I haven't seen him since he was very sick with that rare type of flu."

Craw tried to hide his impatience. He needed Vaux's answer. "He's just fine. Just got engaged, by the way. He's in great form, but we're just not satisfied with his efforts. It's probably too much for one man. We need a team out there, Vaux. And you'll be the point man. We have to find the leaker, the mole within."

"What about the Americans? I thought they pretty much dominated the scene over there?"

"They're big. The CIA operation is huge. Likewise Mossad. Both agencies keep close tabs on us, and they know we've undergone a series of fiascos. We can't afford to give the Brit-bashers at Langley any more easy ammunition to sabotage what mutual trust still exists between us and the Cousins--post the Iraq debacle. So time is of the essence. What do you say, Michael?"

As far as Vaux could remember, this was the first time he had ever heard Craw address him by his first name. "I'll have to think about it. Give me a few days."

Craw stood up, wove his long, slender fingers into his Italian lambskin driving gloves, and looked satisfied with himself. But he had one more question. "How about dear Anne. How is she?"

Vaux knew that Craw had always nursed a strong attraction and affection for the beautiful Anne, secretary to Sir Nigel and permanent dogsbody at the shabby Gower Street offices of Department B3.

"She's had to move back in with her father. He's alone and sick. Other than that, she's fine. You see her every day in the office, don't you?"

"Yes, yes, of course."

If Craw was fishing to see whether Anne's moving out meant the end of their relationship, Vaux had left Craw none the wiser.

Chapter 2

BEIRUT, LEBANON
JULY 2010

Anthony Mansfield's favorite watering hole was aptly named Checkpoint Charlie, an over-decorated, gimmicky bar on Rue Uruguay in what tourist guide books call the bohemian district of downtown Beirut. Along with nearby Rue Gouraud, the popular bar was in the heart of Gemmayzeh, a neighborhood saturated with bars, elegant restaurants, and small cafés, yet within walking distance of the sedate British embassy, the spectacular Al-Amin mosque and the enduring Saint George's Cathedral. For Mansfield, who loved London, the Gemmayzeh district was a poor man's Soho.

It was quiet at this time of the morning when the few waiters and barmen outnumbered the customers. Mansfield maneuvered himself around the small ersatz border—crossing guards' hut into a dark corner where he could see who entered the bar and observe the frenetic comings and goings of the early-morning skeleton staff. Despite the gloom, he opened the newspaper that had been flown in from London just yesterday. As was his habit, he turned first to the *Times*' obituary pages.

He scanned the headlines for any recognizable names: former diplomats, agent-runners, and undercover operatives whose careers had spanned the Cold War years in Berlin and who now seemed to be dying off like flies. Mansfield's first assignment as a young MI6 probationer had been on the graveyard shift at Checkpoint Charlie, monitoring the major crossing between capitalist West and communist East Berlin.

Mansfield, a stocky man now in his early sixties, had thick brown hair graying at the temples and the cultivated scruffiness of rumpled linen suits, creased cotton shirts, and well-worn Gucci loafers. He wore no socks because of Beirut's clammy heat rather than any heed to high fashion. He had called for a meeting this morning with Chris Greene, Department B3's man in Beirut. And he had no intention of giving him an easy time.

Greene, as usual, showed spot-on the appointed time. Before he had decided where to sit—on the banquette at Mansfield's side or opposite him on an upright chair?—Mansfield had blurted out the question that had been on his mind since learning of the imminent arrival of Michael Vaux, a nonprofessional, part-time spook who had featured too often for his liking in the recent institutional history of the service.

"What's this I hear about a pending visit from your associate and colleague Vaux? Fill me in, dear boy. And what's your tipple at this early hour of the morning?"

Chris Greene, in a dark-blue blazer and khaki chinos, looked around the empty bar as if a drink would suggest itself by another customer's choice. "Oh, I'll have a Flensburger. It was on special the other day—a good German beer, I might add." Mansfield ordered two bottles of Flensburger.

"I have friends who have refused to buy Mercedes cars since the end of the war," said Mansfield without elaboration. But Greene knew of the older man's past—he had studied his file along with those of every other official at the embassy complex, including his fellow undercover agents who posed as legitimate diplomats.

Greene played the conventional role of a junior officer. "But they're our allies now, Tony. Have been for decades. We have to move on, as the ambassador is always saying." Greene knew this provocation could spark a long exposition on the talents or lack of them of the many ambassadors Mansfield had encountered during his long clandestine career.

But Mansfield didn't respond. He waited for the drinks to be planted on the table and then for the waiter to return to his post at the bar.

"Look Greene, I don't want any evasions from you. I need straight answers. I haven't got time to play games nor do I give a tinker's cuss about the internal politics of this situation. I'm too close to retirement to give a damn, if you want to know the truth. But I insist on full disclosure, all right? I have been fair to you since you arrived here three months ago. I didn't like B3's interference and meddling then, and I don't like it now. Never understood the DG's fascination for your rump outfit, anyway. Always maintained we could do the job ourselves." Mansfield, who operated under the official cover of deputy commercial attaché, took a long pull of the blond German pilsner and waited for Greene's report.

Greene stood up to take off his blue blazer with London's SOAS college crest emblazoned on the top pocket. He had semi-prepared the briefing. In this case, he told himself, attack was the best defense. "First off, the plan was for Vaux to come here under 'deep cover' status. No one other than Department B3 personnel was supposed to know about his assignment. So, right off the bat, we have a serious internal leak that needs an in-house investigation."

Mansfield drank his beer slowly as he watched Greene deliver his foreseeable opening gambit. He had prepared his counter move. "Don't give me that codswallop, Greene. You not only insult my intelligence but my competence. What do you think I've been doing all my life but honing the skills of penetrating other buggers' secrets? I have my methods, and your idea of 'deep cover' has as many leaky holes as your mother's colander."

Greene's face flushed while he struggled to regain a calm demeanor. In similar situations, he had often disguised his concern with irony. "Perhaps if we could reconstruct the channels that leaked this information about Vaux, it would be a step toward finding our double agent."

Mansfield took a deep breath as if he needed an intake of oxygen to give him strength. Then, with a theatrical sigh, he said, "Just tell me the gist of Vaux's mission before I tell you myself."

"Go on then. Tell me what you know," challenged Greene.

"It's obvious. Old Sir Nigel, bless his soul, saw that after several months, you had achieved bugger all in so far as finding the source of the leak, so he took the easy option and persuaded the D-G to send over his champion part-time secret agent to complete the job. All I would like to know, as a matter of courtesy, is why you didn't tell me yourself. Why did I have to find out about Operation Cedar through my own exclusive grapevine?" Plaintively, he added, "I thought we were mates."

Greene, who on his arrival in Beirut had adopted the cover of deputy cultural secretary, felt a short-lived pang of sympathy for the senior MI6 operative. But he wasn't on his team and his loyalties were now commanded by his old friend Vaux. Mansfield's intelligence-gathering talents could torpedo B3's efforts to uncover the leaker. If Mansfield knew about Operation Cedar, how far had it been compromised before it had gotten off the ground?

"Look, Tony. You obviously have your methods and your networks, and I admire you for it. But if our plan gets out to all and sundry, then it's stillborn from the word 'go'. Who else do you think knows about the project?"

Mansfield looked at the young man—midthirties, he supposed, light-brown hair, lean and handsome, one of the non-Oxbridge career staffers he liked to encourage. The success or otherwise of Operation Cedar would clearly have an impact on Greene's career prospects.

"I'll give you some advice, Greene. There are all sorts of rumors flying around, and your outfit, not for the first time, has put a few backs up. My staff learned about Vaux's imminent arrival from Vauxhall contacts, OK? Do you really think the DG can keep everything under wraps? He has a big personal staff. Housekeepers, janitors, mothers, not to mention wranglers—nothing's watertight, especially among colleagues.

"So the best thing you can do, my boy, is go about your day-to-day business after you have completed your first move in what promises to be an intriguing game of chess: bury Vaux as soon as he puts foot on Lebanese soil. Do you understand me? Put him some place where nobody will suspect he is staying—not our people; not yours; and God forbid, not the prime leaker, the traitor in our midst."

Greene knew Mansfield was a spy fiction enthusiast and liked to adopt John Le Carre's fanciful jargon for various MI6 functionaries. But he had a point. Bureaucracies, by their nature, undermine total security. "Remind me again Tony, who are the mothers?"

"The bloody secretaries and typists, for God's sake."

"Ah, yes."

Mansfield got up to leave. "I'll see you later."

Out on the street, Mansfield quickly donned an old pair of dark-lensed horn-framed sunglasses to protect his eyes from the sudden change in light from the dimness of the bar to the sun -glare of the street. He walked briskly toward bustling Martyrs' Square, looked back down the narrow street to Checkpoint Charlie, and pulled from his sagging jacket pocket his cell phone along with a piece of paper, the one-time pad that showed today's number for his personal lamplighter—Le Carre parlance for the freelance field agent who worked exclusively for him whenever he needed round-the-clock surveillance of a target in which he had a special interest.

"Citron," murmured a scarcely audible voice.

"Orange," said Mansfield softly. "I have another job for you. Meet me at the usual place in one hour exactly."

"*Oui*, monsieur," replied Citron.

Mansfield smiled to himself. He had hired the young man after he had been talent-spotted by a lecturer in computer science at Beirut's Business and Computer University. The professor, in his early forties, had for some time worked for British intelligence in return for substantial cash payments plus the dangled promise of a senior technology position with a major high-tech company in the UK. Mansfield liked to keep code names simple, so he had named the professor's newfound asset Citron.

Chapter 3

Astench that combined the odor of human sweat with the cheesy stink of unwashed feet jolted him awake. He was almost on the point of retching as he pushed the thick woolen blanket away and sat up to survey the room: the yellowed ceiling displayed a large oval water stain, and the faded white walls were pockmarked by large patches where the plaster had fallen away.

He sat at the side of the bed and observed the bottle of mineral water that had been placed on an upturned cardboard box that served as the bedside table. The bottle was only half-full, but he couldn't remember drinking from it during the hot night. All he remembered was collapsing on the bed, exhausted by the five-hour trip from London and the late-night meal in a dimly lit shawarma joint. He took a swig of the flat sparkling water and recalled how a cheerful Chris Greene had met him at the Rafic Hariri International Airport and hustled him quickly into a waiting taxi.

He heard a light tapping on the door. A burka-clad woman in an ankle-length black cotton robe gently opened the door and gestured a greeting as she walked quickly to a pile of clothes stacked in the far corner of the room. Vaux watched her as she gathered the bundle into her arms, turned, and walked toward the door. She nodded and left him as quietly as she had come. Vaux suspected she had removed the source of the fetid odor. His attempt to collect his thoughts was thwarted by the sudden loud ringtone of the burner Greene had given him over the lamb kebabs: the incongruous first few notes of "The Star Spangled Banner."

It was Greene. "Has Mahmoud arrived yet?"

"Who's Mahmoud?"

"Never mind, I'll be there in twenty minutes."

Vaux stood up, slid his legs into the blue jeans he had worn for the trip, and looked in vain for his luggage. He went to the door, opened it slightly to survey the crepuscular hallway. A long passage led to several other rooms, and he wondered if they were all as insecure as his. The dark brown walls of the corridor were covered in Arabic graffiti, sketches of militants wielding MK-47s, and an effigy of an evil-looking cigar-smoking Uncle Sam in a garish stars-and-stripes top hat. Vaux navigated his way to a smelly seatless toilet. Then he looked hopefully for a shower room. But all the other doors were locked, so he returned to his room. His cell phone was loudly chiming America's national anthem.

"Hello?"

"Mike! Come and join me for a Coke," said Greene.

"Where?"

"At the place where we were last night. Turn left outside your building and it's about ten yards down the street."

Vaux rushed down four flights of concrete stairs into a narrow street where young men on noisy motor scooters frenetically wove in and out of clusters of women and children. A canopy of high-voltage power cables and telephone wires sagged over the street, linking the decaying tenement buildings on each side. Some of the apartments featured narrow wrought-iron balconies cluttered with makeshift TV antennae and satellite dishes. Threadbare carpets, broken cane chairs and old boxy televisions made up the rest of the detritus of the residents' everyday existence.

The small café was loud and busy. The sweet smell of roasting lamb mixed with the fragrance of hashish and other exotic perfumes produced by the bubbling hookah pipes. Vaux saw Greene at a corner table as he stood up and waved to him. He was with a man in his midtwenties, presumably Mahmoud. But after Vaux shook hands with them, Mahmoud walked over to a group at the bar and went through an elaborate ritual of air-kissing and back patting.

"This is an ideal place to talk, Vaux. So don't look so uncomfortable," said Greene as he slid a glass of hot mint tea toward him. "And this is better for you than Cutty Sark."

"I'm sure it is," said Vaux. He sipped the tea. Then he got up, pulled the table out a little, and moved around to sit with his back to the wall. Greene smiled as he observed Vaux's instinctive compliance with one of the basic and eternal rules of Portsmouth's training manual: never sit in a bar or restaurant with your back to the entrance.

"This is probably the most secure place we could meet, Vaux. So relax. We're very close to the Shatila and Sabra refugee camps here, and I've built up a lot of contacts since I arrived three months ago. It's my own private network, if you like. And by the way, I have Shia, Sunni, and Christian informers—even a Druze. Believe me, I feel safer here than in some of the more cosmopolitan areas of the city."

Shatila! The massacre of hundreds of Palestinian men, women, and children by Christian militias in the long agony of the Lebanese civil war.

"Tell me something. How long do you expect me to stay in that slum of a rooming house or whatever it is? We're going to have to do better if I'm to function as a normal, reasonably efficient human being. And don't give me that claptrap from Craw about the necessity of deep cover. Cover is one thing, but I can't operate out of a rat hole. We'll have to think of something different. Somewhere else to base the operation."

"'Operation Cedar' is the latest label, Vaux."

"So I understand. Who's your friend?"

"Mahmoud is a university grad who, like so many others here, can't find a job. He's honest as the day is long. And he's tuned in to everything that's going on in this hornets' nest."

"How do you know he can be trusted?"

"I've tested him time and again. He's a Sunni—but that's like calling you a Christian or an Anglican. It means nothing."

"Nothing means nothing in these parts. They all have different loyalties and agendas. I don't have to tell you that, surely."

"Of course, I know that. But cool hard cash counts for an awful lot in this part of the world, and I have every confidence in him. He's married, and his wife has just given birth. So he needs the moola. He's got me out of a few scrapes, too."

On the British Airways flight from London, Vaux had decided to treat all sources and contacts with the utmost suspicion—whether Lebanese or embassy personnel, including undercover MI6 field agents. He was beginning to wonder now whether to work solo—without Greene's help and assistance. He could build up his own sources and his own team of informants. That, after all, was the mandate given him by Sir Nigel.

"So I'm moving out of that hellhole this morning. Where's my luggage? "

"Don't worry. It's been taken care of," said Greene.

"But I do worry, Chris. I have to find alternative accommodations. I can't operate out of a virtual doss-house, OK?"

"It's just a stop-gap. I was watched at the airport by one of our people, and I had to shake the tail. It wasn't too difficult. The taxi driver is a friend and helper and knows this maze of a city like the back of his hand. Plus he drives like a madman."

"You were followed by one of our own?"

"Yep. I'll fill you in later. Your suitcase is in the car. Let's go."

* * *

Vaux sat behind the steering wheel in a rented black Citroen C4 Picasso. A string of colorful prayer beads hung from the rear-view mirror. He had parked on a narrow street opposite the Jamaica Inn, a small bar with no windows and a black metal door with a spy hole. It was the frequent late-night destination of Hammond Seward, senior diplomat at the UK embassy in Beirut. Vaux has decided to make Seward the first of the embassy staff to put under close surveillance. Chris Greene's report pointed to Seward as a major suspect in the search for the leaker. Vaux is skeptical but has to go through the process of elimination. Greene's notes are mercifully brief:

> Seward, Hammond
> Rank: Second Secretary
> Age: 37
> Education: Eton, Oxford (Merton)
> BA Ancient & Modern History (a First)
> Personal profile: Single. Bon vivant (likes the best restaurants), heavy drinker (preferred beverage: large gin and tonic), history buff, (reads voraciously when drying out). Sexual preferences: Seward is unmarried and clearly homosexual. Observed as a regular at some of Beirut's numerous gay bars.

Vaux fished in the glove compartment for the Mont Blanc fountain pen digital camcorder the tech crew in London had supplied, along with his newly-doctored Derek Westropp passport. Other handy furnishings included a set of stainless steel lock picks supplied by Defense Ministry locksmiths and, Vaux assumed as testimony to tradition, a book of one-time pads from Vauxhaul's encryption experts.

He recognized Seward from Greene's photo. Now in white shirt and blue jeans, he sported an Australian wide-brimmed cowboy hat and wire-framed speed-cop sunglasses. He pushed on a bell pull and stood facing the spy hole for a few seconds, then the black door opened, and Seward sidled into the gloomy interior. For a moment, Vaux detected the raucous vibrations of a Mick Jagger number. It was just past midnight, and Vaux guessed the few couples sauntering up and down the street were bent on the same sort of Friday night entertainment as Seward. He opened the car door, got out and pressed the key fob.

It seemed to Vaux that he had been made to wait longer than Seward had while the bouncer checked him out through the judas. But the door eventually opened and he was beckoned in. Vaux was surprised how empty the place was. He looked at his ancient Accurist: 12:30. Early for Beirut's nightlife, apparently. He chose to sit on a tall, leather-covered stool at the small bar. From this vantage point he could see Seward at a corner table talking to a young-ish man who kept shielding his mouth with his hand as he talked to him. A few other male couples sat at isolated tables. He observed that, from time to time, they would saunter over to where a beaded curtain presumably led into another part of the establishment.

"*Oui*, monsieur, *vous voulez?*" A man in his forties, wearing a red fez and a black European suit that shined with wear. Vaux surveyed the scant collection of bottles on the dusty glass shelves, saw no whiskey, so asked for a beer. Without a word, the man bent down to a cooler below the bar and produced a bottle of Almaza, the local brew. No glass was offered. Vaux took the bottle to where he had seen a wall shelf that served as a bar for those patrons who preferred to stand while surveying the room. Mick Jagger had retired for the night, replaced by a noisy Arabic pop band. And now he had a head-on view of Seward's companion. The two men seemed totally absorbed in each other, oblivious to anyone else in the bar. Vaux casually took the fountain pen from the top pocket of his khaki safari jacket and started to write something on a cardboard coaster. Nobody saw him lift the pen to the angle that would produce a perfect video image of the British diplomat and his young Arab companion.

Chapter 4

Anthony Mansfield, his feet perched on the edge of a long mahogany desk, leaned back in his black leather swivel chair and scanned that morning's edition of *The Daily Star*, Beirut's only English-language newspaper. The front-page lead story was unsettling: fighting had broken out between the Lebanese army and the Israelis in the sensitive "blue line" area of south Lebanon. The *Star* reported that it was the most serious outbreak of hostilities since the two countries fought each other in 2006. There were fatalities on both sides.

Was this skirmish on the Israeli-Lebanese border an ominous precursor of further escalation and another bloody round of hostilities between the two enemies—or just a flare-up that could be dampened down by a quick diplomatic intervention by the United States and its western allies? Before Mansfield could answer his own question, his cell phone gave out a truncated rendition of Big Ben's hourly chimes.

It was Peter Browne, his newly posted field officer, a fully vetted operative of MI6, a young Turk, he had been told, who had passed the robust training course at Portsmouth with flying colors after graduating from Cambridge with a mediocre degree in classical Greek and Latin. Another well-connected recruit from the establishment. But Mansfield, two or three years from retirement and in the throes of a major crisis within his bailiwick, had decided to take no one at face value. Browne said he needed to talk.

He put the newspaper aside as Browne, in a tight-fitting navy-blue lightweight suit and polished black brogues, made himself comfortable in the Windsor chair. "Well?" said Mansfield, eager to hear the latest surveillance report from the field.

"Vaux did a bit of reconnoitering last night, sir. He was watching the actions of our Mr. Seward well into the early hours—"

"So? Did he learn anything we don't already know?"

"I doubt it."

"I want you to make a full list of B3's assets here. The more we know about Vaux's field operatives the better. I'll want details on their backgrounds, their current occupations or covers—whatever applies."

"Yes, sir."

"Did you see this?" asked Mansfield as he hit the *Star*'s front page with the back of his hand.

"No, sir, I haven't had time to read the morning papers—"

"Well, make time, for heaven's sake. It's part of the job. If we wait for a memorandum from Tom Burns, the skirmish will be over and done with. You know how bloody slow the 'current developments' people are." Burns, the embassy's military attaché, had only recently been given the task of summarizing the regional news on a daily basis. The memo was then circulated to embassy staff deemed important enough to receive the elegant fruits of his efforts.

Browne blushed slightly. "I don't think I'm on their circulation list, sir. I'll have to rectify that."

Mansfield grunted—whether with approval or not, Browne couldn't tell. "So where are we with Vaux and company? We now know where he's shacked up and we know he liaises with Greene every morning. Any new contacts, any Lebanese in the picture— Muslims, Christians whatever?"

"I think the answer to that question is a cautious yes. I've put my field agent on a twenty-four-hour surveillance of one Ahmed Hussein, a twenty-something student at the American University. He's been seen in the company of Vaux several times—mainly in the odd coffee house or small café."

"So Vaux has hired his own lamplighter."

Browne indulged the older man. "Yes, but that term, is purely fictional, as you know—"

"All right, we'll stick with your colorless *field agent*. What's he got to report?"

"We'll know more about that when the intercepts come in. Our electronics people have succeeded in hacking Vaux's cell phone, and his small apartment is now wired."

"So much for the super-encrypted mobile phones the boffins at Vauxhall Cross were supposed to have come up with."

"Yes, sir," said Browne, as he got up to leave.

"One moment, old boy. I presume this skirmish in South Lebanon is as much a surprise to you as to me?"

"Yes, sir."

"Does it ever occur to you that because it's such a surprise, both of us are derelict in our duty? That we've dropped the ball? For Christ's sake, man, what have our well-paid informants been doing recently? This is just the sort of intelligence we should have had in our hands weeks before it happened."

"As you know, sir, several of our key informers have been eliminated—"

"Yes, and that's why we have our Mr. Vaux in town. Tell me something I don't know."

Silence enveloped the two case officers.

Mansfield brought his feet off the edge of the desk. He threw the newspaper into the nearby waste basket. "You'd better get the second eleven organized—and quickly. Otherwise Vaux will report back that we haven't moved fast enough to fill in the gaps left by several regrettable disappearances."

"Do we still prioritize the search for the leaker, sir?"

"Surely to hell we can walk and chew gum at the same time, Browne. Now leave me to think."

Browne headed toward the door, feeling a little less confident than when he came in.

After Browne had left the room, Mansfield picked up his phone and called Kamal Moussa, a.k.a. Citron. He kept his question as cryptic as his creative powers could muster. "Ever heard of one Ahmed Hussein, currently a student at the American University?"

"*Non*, monsieur," replied Citron.

"See me at the usual place tonight at the same time."

"Very well, Monsieur Orange."

* * *

Mahmoud Gaber, Greene's field agent, told him that he had managed to persuade his old uncle to move out of his cramped one-room flat in the bustling Hamra district, close to several colleges, including the American University of Beirut. Greene agreed to pay the old man three times his monthly rent for the first month and what Vaux had called "the duration."

Vaux surveyed the narrow room. The gloomy prospect of spending any serious time in the shabby confines of a stranger's unadorned, disorganized living space produced an unfamiliar sensation of compassion and unease. And the semi-permanent arrangement only intensified his occasional pangs of yearning to be back with Anne again. He sat down on a rickety cane chair beside a small, greasy two-ring gas stove. He tapped his scuffed brown suede shoe against a fifteen-kilogram cylinder of Calor gas as he tried hard to listen to Greene's summing up: "And those," he said, "are the reasons I place him as the number one suspect for the string of fatal security leaks."

"Yes, he's gay," said Vaux. "But there's no evidence in this dossier to suspect he may be passing on top secret information. I followed his boyfriend that night. And after presumably having sex at the gay club, they parted company and the hustler, or whatever he was, ended up at a local McDonald's. A group of his cohorts gathered around him, and he seemed to be standing them drinks of Coke along with the odd joint.

"So I made a move on him. He got up to leave, and I propositioned him—an English tourist out to get laid. He took me to a nearby parking lot and before we got down to anything, I put a half- nelson on him, told him I was a security investigator, and if he didn't tell me what he did for the English friend at the Jamaican Inn, I'd blow his head off with the Sig Sauer you so kindly loaned me. Cut a long story short: he was just a young kid out to make some cash. Said he'd known Seward for about six months. They had no other relationship except sex. And if he was lying, he deserves an Oscar. I believed him and let him go."

Greene looked shocked, his thick eyebrows raised as Vaux pronounced his prime suspect eliminated. He was even more taken aback that Vaux had ever heard of a nelson. But he was also mortified: why hadn't he used such an obvious ploy to confront the youth? Before he came up with an answer, he heard Vaux suggest they should move on.

"Who else is there on your priority suspect list?"

"Before we go there, let's not so easily dismiss Seward. Don't forget his heavy drinking. Every embassy get-together, he ends up plastered. He's known as a drunk, for heaven's sake. He's been arrested three times for drunk driving—and that's only in the past year. He's a reincarnation of our supermole Guy Burgess."

Vaux ignored the young man's reference to Britain's notorious Cold War double agent who fled to Moscow on the eve of his pending arrest. "Do you realize, Chris, that the Foreign Office now tolerates and even recruits gay personnel? That a recent French ambassador happened to be gay and lived openly with his partner in Washington? We can't exist in a time warp. We'll have to look at this whole situation in a new light. Let's drop your obsession with Seward. Yes, he's a drunk. But he has lots of company in the diplomatic corps and every other government department I can think of."

Vaux stood up and moved toward the long arched windows. He opened the exterior metal screens that blocked out the searing midday sun. In the distance, the sparkling azure blue of the Mediterranean sharply offset the foreground of bombed-out buildings, pockmarked concrete walls of high-rise apartment towers, the steel skeletons of former luxury hotels, the sagging balconies of abandoned Ottoman-era houses. The panorama of derelict ruins was punctuated by gaping bomb craters filled with garbage and sewage that seeped from broken underground pipes and culverts.

Vaux said, "The civil war ended in 1990, twenty years ago. It's unbelievable how little progress they've made in rebuilding the city."

Greene moved toward the window. "As I understand it, they were making good progress until the Israelis bombed the hell out of the place in 2006—"

"Because they feared Hezbollah was taking over, I gather."

"I understand they *have* taken over."

Vaux said, "But the prime minister is a Sunni and Suleiman, the president, is a Maronite Christian. Hezbollah is a Shiite movement, surely."

"This is Lebanon. Go figure," said Greene.

Vaux looked out at the frenetic traffic streaming in both directions along Beirut's landmark Corniche that clung closely to the shoreline. He needed a cool beer and was about to suggest they both head for a bar when Greene suddenly returned to the subject Vaux thought they had exhausted. "The point is, Mike, doesn't someone like Seward who pounds the streets most evenings run a high risk of blackmail? As soon as any of his sexual partners, and God knows how many there are, learns of his position at the embassy and all that—won't someone sometime exert pressure on him to supply information they want, threatening to expose his 'extracurricular' activities if he doesn't do as they ask?"

"Yes. But you have to ask yourself whether, in this day and age, he really gives a jot. I'm sure everyone at the legation knows about his sexual preferences, but who cares anymore? That's the point I'm trying to make."

They left it at that. Greene hailed a taxi, and they headed east for Gemmayzeh and a small, dark bar called Awesome on the Rue Gouraud.

Chapter 5

The UK's ambassador to Lebanon personified a public relations victory for the Foreign and Commonwealth Office. Long criticized for recruiting only from the upper classes who could afford to attend posh private schools and the two ancient English universities, the FCO had quietly extended its invitation to more diverse and less opulent members of the intelligentsia: John Eccles, in his late forties, had graduated from Sussex University (founded in 1961) and in his early adult years had been a professional pianist for an obscure Brighton blues band. Previous postings: Maputo, Yaoundé and Kabul.

At 5:00 p.m. on weekdays, Eccles would summon his fictional deputy commercial attaché, MI6's head of station in Beirut, for the daily intelligence briefing. Eccles, a rotund, heavy man with sparse graying hair, sat at the head of a long rosewood table in what the embassy's employees called the conference room. It was a big room with french windows that looked out to a long, manicured garden, shaded by tall pine trees and bordered by large clumps of pink bougainvillea, where several brass gooseneck sprinklers swirled all day in a losing battle to keep the parched lawn green.

For some reason, perhaps a subconscious desire on Mansfield's part to claim equal diplomatic status, both men always sat at either end of the long, highly polished rosewood table. Today, Mansfield had brought the folder that usually indicated that the meeting would have some substance rather than the usual complacent "Everything's under control" update that Eccles had become accustomed to.

Before any official discussion could begin, Eccles' private secretary, a portly middle-aged English lady who defied Beirut's broiling summer heat by wearing a heavy two-piece Scottish tweed suit, white embroidered silk blouse, and sensible flat shoes, placed a tray before Eccles. The ritual never changed: English tea (Earl Grey) accompanied by chocolate-covered digestive biscuits. Despite Mansfield's mimed efforts to say hello, Nancy Sheridan never acknowledged his presence. She left Eccles to perform the rituals while Mansfield walked the twenty-five foot length of the table to pick up the blue-patterned Spode china cup and saucer and the biscuit.

In silence, the two men sipped the tea and nibbled on the biscuits. Then Eccles' cell phone gave off a conventional late-twentieth-century British Telecom ringtone.

"Yes, darling. I understand. But don't forget I can't get away until around seven p.m. All right, Miranda, I'll see you then."

Mansfield decided to let the ambassador start the conversation. It was, he told himself, a sort of silent homage and respect to the man and wife who had tragically lost their nine-year-old daughter in a terrorist outrage three years earlier. It was just outside the southern port city of Tyre. Yasmin, then just nine, had been killed along with her teacher and eleven other schoolgirls when unidentified militants fired a shoulder-launched RPG-7 rocket into the school minivan. It was some time before his Beirut posting, but Mansfield could only imagine the grief their daughter's death had caused father and mother.

But Eccles remained silent. So Mansfield opened his folder and adjusted his half-moon glasses. He shuffled a few papers, looked up to meet the ambassador's watchful eyes and launched into what he knew would sound like a mea culpa. "You've no doubt been informed of the sudden flare-up on the southern border—"

"Yes, Tony. At three this morning. Nobby called on the secure phone to wish me sweet dreams and then broke the bloody news. Where were your boys these last few days? How come we hadn't a clue about this planned attack on the Israelis?"

Mansfield was not surprised his boss on the Mideast and North African desk had lost no time preempting his own job to keep the ambassador fully informed. Clark would have known it would be interpreted by Mansfield as a passive rebuke. "I haven't got all the facts yet. But the Lebanese Armed Forces say they opened fire on Israeli soldiers who crossed the border into Lebanese territory. One Israeli and two members of the

Lebanese Armed Forces were killed and apparently a Lebanese journalist."

Eccles declared, "I don't have to tell you, surely, that I would much rather have heard about this disturbing incident through you than from the timeservers in London. What the hell are these field agents you run doing in return for the large wads of cash they cost us? What's the point if they can't even get close enough to their sources to be able to predict this sort of aggressive act on behalf of the Lebanese Armed Forces?"

"That's a moot point, Ambassador. The Lebanese claim the Israelis crossed into their territory and used artillery and air strikes against them north of the border where they had every right to be."

"Your people missed this. That's the bottom line. This is the sort of intelligence we should have had in advance. Who knows, maybe we could have warned the combatants and prevented the flare-up."

Mansfield had to field that one. "The team's depleted. You know we have a problem. Two of my agents have been eliminated in the last six weeks. That brings the total to fourteen over the last year. So what few are left are lying low—reluctant, shall we say, to go out, find out what the hell's going on, and feed us the intelligence we need on a day-to-day basis."

Both men fell silent. Each wondered who would reference Department B3's now perhaps even more urgent Operation Cedar. The ambassador took the plunge. "Is this man Vaux making any progress on the source of the leaks?"

"How can I answer that when I'm supposed not to know he's here to conduct an undercover investigation of the embassy staff?

I can't liaise with the man because I am told it would compromise the investigation. Am I on the suspect list, for God's sake?"

The ambassador stood up, pushed the elegant Chippendale chair back, and walked toward the french windows. It was his usual signal that the meeting had come to an end.

Mansfield closed the manila folder, drank the dregs of the tea, and heaved himself up. "See you tomorrow John—when hopefully we'll have some better news to discuss." As he made his way to the double doors that led to the expansive foyer of the fortified complex, he heard Eccles ask him to hang on a minute. Eccles approached him and took his hand for a friendly shake. "Never mind. You can't always have your eye on the ball, old boy. But I wonder who reported the border fracas to Vauxhall in what I suppose they now call 'real time.'"

"That's my first priority, Ambassador. I'll get to the bottom of this if it kills me."

"Don't tempt fate. Can't afford to lose you."

Eccles put a hand on the veteran agent's shoulder. "I'd like a comprehensive report from you tomorrow. Perhaps you can touch base with Nobby Clark in London and give me the full picture at tomorrow's meeting."

"The report will be in your briefing documents by five p.m. tomorrow. Then you can, as usual, take them home and study them at your leisure," said Mansfield reassuringly.

"Oh, and from now on I'd better be informed about the activities of this agent Vaux and his merry men at B3—their plans to uncover the mole, names of their newly hired sub-agents and the like."

"Yes, sir. Absolutely," said Mansfield with a sigh to indicate his steadfast resolve to accept any further burdens that duty to queen and country might entail.

* * *

At about this time of the afternoon, Michael Vaux usually tried to take a nap before his evening excursions. He lay on an ancient and stained silk-covered chaise longue he had discovered behind a faded Chinese folding screen.

He had now been in Beirut six days. Chris Greene, whose energy and loyalty he admired, had virtually disappeared since handing over seventeen personal and confidential files on the embassy staff—from the ambassador down to a locally employed chauffeur and a filing clerk, both Sunni Muslims who prayed the obligatory five times a day.

But he had come up with nothing. In a nod to Greene's paranoia, Vaux had carefully studied the profiles and lifestyles of Seward and four other unmarried career diplomats. In their surveillance efforts, Greene's team of hired helpers had found nothing to implicate or compromise any employee of the embassy—including the two English females who ran the twenty-four-hour cipher-decrypt office and Ms. Nancy Sheridan, the ambassador's personal private secretary.

So where did he go from here? He felt that a major shift in strategy was needed. Should he go against Sir Nigel's deep cover imperative and adopt a more empirical approach? That would probably mean some liaison with MI6's Beirut station chief, some coordination and cooperation between Department B3 and the spooks run by Vauxhall Cross. It would no doubt cause a major blow-up at Gower Street—but Craw and Sir Nigel were not in the field. How could they know the best way forward?

Vaux was about to answer his own question when he heard a light tap on the door. He had forgotten that Ahmed Hussein, the AUB student he had met on his third day in Beirut, had called to say he needed to see him. Hussein was in his mid-twenties, tall and lean. He had started up a conversation with Vaux as they sat at the counter of a fast-food eatery on the Avenue de Paris, just off the Corniche and close to the AUB campus. At first, Vaux had been wary of the young man's approach. They talked about Beirut and Lebanon's complicated politics and of the endless war in Iraq. And ever-cautious Vaux decided that Ahmed Hussein was not a plant but just another affable young Arab, interested, as he kept saying, in improving his English. But as the conversation ran its desultory course, an idea began to grow in Vaux's mind: perhaps he could be used. Here could be a potential helper, an aide-de-camp, a hidden asset in what looked like becoming a complex spy game in which the key players were all too well known to each other.

Hussein stood at the door. He was dressed like most of the city's college students: blue jeans, sneakers, and a black T-shirt. He walked to the tall windows and looked out to the Corniche and the hinterland of bombed out sea-front apartments and skeletal hotel towers. "Look! You can just see the campus from here on the extreme left," he said enthusiastically.

"Yes, it's a great view of the American University—almost as if some city landscaper had taken advantage of the devastated waterfront to give the campus a more prominent setting. The hill helps, I suppose." Vaux chose to keep his opinion about the bland nineteenth century architecture of the main buildings to himself.

"College Hall, the main building, was bombed back in the war. You're looking at the rebuilt replica," said Hussein with a tinge of pride.

Both men absorbed the wasteland, now peppered with tower cranes and giant bulldozers that heralded the city's slow resurrection. Vaux had placed a battered laptop computer he'd picked up in a nearby souk a few days earlier on the small table in front of the windows. It helped to back up the cover story he had given Hussein when they met.

"How's the research going?" asked Hussein.

"Slowly. Can I get you anything? Tea, coffee?"

"No thanks. I have a lecture in an hour, and I only came to tell you about an uncle of mine who could help in the series you're writing. He's my only surviving relative. My whole family—two brothers and my father and mother—were killed in the war. A massive rocket landed close to Saint George's Cathedral where they had just attended the Divine Liturgy. My uncle was then in his twenties—fought with the Christian militias in downtown Beirut and has loads of stories to tell. He lives close to an ancient village called Aanjar in the Bekaa Valley. You could get there in less than two hours by car."

Vaux realized that his cover story had worked too well. Now he'd have to find all sorts of reasons why he couldn't make the trip. "I take it then that you're Christian."

"Maronite, yes." The young man was writing an address on the back of a tattered visiting card. He slid the card over to Vaux who picked it up and put it in a china mug full of ballpoint pens.

"My filing cabinet. Thank you, Ahmed. I'm grateful. Your uncle could be helpful." He was about to ask Hussein if his uncle had a telephone number but quickly dropped the idea. He probably didn't, and if he did, it would only complicate matters when Hussein realized Vaux had failed to follow up.

Then they heard a knock at the door. Hussein got up to leave as Vaux ushered Greene into the room. Greene and Hussein shook hands after Vaux introduced Greene as a Mr. Robert Menzies, a freelance journalist who happened to be passing through the city.

After Hussein had dashed down the dusty marble staircase, Greene began to search the room, looking into old dust-clogged vents, under the chaise longue and the small dining table, even the base of the laptop.

Vaux said, "Don't you think I've already searched the place for bugs?"

"You could have missed something. Ah! What's this little blighter?" Greene pulled out a tiny square listening device about the size of a cell phone's SIM card tucked under the grille of a defunct air conditioning duct. "These are like cockroaches. Where there's one, there will be others."

Greene went about his business with frenetic enthusiasm. He uncovered four more: one under the cistern in the cramped toilet, another attached to the butane gas cylinder, and two hidden in the folds of the Chinese screen.

Vaux looked on with passive interest and some bewilderment. "Who the hell would be interested in eavesdropping on my life in this slum? And more to the point, who knows I'm here, except you?"

"That's a silly question, Michael. The CIA for starters. They're now working closely with Lebanese security and have tabs on every foreigner who arrives here—especially someone who's in their files already for having worked for British security. They could have liaised with the supersuspicious Mossad, which we know has a grudge against you, anyway. Then there's the GSD, Lebanon's own intelligence outfit—they could be very interested in the sudden arrival of journalist Derek Westropp, a wanted man in Syria, thanks to your association with one Ahmed Kadri, whom they shot as a traitor. Even though their troops have withdrawn, the Syrians still have enormous influence here."

"You talk like a conspiracy nut."

"No, Mike. I'm a realist. You've been out of the game too long. You're getting rusty."

Vaux sighed. "And what's this about the Israelis having a grudge?"

"Operation Saladin—remember? Do you think they didn't know you were pushing the theory that the Syrian scientist you were babysitting had been the victim of one of their targeted assassination networks? Whitehall, at the D-G's urging, whitewashed the shambles by blaming Syrian intelligence. But the Israelis never forget an unfriendly act."

Vaux knew his colleague was probably right. Now was a good time to tell Greene of the decision he had come to in a fleeting moment just before his arrival. "I've decided on a new strategy, Chris. I want to work with Mansfield. There's no way I can trace the leak without face-to-face interviews with all the embassy personnel. It's as simple as that. I want to talk to all of them. To do that I'd have to have Mansfield's cooperation.

"You can't get the feel of a man by reading an anodyne personnel file, even with brief notes on their social lives, marriage status, leisure habits, and the rest of it. What they did at university—political party affiliations, any demonstrations they participated in. Yes, it will be a complete about-face in B3's strategy. But it's the only way forward as far as I'm concerned. If I can get the feel of a person, I can usually figure out what makes him or her tick. We'll have to report to Sir Nigel and Craw within twenty-four hours. I want your support, obviously."

"I've already interviewed members of the staff who I thought were potentially suspect, Mike. But if you want to do the whole thing over again, that's your privilege."

Now Greene felt a confession would help clear the air. "But there's one thing I should tell you. Mansfield already knows you're here and what your remit is. I had to confirm his suspicions."

Vaux felt suddenly vulnerable—stripped of his comfortable cover, betrayed by a colleague, shot by friendly fire. The two field agents looked at one another. A faint blush appeared on Greene's tanned cheeks He sat on the end of the low chaise longue, the small listening devices in the palm of his hand. He looked at them carefully. He couldn't yet look Vaux in the eyes. "Mansfield was tipped off by one of his disciples, fans, contacts—call them what you want—at Vauxhall Cross. You know the place is a sieve. I'm Department

B3's rep in the embassy, so he demanded a meeting. He said I was to keep you out of sight and suggested he didn't want to know about any progress or otherwise we might make in our probe into the leaks. Of course, he was bloody skeptical we'd make any."

"What harm would it have done if you'd informed me?"

"None, I suppose. But my old Portsmouth training came to the fore: the sacrosanct rule—need to know."

"But I did bloody well need to know! I'm supposed to be running Operation Cedar. Surely you can see that?"

Greene got up. "I'm sorry. I made a mistake. But I'll support the new strategy one hundred percent. I don't know what else to say."

Vaux said, "Just treat me as a colleague, a trustworthy friend. Tell me everything you know. You're the career guy, not me. I'll be glad when this is all over, to be frank. But it's not going to be over until we find out why we are losing these young field operators. Let's work together and not at cross purposes."

Greene was about to take issue with the last comment but let the matter drop. He went over to Vaux and shook his hand. "It won't happen again."

"A beer?"

"Sure. But first, who was the number I met when I got here?"

"Need to know…" smiled Vaux.

Chapter 6

The two men took an ancient Renault taxi whose heavily bearded driver had been waiting hopefully outside Vaux's building.
Greene gave the instructions in passable French and they sped off
down a network of narrow streets that brought them to the Avenue
de Paris, a southbound extension of the Corniche, and then into
the Raouche district.

Greene thought a bit of tourism could help change the tense
atmosphere he felt he had created by telling Vaux of Mansfield's
penetration of Department B3. He had always sensed that Vaux got
his kicks by outwitting Vauxhall's pompous professionals. And now
he probably felt betrayed by a colleague within B3.

Greene paid off the taxi and they walked a short distance before crossing Avenue General de Gaulle to a modern, low-slung
building perched on the cliffs overlooking the becalmed, cobalt-
blue Mediterranean.

Greene became an ardent tourist guide. "This is the Bay Rock Café, an excellent place for lunch, but the best time is at sunset. See those rocks ahead of us? They're naturally formed arches and are known as Pigeon Rock (don't ask) but the view is *magnifique!*"

Vaux was persuaded to order *mezze*, Lebanese appetizers, along with a bottle of the local Almaza beer. There were few lunch-time customers, which was perhaps why Greene had chosen the tourist trap. In a large room closer to the long bar, a cluster of middle-aged men in shabby dark suits smoked *shisha* pipes in silence. Greene played the flawless host by paying the bill after he ordered a cab on his cell phone.

"I want you to meet one of my best field agents. He lives in a bombed-out apartment building quite close to my hotel. Are you game?"

"Of course," said Vaux. "But didn't I meet him on the first day? Name of Mahmoud, I recall."

"No, Mahmoud's had to go to Tripoli. Death in the family or something. This guy prefers to have just a code name. Calls himself Azimi. He's a Shiite and probably a member of Hezbollah. But don't hold that against him. He just wants to survive, and with what I pay him, I think he's found a way to do so."

The taxi driver went north on the Corniche, which now resembled a cacophonous two-way racing track as drivers sped home for late lunches and the traditional siesta. Vaux observed that Beirut drivers used their blaring car horns as signals for quick lane changes or warnings to dawdling vehicles to clear a lane.

When Greene suggested in faltering French that the route chosen was the long way to their destination, the driver spoke rapidly in Arabic and gestured to the traffic. Greene gave up and looked at Vaux, who had decided to take a heat-induced, post -lunch snooze.

The ancient Mercedes turned right at the ruins of the storied Saint George's Hotel and headed north to the Radisson, a modern American-style hotel built just after the Israeli bombardment of the city in 2006.

Vaux scrambled out of the low back seat and looked up at the ritzy building. A liveried doorman greeted Greene and came over to usher them into the low-lit, cool foyer, but Greene interceded and promised they would return soon. Greene started to walk ahead of Vaux up a neglected side street where the narrow crumbling pavements forced them to walk single file. They passed wide arid spaces, fenced off by concrete bollards, where apartment buildings had been blown up by mortar shells and rockets. The surviving edifices, pockmarked and shattered by shrapnel, showed evidence of day-to-day life: damaged stucco balconies, often furnished with an upright chair and table, were covered with roughly hung tarpaulins against the heat and the sun.

They climbed a chipped and scarred concrete staircase to the second floor. Greene gave three slow knocks on a glossy varnished brown door. He waited about thirty seconds, then gave two heavier knocks in rapid succession. But there was no response. Both men listened for some movement from inside. Greene repeated the coded signal. Still nothing. Greene looked at Vaux, turned the metal door knob and the door swung open. The room was dim, thanks to the black canvas tarp that hung from the balcony's ceiling, but the two men could see that the place had been ransacked: the doors of an antique armoire had been thrown open, the clothes—jeans, sweaters, shirts—scattered on the worn parquet floor, the drawers of a bulky Victorian chest hung open, their contents scattered.

Greene instinctively went through to the bedroom. On the bare blood-soaked mattress lay his star cutout, face down, blood still trickling from his open mouth. Vaux went over to perform the ritual of taking the young man's pulse. He looked up at Greene and shook his head.

Vaux could see Greene was stunned. He leaned farther over the naked body. "His throat's slashed—with what looks like a pretty primitive knife with jagged or serrated edges. Doesn't look like there was any struggle or fight."

Greene couldn't bring himself to comment. He looked around the bedroom. Here there were no drawers to go through, not even a wardrobe—just the bed against the far wall, a bedside table on which stood an ancient Tiffany lamp whose multicolored glass shade had several missing panels.

Vaux went through to the small kitchen and flipped on the dull ceiling light. In a filthy sink, rapidly evacuated by several scuttling cockroaches, lay the probable murder weapon: a bread knife. He took a Kleenex out of his pocket and picked it up. The blood had coagulated and the serrations showed traces of the victim's olive skin. The "Made in Sheffield 1934" hallmark had survived the decades.

Then Vaux heard raised voices. A mixture of guttural Arabic and English. Someone was talking to Greene. And it didn't sound like a friendly conversation. Heavy footfalls came from the living room. Vaux, from somewhere in the recesses of his memory, recalled that oriental apartment houses often had a servants' door in the kitchen. He looked for a door. Nothing—but then, on the far wall, he saw a long greasy oilcloth curtain that covered a narrow area. He pulled it aside and discovered what could offer him a quick exit: a shabby plywood door whose top half featured a panel of frosted glass. He tried the metal handle. It turned, but the doorjamb had warped with age or bomb blasts, and the door wasn't going to give way easily. On his third strong tug, the door creaked opened. Vaux caught a whiff of the stale, stagnant air and plunged into the dark well whose narrow stone stairs would, he hoped, lead to an exit onto the wasteland below.

Chapter 7

Kamal Moussa, a twenty-seven-year-old student at Beirut's Business and Computer University, was what Anthony Mansfield called a "professional student." He had graduated from Beirut's Arab University in classical studies and his tutors had pigeonholed him for an academic posting at an institution of his choosing. But he had opted for a course in computer literacy because he felt challenged by his younger brothers, whose laptops and tablets were as unfathomable to him as quantum physics. In Mansfield's world-weary eyes, he was a procrastinator, forever putting off the day he would join the work-a-day world.

Mansfield had combed the staff lists of every college in Beirut for possible sympathetic talent spotters whose loyalty could be counted on by any leanings toward Anglophilia or avarice or both. A certain Dr. Fahmi, a part-time lecturer at Beirut's Business University, Lebanon's top computer science college, who—owing to Mansfield's handy corporate connections—had been placed on the short list for a lucrative IBM posting in London, volunteered his services. He convinced himself that to assist the British in their efforts to gather intelligence about his own countrymen could only boost his appeal to top IBM executives who, he was certain, were in cahoots with the sinuous arms of the British government.

Dr. Fahmi had closely monitored the activities of one Kamal Moussa, a diligent student, older than the rest of his class, keen on joining various political societies but ideologically hard to pin down. Crucially, he had been seen in the company of a sophisticated lady who headed up the newly opened Gucci boutique at the city's elegant downtown shopping center called simply Beirut Souk. What's more, he discovered that Moussa had incurred the wrath of his elderly father, a humble taxi driver, for not contributing to the increasingly burdensome family budget. The last straw, his father had reported to his son's tutor on the college's open house last fall, was evidence (discovered in a diligent pocket search while Kamal enjoyed an afternoon siesta) that he had recently bought a fancy handbag for the mind-boggling sum of $250.00, equivalent to no less than 375,000 Lebanese pounds. Dr. Fahmi calculated that the promise of generous "reimbursements" of the size to which Fahmi himself had become accustomed would tip the scales in favor of a successful recruitment.

So a delicate approach was made in the relaxing atmosphere of the refectory over a mid-morning cup of coffee and a slice of stouf. To his delight, Dr. Fahmi discovered that bright as he was, Kamal Moussa was not only pretty much apolitical, but as a denizen of politically chaotic Beirut, willing to take any side in any argument—for the sake of his Lebanese ancestry, if nothing else.

Moussa was duly summoned to serve queen and country. Mansfield, who had no knack for Arabic names, bestowed on him the code name Citron for no other reason than Moussa's second language was French. And so, on the day that Chris Greene had taken Michael Vaux for a little field tour, as he had put it, Kamal Moussa, whose remit was to tail Vaux around the clock, found himself searching among the rubble for a shady spot to loiter and await developments.

He lit up a Byblos and sat on the crumbling remains of a brick wall, shaded by a stand of hardy cypress trees. After about ten minutes, he heard the wail and yelp of police sirens. Then two Dodge Chargers of the Interior Security Force (ISF), screeched to a dusty halt just twenty feet from where he was sitting. Four figures in brown camouflage uniforms and maroon berets scrambled out of the vehicles and rushed toward the gaping entrance of the building, their AK-47s at the ready. Three others nursed M24 sniper carbines as they walked around their vehicles and kept a watch on the building's entrance.

Moussa felt conspicuous. He lit up another cigarette to feign indifference. Then shouts from a balcony above him prompted one of the guards to pick up a cell phone. Five minutes later, distant sirens signaled the imminent arrival of additional ISF vehicles. But a white low-slung ambulance emerged from a side street. Two men in dangling surgical masks and blue scrubs jumped out and ran toward the entrance to the building.

By this time a small crowd had assembled on Rue Ruston Bacha, the narrow street that faced the squat. Moussa felt less conspicuous and waited. The two ambulance men reappeared above the stone steps that led to the building's entrance. Between them, they carried something bulky on a stretcher. A man's arm dangled from a blood-stained woolen blanket, the hand scraping the stony ground as they carried the body to the ambulance.

Moussa watched and waited. He had tailed Vaux and another man. Who was the dead man on the stretcher? And where was the second man?

* * *

Anthony Mansfield, MI6's head of station, always relished the routine weekly meeting with his CIA counterpart, one Alexander Mailer. Months ago, they had suspended the overstaffed and, in their view, ineffectual six-man liaison committee for this one-on-one Tuesday morning chat. And from the day they first met, they figured that having identical initials could only herald a new era in Anglo-American cooperation. But their shared initials were pretty much the only thing they had in common.

Mansfield's unshakable take on the US presence in Lebanon, before and after the devastating civil war, had only served to exacerbate the political dynamics of the small nation. The fatal frictions among the various religious parties, the eternal tensions between the Maronite Christians and the majority Muslim population, split as it was between the Sunni and the Shiites, were comprehensible only to seasoned colonial powers like the Brits and the French who had been in the region for centuries.

But Mansfield never considered Mailer personally responsible for the perceived missteps of the world's most powerful nation. Paraphrasing an old Churchillian observation, he often reminded him of England's role as "the wise old Greeks to you warlike Romans." Mailer, for his part, was soothed whenever he heard confirmation that he represented the strongest nation the world had ever seen.

Alex Mailer, in his late forties, six feet- three inches tall, heavy-set, shaven dome of a head, in a seersucker suit and highly -polished wingtips, navy-blue shirt, button-down collar and Princeton's orange-and-black-striped silk tie, sat down in the hard-bottomed Windsor chair in front of Mansfield's big desk. "All quiet on the western front?"

"Maybe on the western front, but not bloody well here in the eastern theater," said Mansfield. "Right now, we have an internal investigation going on about various developments affecting us." Mansfield was pleased with his choice of words, obfuscation being the name of the game when it came to dealing with the great ally. "I can't go into details, old chap, but until the probe is over and over successfully, I can't say more."

"Understood," said Mailer as he clicked his shiny Zippo to light the morning Camel. "We have a similar situation going on. Perhaps similar. I don't know because you're being chary as usual."

They smiled at each other. Mansfield sensed that the CIA chief was about to throw caution to the wind. "All I can tell you is that we've detected a massive breach of security affecting our stringers and field agents. Seems the Hezbollah network is much more so-phisticated than we ever imagined."

Mansfield's ears pricked up. Could this in any way help him find the mole within his own intelligence outfit? He asked, tenta-tively, "What do you mean by sophisticated?"

From the left side of his mouth, Mailer blew a cloud of blue-gray smoke toward the steel filing cabinets. "We hear they've re-cruited some first-rate counterintelligence, computer-oriented experts. They've embarked on a wide-ranging fishing trip—trac-ing cell phone calls to and from our informants, communication patterns etcetera. These guys can follow data trails like terriers sniffing out foxes. Apparently, electronic communications can be reverse- engineered to detect certain patterns that expose who talks to whom. These nerds are highly sophisticated—probably learned their computer skills in the West. God knows there are enough Arab students at our colleges and universities."

"Don't like the sound of it."

"I think we're dealing with a dangle."

"A dangle?"

"Someone we probably recruited in the past who's a double agent and feeds stuff to the other side—in this case Hezbollah."

Mansfield now wondered whether he should adopt the same nomenclature for his mystery mole. There had been leaks, fatal leaks for some of his major assets, but had they been electronic breaches of security or just plain simple human betrayal by internal personnel? In any case, the results were the same—a devastating attack on both nations' efforts to get a handle on the unpredictable maelstrom of Mideast politics.

"Cup of tea?" suggested Mansfield.

"No, thanks. I'll have a coffee if you don't mind."

These were the silent mutual codes for agreeing that business was at an end.

A young Lebanese assistant to Nancy Sheridan brought in the refreshments. She wore a royal-blue hijab over her head, white jeans, and a black silk blouse. Laying the large mugs down on the table mats pushed forward quickly by Mansfield, she then plonked down two ministrips of KitKat. "Sorry. Ms. Sheridan says we've run out of biscuits."

Mansfield nodded, and in the silence that ensued, both men quickly stripped the small chocolate bars of their cellophane wrappings. Then Mansfield's encrypted cell phone rang out the first few bars of "Land of Hope and Glory." While he was happy to have imposed his patriotic ringtone on Mailer, he now showed his impatience at his continuing presence by several nods and a wave of his free left arm. Mailer quickly drank the dregs of his coffee, picked up the KitKat bar, and headed for the door.

Mansfield wondered why Citron was calling at this hour. It had been agreed that he would check in twice a day at 7:00 a.m. and at 7:00 p.m. if there was nothing exceptional to report. They had discovered that Vaux's daily habits were pretty much routine and far from frenetic.

"Yes," said Mansfield curtly.

"Citron here."

"I know. I can read my own display screen. What's on your mind?"

"Vaux has disappeared. He was with Greene. Someone has been killed, sir."

Mansfield said nothing. In the background he could hear the hum and clatter of the Beirut traffic. In view of what Mailer had just told him, he wondered whether he should meet with Citron face-to-face rather than any more phone talk. But curiosity got the better of him.

"You said *killed*. Who, for God's sake?"

"I can't tell you that. Perhaps Vaux. I saw Greene—how you say?—frog-marched, yes, frog-marched out of an abandoned building. He was handcuffed, anyway, and more or less thrown into the back of the police vehicle. Before that, I saw a body being taken away on a stretcher—"

"A body? Whose body? Do you mean Vaux was taken away on a stretcher?"

"Can't be sure, sir. The corpse was covered with a blanket, head to toe."

"Meet me at the usual place—in thirty minutes. And watch your back."

Mansfield dialed a three-digit internal office number. "Browne?"

"Yes, sir."

"Get down here as soon as you can. There's a major bloody crisis. And bring your little toy with you."

Browne, two floors up in the embassy compound, pulled out his desk drawer and picked up the Glock 17. He checked the magazine and slipped the small handgun into a shoulder holster. His pulse raced at the thought of finally some action at the sharp end.

Chapter 8

Vaux saw daylight streaking in from the gaps between the thick steel door and its sturdy frame. He had clambered down four flights of stairs, often stumbling on stinking garbage that had been thrown into the servants' stairwell by transient residents. He plunged toward the door and pushed. But it didn't give way. He pushed again and looked for a crossbar that might trigger a release and open the lock. There was no bar. He pushed hard again, shoulder against the door, but the door wouldn't budge. He listened carefully for any noise that would indicate he had been followed by the men who had entered Azimi's apartment. He felt in his pocket for Greene's Sig Sauer P226. Greene had told him it was suppressed and the magazine fully loaded. Reassured, he began to mount the concrete stairs. He cursed when he stumbled on a couple of empty beer cans. He stood still as the cans clattered down the steps. The stench of stale urine propelled him upward to the second floor. He had closed the hidden door when he left and it remained unopened. He listened for voices. Nothing. How many minutes had passed since his escape down the stairs? He looked at his old Accurist. He reckoned he'd been in the stairwell about thirty minutes. He put his ear very close to the narrow plywood door but there was complete silence. Through the frosted glass, he saw no movement of any kind. The men, whoever they were, had left and had taken Greene with them.

Slowly, quietly, he opened the door. The cockroaches had returned. Now they scarpered from the countertops to crevices between the large, deep sink and the chipped tiled backsplash. He stood and listened. But there was a deep, telling silence. He walked slowly and tried to be as light -footed as his 190 pounds would allow him. He headed for the french doors whose windows had been blown away one brutal night long ago. He could hear distant muffled voices from somewhere below: a man talking to someone whose thin, tinny voice had the timbre of a radio. He gently pulled aside the tarpaulin that draped the balcony. He looked down and saw a uniformed police officer standing casually by his car talking through a walkie-talkie. His partner sat in the driver's seat enjoying a cigarette.

Vaux turned back to the ransacked room. It had all the signs of a hurried search—the office desk whose drawers had been flung open, their contents strewn on the floor; the doors of the old armoire gaping wide; Azimi's few garments—two cotton bomber jackets, shirts, jeans—kicked away to the center of the room.

In the corner near the tarp-covered balcony, Vaux noticed an antique, wormholed escritoire. Here, too, the small desk drawers had been opened and their insignificant contents—a few small coins, paper clips, an office stapler—spilled onto the ink-stained blotter. Vaux then walked over to the passage that led to the small bedroom. The door was ajar and he gently pushed it open. The blood-stained mattress now stood against the far wall and the small bedside table lay on its side, its one empty drawer hanging open. Colored shards from the shattered shade of the Tiffany lamp reflected an eerie sparkle on the yellowed, cracked ceiling. Then he saw a pair of white trainers, stained and soiled, in a corner. He had never met Azimi, but to see the murdered man's scuffed workaday shoes caught his breath.

Vaux pulled himself together. There was nothing he could do to help Greene. The police had taken him away because they considered him the prime suspect. But why did the gendarmes suddenly show up? Presumably because someone had tipped them off. If so, whoever killed Azimi must have observed him and Greene arrive at the apartment and seized the opportunity to frame them. Unlike Greene, he had been lucky to escape detection. Azimi's killer or killers presumably suspected Azimi of betrayal. The questions kept coming. But here he was at the scene of the crime. And it happened to be the place Greene's valued cutout had chosen as a makeshift safe house.

Now Vaux's natural talent for tradecraft kicked in. He went to work. He searched every nook and cranny of the dismal apartment. Under baseboards, above door lintels, on his knees crawling along the disused balcony, strewn with bits of shrapnel and cartons from a local Kentucky Fried Chicken outlet. He examined the creases and folds of the soiled and bloody mattress. He looked under the escritoire, searched the small drawers and the pigeon holes, examined every item from boxes of paper clips to stapler refills. He found an ancient Remington portable typewriter in a cupboard under the kitchen sink. Cockroaches and several centipedes scampered for safety as he lifted the machine above his head to examine the base. He carefully rewound and pocketed the red and black typewriter ribbon for the cryptology geniuses to work on.

Just as he thought he was done, his eyes caught the small metal flaps of a fuse box, flush to the wall beside the narrow servants' exit. He pulled the small doors open. And there, stuffed in front of the glass-topped power fuses, sat a black leather–covered diary. He opened the first pages—names in Arabic and English and French, telephone numbers, e-mail addresses, indecipherable letter-and-number combination codes. Vaux mumbled, "Eureka."

* * *

The police car sped through the busy downtown streets, sirens blaring, lightbars flashing. Within ten minutes of Greene's arrest, he was sitting in a cramped office in Beirut's central police station on Verdun Street in the Hamra district. The handcuffs had been taken off; he had been patted down and then relieved of his blue blazer.

He planned to brazen it out by not claiming diplomatic immunity. He had to conceal the real purpose of his presence at Azimi's pad to prevent unfriendly parties from coming to unhelpful conclusions. They had taken his passport, so Greene occupied his mind with trying to recall his alternative cover story.

He heard the door open behind him, and he turned to see two uniformed men: the younger brandishing an AK-47, the other, a corpulent man in his fifties who held Greene's passport in his hands along with a typewritten copy of the short statement he had given. The man with the weapon stood at the door. The older man sat down heavily in a scuffed leather chair opposite Greene. The room was hot and quiet. A silent, three-blade ceiling fan twirled slowly with little effect.

The officer scanned Greene's short statement. He looked up and took off his steel-rimmed half-moon glasses. "I am *Capitaine* Freige." He smiled benignly. Greene felt heartened. "Let us get down to business, as I think you say in England, *non?*"

Greene smiled back. Freige wore a light-weight green chino uniform with a traditional French kepi that he now removed and put on the desk between them.

"Yes, absolutely," stuttered Greene.

Captain Freige flipped through the pages of the passport. "So, Monsieur Menzies, you claim that you discovered the body of your friend just minutes before the police arrived."

"That's correct, *Capitaine*." Greene figured there was nothing to lose by going along with the sort of Franglais the captain had chosen to use.

"And you claim you were just paying a friendly visit to this man. May I ask, monsieur, what exactly is your relationship with the victim? Did you have business dealings with him?"

"No, no, *Capitaine*. I'm just a tourist. You can check with my hotel. I've been here a few weeks now, and I'm fascinated with the city. I try to meet as many Beirutis as I can squeeze into a day. I'm thinking of writing a travel book, you see."

Captain Freige looked skeptical. "But 'ow can this man who lives like a—'ow you say?—vagrant, vagabond, *non*?—possibly be of any interest to you?"

"Well, when I visit different countries I try to meet all sorts of people, *Capitaine*. That's what writers do." Greene thought it would pay off to sound socially progressive.

"Umm, I see. No drugs or sex involved, I assume, monsieur." Freige looked coldly into Greene's blue eyes. He detected a slight flush on the young man's cheeks.

"No, absolutely nothing like that, *Capitaine*."

"So please stop wasting my time and tell me what you wanted from him." The captain's voice had hardened, a signal perhaps that his patience was not inexhaustible.

"Color! Reportage, stories from real life, real people—their experiences, perhaps, in the long and bloody civil war..."

"Ah, I see. Politics, eh?"

"In Lebanon, it's hard to avoid politics, sir."

"Very true. You know per'aps to whom the dead man had pledged political or religious allegiance?"

"I have no idea," lied Greene.

Freige looked unconvinced. But Greene was saved from further evasions by the jangle of the captain's cell phone.

"*Oui*? Ah, *oui*. *C'est bien*. OK, it is good. *Tout de suite*." The Captain's thick lips curled into a benign smile. "Seems you have friends in high places as well as in the city's squats."

He rose, picked up his kepi, tore Greene's statement into four pieces and put them in a shredding machine behind his desk. He handed the passport back to the former prisoner. "You may go now. And be sure to send me the book."

"Thank you, sir." Greene hurried past the sullen armed guard and left the grim old building. He walked swiftly down Verdun Street, patting his inside pocket occasionally to make sure his sham passport was still intact.

* * *

The liveried doorman greeted Vaux as he entered the swing doors of the hotel's air-conditioned lobby. He was confronted by a uniformed security guard who ushered him through a metal detection scanner. As he went through the narrow monitored passageway, he set off a screeching intermittent *bleep* that echoed through the quiet lobby. Vaux had forgotten about Greene's Sig Sauer. He handed it over to the guard. The scanner operator pressed a silent alarm device, and three burly armed men of indecipherable nationality trotted over from somewhere behind the hotel's reception desk. Vaux was ushered into a back office and asked for his passport.

A senior officer, bald and overweight, flipped through the pages, looked at the recent photo, looked up at Vaux, and slowly tapped the blue-and-gold hard-covered document on his desk. The other three security guards stood behind Vaux who was invited by the senior man to sit down on a high-backed chair in front of his desk.

"Well, Mr. Westropp. British, I see. You speak Arabic?"

"Very little," said Vaux. "But if you prefer French—"

"No, no. English will do. You are a tourist? Or are you working here in Beirut?" His accent was heavy and guttural. Small beads of sweat covered his high forehead.

Vaux delivered his cover story. "I'm a freelance journalist working on a series about the Middle East," said Vaux calmly.

"For which publication?"

"*The Economist* magazine," said Vaux.

Department B3's Sir Nigel Adair, who had sat on the board of the magazine for twenty-five years, had told Vaux that *The Economist* would vouch for him in any identity crisis.

The senior man signified that he recognized the name of the publication. His eyebrows rose in silent respect.

"And do you usually carry a handgun?"

Vaux heard a shuffle behind him. Perhaps the security guards were getting impatient, or they were reminding the chief of their competence in detecting the offensive weapon.

"Because of the areas I have to go to for background material, I was advised to carry a handgun for my own safety. That's all."

Vaux saw that none of the security team wore a uniform. They were all dressed casually in jeans and dress shirts, their gun holsters clearly visible. He was not dealing with the official Interior Security Forces, the ISF.

"What areas? Why do you think you need a gun in Beirut?"

Vaux suppressed an urge to introduce some humor to lessen the tensions he felt were slowly building. Of all the capitals around the world, lawless and sect-riven Beirut would be just the place most people would feel safer with a gun. He wondered whether the security chief was just playing with him, enjoying the conversation, showing the usual pleasant Arab hospitality. Or was it more a sadistic cat-and-mouse play that would end in a speedy trip to an ISF detention center?

Vaux now appreciated the short morning briefings delivered by old-hand Arabists at Vauxhall Cross. "I am thinking of places like Shatila and Tal el Zaatar, Palestinian refugee camps where tourists—which I would be mistaken for—have to be cautious."

The man facing him shrugged. He closed his eyes and squeezed the bridge of his nose between thumb and finger while he came to a key decision.

"Are you staying here in the hotel, Mr. Westropp?"

"No. But I am thinking of checking in, and I wanted to ask about vacancies and room rates."

"Ah, so. And where are you staying now?"

"With a friend at the American University," said Vaux, hoping there would be no follow-up to this piece of disinformation.

"You may go now. Collect the gun when you leave. And if you return, you will have to deposit the piece with the front desk."

Vaux made a quick exit, nodded to the three security guards, and headed for the lobby bar. On the mirrored back bar shelf, he saw the bright yellow label of his favorite whiskey. The young lady behind the bar smiled broadly, delighted at last to have a customer.

"Cutty Sark. A large one."

Chapter 9

Vaux grabbed a taxi that had been waiting in the small fore-court of the hotel. The doorman opened the rear door for him and repeated Vaux's declared destination to the grizzled driver. It was now early-evening, and the traffic was light.

Vaux handed the driver a bundle of notes. With the Cutty Sark coursing through his veins, he knew he had probably over-tipped—the lop-sided dollar-Lebanese pound exchange rate took time to master.

From the cross-section of the Rue de Rome and Rue Hamra, it was about ten minutes' walk to the small apartment. Today the ancient grilled elevator was out of order. Vaux headed for the narrow marble staircase. He climbed three flights and was out of breath when he got to his landing. He saw that the apartment's solid front door had been left slightly open. He heard no voices and wondered if Ahmed Hussein had let himself in with a duplicate key. So he gently pushed the door open, ready to pull back if there was the slightest hint of a squeaky hinge. But the door swung silently and he opened up enough of a gap to see through to the tall windows. A man was splayed out on the parquet floor, his face turned to the side, eyes wide open. Blood oozed from his gashed throat. Vaux knew he was dead and knew that it was Ahmed Hussein.

He looked up and down the corridor and listened closely for any movements. Only the kitchen provided any cover for a killer. He took out his Sauer and moved slowly and quietly forward. The kitchen door was wide open. He strained to hear any signs of breathing, any sound or shuffle that would indicate someone's presence. But he heard nothing. He slowly advanced toward the kitchen, listened more closely, then dived through the door, swinging the handgun in a wide swath to take advantage of surprise.

There was nobody. He quickly went back into the main room and closed the door. He bent over Hussein's body, and for the second time that day, he checked a young man's pulse. He was dead. His wrist was as cold as his forehead. Vaux closed the gaping eyes—eyes that suggested the sudden shock of a surprise assault. Suddenly, Vaux wanted to vomit. He went through to the kitchen sink, which also served as his bathroom washbasin, and threw up the Cutty Sark along with the dry club sandwich he had ordered at the hotel bar.

He wiped his face with a paper towel and went through to the main room. Before he could collect his thoughts, he heard a heavy knock at the door. Perhaps the police. Another frame-up? He moved quietly toward the door. He would finally get to use the old-fashioned fisheye he had noticed when moving in. He saw two distorted, rotund men waiting for some response. But they weren't in the camouflage fatigues of the ISF. One burly man wore a tropical beige lightweight suit with a striped tie; the other wore a white shirt with ballpoint pens sticking out of the top pocket.

Like all Englishmen, Vaux recognized his own tribe. But he decided to make double sure by shouting from behind the door. "Yes! What is it?"

Mansfield, who had never met Vaux face to face or heard him speak, guessed it was Vaux.

"We're from the embassy, Vaux. Can we come in?"

Vaux, still holding the Sauer, pulled the door chain from its socket, turned the Yale lock and opened the door.

"My name's Mansfield, and this is my colleague Peter Browne."

"You've come at what in polite society they call an inopportune time," said Vaux coolly. He opened the door wide to see how the two men reacted to the sight of the corpse.

"My God, Vaux. Have you called an ambulance?" asked Mansfield. Browne had already fished out his cell phone.

"I only just arrived here myself. And please put the phone away. There's something I have to tell you." Vaux then related what had happened to Greene and how he had probably been framed for killing one of his key field agents. How he had spent some time at the hotel before returning just minutes before their arrival.

Vaux's report confirmed what Citron had already told Mansfield. He turned to Vaux. "Don't worry about Greene. The ambassador has a direct hotline to the minister of the interior. He runs the ISF. I'll get on to Eccles as soon as I get back. Greene will be released before midnight, I guarantee it."

"Meanwhile, we'll have to call the authorities," said Vaux.

"May I make a suggestion?" said Mansfield.

"What?" asked Vaux.

"Let them get an anonymous call. While you do a runner, skedaddle."

"But where to?"

"The hotel you just told us about. The bar with the Cutty Sark."

"But Hussein has an uncle. This is his place, for God's sake."

"The worthy men of the ISF are used to dealing with this sort of thing, Vaux. This is Beirut, for heaven's sake. Now go. And let us tidy a few things up here while you go and check in at the Shangri-La or whatever it is.

"Radisson."

"Go!"

Vaux gathered up a few clothes and toiletries to put in his leather holdall while Mansfield paced the room. Browne worked diligently on his cell phone. As he opened the door, Vaux turned to Mansfield. "By tidying up I presume you mean you will deactivate the bugs?"

"We think Greene did that for you," said Mansfield, as he nonchalantly gazed through the windows.

* * *

Vaux checked in to the newly -built hotel only some three hundred yards from the bombed-out building where Greene had taken him to meet his cutout. He deposited the Sauer, wrapped in a bubble envelope, in the hotel's back office safe. The room, on the fifth floor, was spacious with two double beds and what Vaux called "all the mod cons"—glittering bathroom with marble bath and a stand-up shower big enough for three people, a minibar filled with small whiskey bottles (no Cutty Sark), gin, vodka, potato crisps and several cans of Heineken. He had a quick shower, shook himself into the hotel's white cotton bathrobe and lay on the bed nearest the large picture window.

Despite the devastation and the construction sites, Beirut at nighttime was a sparkling jewel set in the velvety dark blue of the Mediterranean. He tried to stay awake, but it was hard. He thought of Ahmed Hussein, a well-meaning, bright student just about to start out in life. Who would want to kill him and why? Greene's man was another story: he was involved in the great game, risking his life every day, serving perhaps several spymasters. Greene had told him that Azimi was an agnostic. But who in this country of seething sects, irreconcilable faiths, and family feuds could be called agnostic?

Vaux's eyelids were closing and he fought the urge to sleep. Then his bedside phone tinkled.

"Mr. Westropp, we have a long-distance call for you." The operator sounded soft and soothing and spoke with a BBC accent.

"Hello?"

"Craw here, old boy. Hear there's been a bit of a setback over there. Want you to get down to the embassy ASAP where we can speak on the secure line."

Vaux looked at his old Accurist. It was 12:30 a.m.

"I've had a long day, Alan. Can't it wait till the morning?"

Predictably, Craw caved in. "I'd prefer to speak to you tonight. However, it's getting late here, too, so we'll do it in the morning."

Vaux calculated London time at 10:30 p.m. Though he'd deny it, Craw was probably happy not to have to order a taxi for the gloomy Gower Street offices at this time of night.

"But it's crucial we talk tomorrow. I'll try and arrange a conference call with Sir Nigel. You understand that the operation has been aborted, I take it."

"So Vauxhall has won the turf battle."

"I wouldn't put it that way, old bean." Craw employed Wodehousian phraseology whenever his professional competence was called into question.

Craw continued: "We may have lost round one, Westropp, old boy, but the fight continues. I shall be coming over there within a few days for a debriefing. Prepare for it, my boy. Bye for now." Craw rang off.

Vaux finally closed his eyes and thought of the two young men who were alive and well this time last night but now lay on a slab somewhere, cold as stone. "God rest their souls," he murmured. It was a supplication he made to a mysterious God whenever he mourned the unexpected and untimely deaths of loved ones and strangers.

Chapter 10

Vaux had to admit that Alan Craw, deputy director of Department B3 and seasoned alumnus of Britain's Secret Intelligence Service, had a talent for housekeeping. Within two days of his arrival in Beirut and the official debriefing sessions, he had found a safe house for the small B3 team. It was an unoccupied, ornate Ottoman-style mansion in Achrafieh, a leafy residential quarter, not far from central Beirut. The old house had been due for demolition to make way for a high-rise apartment block. But in the face of fierce opposition by conservation groups, the city fathers had given the architectural gem a stay of execution.

Solidere, a construction company founded by a Beirut denizen named Rafiq Hariri, had been given the virtual monopoly to rebuild Beirut after the civil war. The long process of reconstruction continued over the years, along with the unresolved debate between the modernists and those who wanted to preserve the dwindling examples of classic Byzantine architecture. Hariri became Lebanon's prime minister while he still ran and owned Solidere, the legal precept "conflict of interest" having no echo in the halls of Levantine politics. Hariri was later assassinated in a car bombing.

Nuri al-Hamid, a wealthy friend of Hariri's and now vice-president of the company, had known Alan Craw since they were schoolboys at Westminster School, a private institution in London, catering to the offspring of the wealthy elites, English and international. Craw saw it as his professional duty to keep what he called his "gold-plated list" of the well-connected people he had met on his academic ascent at school and later at Worcester College, Oxford. Christmas or New Year's cards and occasional get-togethers cemented the relationships.

And so within two days of his arrival in Beirut, Craw had contacted Nuri al-Hamid, and they had signed an expensive short-term lease on a semifurnished, decaying mansion whose ultimate fate hovered in a legal limbo.

The three secret agents were sitting amid unruly vines on the second-floor pillared balcony that overlooked the unkempt gardens of the big house. A high espaliered brick wall insured privacy from the street; date palms lined the curved crumbling driveway to the villa's rusting wrought-iron gates.

"The only thing this place lacks is a servant or two," said Craw with a sigh.

"An air conditioner would be nice, too. I take it you don't trust anyone to come here and help with things domestic," said Vaux.

"Not even to make the beds?" asked Greene.

Craw said, "I'm surprised I have to justify myself. Both of you have recently lost vital contacts—two of them to be exact, both brutally assassinated. Do you mean to tell me that you feel no responsibility? The fact they were detected and chased down by the enemy means that your tradecraft was faulty. At least, that's what Sir Nigel thinks, and I tend to agree with him."

A long peace-keeping silence ensued. Then Craw came to life. "Oh, I forgot to give you a small gift from Anne, Vaux. He stood up and went downstairs where he had left his new Austin Reed safari jacket. Vaux waited in passive anticipation. Then Craw returned with a shiny compact disk. Vaux looked at the label. Duke Ellington. A 1936 recording. "Reminiscing in Tempo."

Vaux was moved. "Oh my God, that's wonderful. Now I'll have to find a CD player."

"That shouldn't be too difficult," said Craw. "Charge it to entertainment expenses. I'll co-sign. You need something to remind you of home in this god-awful posting."

Department B3's three agents then relapsed into silent contemplation. The embassy had sent over a big box of provisions, including a case of Bass Pale Ale and they now sipped the sparkling lukewarm beer. The kitchen's ancient fridge, a big white GE model, circa 1935, awaited the talents of one of the embassy's handymen.

Vaux said, "I had a long talk with Mansfield yesterday. He told me that in fact the MI6 boys had tabs on both our subagents—if you want to call them that. My guy, Hussein, was apparently not what he claimed to be. All right, I was hoodwinked. He wasn't even a student. In fact he had several masters. He was a Maronite by religion, but he apparently worked for the highest bidder. Mansfield thinks he was probably killed because he was suspected, not surprisingly, of working for me. They may have played him as a double agent, but I guess they figured he had so many masters they didn't trust him. In the end, they resorted to the usual way of dealing with unknown quantities."

Greene said, "But if Mansfield's team had the goods on this character, why wouldn't they forewarn you? They knew you were running him—they bugged your flat."

"Isn't that a silly question? Office politics, for Christ's sake. They don't like B3's interference, our very presence here. And anyway, they deny ever having wired the place. They say Hussein arranged the eavesdropping to bolster his claim that he wasn't working for me but for them—probably one of the Sunni militia groups."

"What's your take, Greene?" asked Craw.

"Well, Michael's right, of course. We've had very little co-operation from Mansfield's people. They gave me the personnel files, and I've had face-to-face interviews with all those whom I had put on my suspect list, but that's about all the help I've ever been offered."

"They look upon us as interlopers," said Vaux.

"Yes, well, we'll see about that," said Craw, his jaw rising in defiance.

Greene opened another bottle of Bass. Craw scrutinized the young man's handsome, tanned face. "And you, Chris? When's the happy day?"

Greene had to think. "Oh, you mean the wedding?"

"Yes, of course. I would have thought it would be very much on your mind."

"Not until we're done here, mate." Greene immediately regretted the colloquialism. "This is a virtual wartime posting, sir. Beirut's probably the most dangerous assignment I've ever had. I can't even think about the future until this job's done."

"That's a very telling remark, Greene. But tell me about this chap Azimi. You swore by him, I hear."

"He was a friend of Mahmoud's who should be coming back from Tripoli in a few days. Again, Mansfield told me they had been monitoring him for months. Apparently, he was very religious and was on Hezbollah's payroll."

"And you were completely taken in."

"I trust Mahmoud. I don't think even he knew where Azimi's loyalties lay."

"Ha! In this bloody country, where do anybody's?" cried Craw.

Taking his last pull of beer, Vaux added, "Including our own team, it seems."

"It's a rivalry we have to put up with, Vaux. Our problem is our success—"

Vaux looked at Greene who looked back at him and then down to a small white concrete cherub that sat in an empty, leaf-strewn garden pond. Craw sensed the skepticism.

"By that I mean we've often outflanked the Mideast desk at Vauxhall. You know that, Vaux—look at your undoubted success in Operation Apostate. We were the right team at the right time. Without you and our back-up, young Micklethwait would have died in some desert redoubt."

Vaux excused himself, pleading fatigue. The big bedroom assigned him by Craw was on the third floor. He climbed the dusty, winding Carrera marble staircase. The room was cool, high ceilinged and shaded by the closed steel shutters. His holdall lay by the side of the bed, and he dug through his clothes to the metal bottom panel. He raised it slightly. It was a tight fit, but what he now called his little black book was safe and secure. He lay on the high four-poster double bed and fell asleep.

* * *

Vaux had noticed that whenever Alan Craw, Sir Nigel's deputy at Department B3, traveled on the firm's business, he showed utter contempt for any budgetary limitations imposed by fickle Parliamentary committees to reign in the overall costs of government. So he was not surprised when, along with Greene, he was summoned to the five-star Phoenician Hotel, in the heart of Ras Beirut and close to the Grand Serail, a sprawling Ottoman palace and home to Lebanon's prime minister.

The grand suite overlooked the busy Corniche and beyond to the golden beaches and the azure calm of the Mediterranean. The hotel had been destroyed in the civil war, hit by Israeli missiles fired from the sea in the 2006 hostilities, taken over in turns by Hezbollah factions, the Christian Maronites, and the Saudi-backed Sunni militias. Now modernized and renovated, the storied pre-war venue of politicians, movie stars, business tycoons and visiting potentates from Saudi Arabia and the Gulf States suffered from only one real problem: the low occupancy rate. But that hardly concerned Craw any more than the heavy discount he was offered due to the hotel's surplus capacity.

Craw greeted the two men at the white, gilt-fluted double doors that opened onto a large lounge with white leather sofas and armchairs, glass and chrome side tables and a wet bar with high stools in the corner.

"What can I get you, gentlemen?" said Craw, who was clearly in a good mood. "Vaux, I know you like Cutty Sark scotch, but you'll have to make do with J&B. Or you can share my Echezeaux 1971— a wonderful burgundy I unearthed in the hotel's wine cellars."

Vaux ignored the question and poured some whiskey into a cut-glass tumbler.

"Chris, what's your poison?"

"A beer will do," said Greene. Craw bent down to a small fridge behind the bar and produced a bottle of Kronenbourg. "Don't mind frog beer, I presume. Can't imagine why they don't stock some good English ale."

"It's been my favorite since my Paris days."

"Ah," muttered Craw. "I didn't know you had a stint in Paris."

"Only because I speak tolerable French. Which comes in handy here, too."

"Sure, sure. But I'm a bit lost, I'm afraid. All this Levantine Arabic. I'm not used to it. I did some time in Cairo where the accent's completely different," said Craw. "How about you, Vaux? You probably understand the Maghreb dialect better, given your soft spot for Morocco."

Vaux felt he and his colleagues were all woefully deficient in foreign languages, so he chose not to answer.

They stood at the floor-to-ceiling windows that looked out to the busy Corniche and the city. In the distant west, a half sun hovered above the straight line of the horizon and quickly sank into the ocean. The city's lights brightened as dusk descended on the coastal city. The scene was breathtaking, and the three secret agents sipped their drinks in awed silence.

Craw stiffened his back, turned around, and headed for one of the plush armchairs. "I met a CIA man today at Mansfield's office. He's their political man. Apparently, the position of political counselor at our embassy remains vacant until they find someone who's presumably qualified. Anyhow, this man, name of Alex Mailer, performs the same function for the Yanks. He knows his eggs, does Mailer. Harvard and all that. He's coming around to talk to us. Fill you in on the current scene."

The response was telling. Vaux raised his eyebrows. Greene smoothed his thick hair and flopped down onto the wide couch. But before either of them could construct an intelligent remark on the sudden reliance on a rival agency, they heard the sonorous notes of the door chimes.

Craw jumped up, opened the double doors, shook hands with Mailer, and clasped his hand like an old friend while he asked him what he'd like to drink.

"A Coke, if you have it, thanks."

Silence ensued while Vaux, Greene and Mailer waited for a formal introduction. Vaux saw that Craw was slowly and carefully pouring the contents of the can of Coke into a tall lager glass with a gold rim. Then, as if it was an after-thought, he introduced Vaux and Greene to the American.

"Alex is an expert on this place, and I think it would be useful to be briefed by a man who's spent his whole diplomatic career in the Mideast, working for Uncle Sam. Would you agree, Vaux?"

Vaux nodded his head in offhand agreement while he went to the bar to pour another J&B. Mailer sat beside Greene who shifted farther away from him to the edge of the couch.

"Well, it's nice of you to say all that, Alan. I appreciate it. We are allies, after all—though when I talk to your colleague Tony Mansfield, sometimes I begin to wonder about the strength of the alliance."

Mailer chuckled to a mute audience. Craw smiled and studied his nails. Earlier, he had noticed that the hairdressing salon in the lobby offered manicures, and he decided he would indulge himself on the morrow while he enjoyed the privileges of his usually un-questioned expense account.

Mailer stood up and followed Vaux to the small cocktail bar. The move was apparently to meet the need for a podium from which to deliver his briefing. He took out a few pages of notes and wrapped a pair of wire-rimmed eyeglasses around his face.

He looked carefully at the three faces of his audience as if to memorize them. "OK, guys. Here's the basic dope I think your Mr. Craw here thinks you should bear in mind during your assignment. I should point out, of course, that I have no idea what the nature of your assignment is. Which is as it should be."

After a dutiful pause, Mailer began. "Lebanon." Here his voice retreated again. Then a deep sigh. Vaux wondered whether it was a gesture of sympathy for the shattered country or a tacit conviction that multifaithed Lebanon faced a bleak future.

"Lebanon's a tiny country, only slightly larger than Connecticut, actually. Population's about six million. Average age—and this will probably shock you—only twenty-nine-point-four years. Muslim population, including Sunnis and Shiites, is fifty-four percent, Christians about forty percent. Over seventy percent of the Muslims are Shiites.

"The civil war broke out in 1975. Combatants were the Palestine Liberation Organization, the PLO, and the Christians who included the right-wing Phalangist movement. Remember that the Palestinians had been here since they left Israel at the time of its creation in 1958. OK?

"Now in 1982, you'll remember, terrorists bombed the US embassy. Since, of course, reconstructed. Sixty-three of our people were killed. Later in the same year, the multilateral force sent to help Lebanon secure internal peace suffered two hundred forty fatalities when its HQ was bombed. The victims were French and Americans.

"In 1984, we quit Lebanon. We considered the country a basket case, quite honestly, and we were wondering why we should back up a country that was playing host to Hezbollah, the PLO and other factions devoted to the destruction of our long-term ally Israel.

"In 1991, the Madrid peace talks ended and some sort of peace was established. But PLO and Hezbollah attacks on Israel continued over the years, and in 2006, Israel went to war again, bombed Beirut, destroyed the international airport, and took over parts of southern Lebanon, then occupied by Palestinians. The ruins you see every day in Beirut are the fruits of both the civil war and the war with Israel in 2006, which included bombardments launched from state-of-the-art Sa'ar four-point-five Israeli missile boats out at sea. Lebanon's small navy is more a coast guard operation than a national defense force. This was a case again where Uncle Sam's hardware helped win the day for Israel."

Greene was eager to move on from history. "And how would you describe the situation today?"

"Faction versus faction, Shiites versus Sunnis, Christians versus Muslims. Have I left anybody out? Yes, Palestinians—there are at least eight hundred thousand of them now—and I would say invisible Syrian agents whose main aim seems to be to protect Hezbollah.

"Hezbollah, in turn, is backed by an increasingly interventionist Iran. And, of course, we have the Israelis and their agents, whose main aim is to protect their border in the south of Lebanon."

Craw got up from his low armchair. "I think we all need refills—a confusing picture if ever there was one."

Vaux and Greene got out of the taxi at an ill-lit crossing about three hundred yards from the safe house. It was dark and they walked in silence. As they came upon the baroque mansion, Vaux saw a glimmer of light on the second-floor balcony. He put his arm out to halt Greene's steps. "Somebody's up there. See the light?"

"God, yes," said Greene.

They stood still while they looked up to an intermittent pinpoint of light. It brightened and then faded, then glowed again. "It's a cigarette. Brightens when someone's taking a drag," said Vaux. "Let's go."

They walked slowly up the weedy driveway to the front doors.

"Wait," said Greene. "Are you still carrying my Sig?"

"Yes," said Vaux.

"Look, could you get the security boys at the embassy to give you your own firearm?"

"Yes, I'll do it tomorrow," whispered Vaux, his hand fishing out the Sig Sauer from his inside pocket.

They quietly crept up the marble staircase to the room behind the balcony. Through the tall glass doors, they could see a man sitting at the big round glass table. Vaux took in the picture: he wore army fatigues, and on the table, a bottle of Evian, a pack of Player's cigarettes, and an overflowing ashtray. English.

"And to whom do we owe the pleasure?"

The man jumped up in astonishment.

"Sorry, sir. I was waiting for you. Mr. Westropp and Mr. Menzies, I presume."

"Yes, but who are you?" asked Greene.

"I'm Sergeant Pitt, sir, from the embassy—Diplomatic Protection Command. Bodyguard. Or minder, if you like."

"Welcome," said Vaux, putting the Sig back in his pocket. "There's food and beer in the fridge. I'm going to bed."

Chapter 11

Vaux sealed the small bubble envelope and handed it over to the mailroom clerk, a fiftyish Lebanese civilian who had passed all the vetting procedures and was considered totally reliable. He was also paid four times the average Lebanese monthly salary, a not insignificant consideration when assessing the man's loyalty. The envelope would be placed among other documents in that night's diplomatic bag on the London-bound Royal Air Force Boeing C-17 Globemaster transport plane.

The envelope, classified at Vaux's request as TOP SECRET, contained the little black book that Greene's informer had hidden away in his kitchen's fuse box. Addressed to SUMNER, BLETCHLEY PARK, BUCKS, the note read:

Dear Jack: Long time no see.
A "little" task for you: please attempt
decrypt of the black book's contents, an

incomprehensible (to me) collection/
collation of numbers and letters,
a mixture of Arabic and Roman.
Clue: cell phone numbers? Base locations
of bad guys, their names in code or plain
text?
Time is of essence. See you next time in
UK. Michael V.

Vaux had met Sumner in Cairo ten years earlier when Vaux was bureau chief for a Damascus-based newspaper. Sumner, who had a doctorate in mathematics from Manchester University, was then a staff sergeant in the Royal Signals Corps, seconded to the Egyptian Military Academy to teach basic cryptanalysis along with digital communications and encryption/decryption methods.

They were two Englishmen eager to investigate the exotic oriental world in which they found themselves, and they became regular nocturnal drinking companions. Some years later, Vaux learned that Sumner had been recruited by GCHQ, Britain's code-breaking outfit at Bletchley Park. Vaux had decided to keep in contact. He thought that one day, Sumner's attributes, apart from partying and drinking, could come in useful. At last they had.

Also traveling to London that warm and humid night were several minor clerical staff from the embassy along with Alan Craw, who felt his stay in Beirut had been useful and should have accelerated Department B3's leaks probe. This he would report to Sir Nigel Adair on his arrival.

* * *

Vaux woke early—the ancient bed was surprisingly comfortable—threw on a pair of khakis and a blue shirt and ran down the winding staircase to the large kitchen. He was surprised to find Sergeant Pitt, a lean man of average height and sunny face, sitting down at the big oak table eating a slice of toast and marmalade. "Morning, Sergeant. Sleep well?"

"Excellent, sir. What can I get you? Bacon, eggs, sausages—a British full breakfast compliments of Her Majesty?"

"Your duties don't include cooking, do they?"

"No, sir. But since we're confined here together for the duration, as it were, I thought I'd muck in and not stand on ceremony."

"Great. I can hardly boil an egg. But I'll just have some toast and marmalade like you, I think. What is it, Robertson's?"

"Right first time, sir. Golden Shred."

Vaux detected a cockney accent. "Comforting to have a Londoner with us in these exotic parts, Pitt."

"Yes, sir. Born in Limehouse. My old lady says she heard the Bow bells chiming just as I came into the world, sir."

"There you go—cockney to the core."

"And you, sir? Where did you see the first light of day, if I may ask?"

"Not that far from you—in a place called Bushey, near Watford."

"Oh, I know Watford, all right. My old man was a Watford fan. Crazy about soccer, he was."

Both men then heard heavy knocking from the second floor where Chris Greene had set up camp—literally. He had to make do with a camp bed because nothing like Vaux's four-poster could be found anywhere in the rambling house. Sergeant Pitt had made do with sleeping on an old, moth-eaten couch in the room that backed onto the large balcony.

"I'll go and see what it is," said Vaux.

He found Greene propped up against a small stained pillow in the corner of the bedroom. He lay on the narrow canvas bed in his underwear, his face shiny from perspiration, his cheeks flushed.

"What's up, old boy?"

"A fever—probably from the tap water or something I ate. It's a bloody nuisance, Vaux. I have to go somewhere every day—a dead drop to check whether Mahmoud's back and where we have to meet. I don't feel like doing anything right now except sleep. Could you go for me?"

"Sure. But where?"

"You've seen Saint George's Cathedral in your travels, I take it. Right next to the Al-Amin mosque on the Place d'Etoile—which you can't miss because of the Rolex clock tower."

"Yes."

"OK. After you go through the big doors, you go up the main center nave until you get to the sixth lateral aisle, turn left. On the first seat place, you'll sit down and kneel on the hassock. Under the seat directly in front of you, you'll find a small but deep gap on the right-hand side between the seat and the wooden arm rest. Dig and you'll find a note if there is one. It will just tell you where to meet him and when."

Vaux said, "Sounds simple enough."

Greene's eyes closed. It had been an effort to talk and concentrate. "Can you get me a bottle of mineral water?"

"Sergeant Pitt will look after you, have no fear."

* * *

Vaux was relieved that the curators of the neoclassical Maronite cathedral put their faith in God above the mundane needs of security. For here there were no metal detectors (he was worried about the alarms that would be set off by the Glock 17 that Sergeant Pitt had loaned him), let alone body searches or pat- downs. Just two elderly Beirutis whose dark blue uniforms resembled those of the veteran British Commissionaire Corps.

Among the wooden pews there were only a few of the faithful. Mostly older women who sat by themselves, a couple here and there who looked like tourists. Vaux walked toward the magnificent gold-domed cedar altar, passing the great marble columns that supported the glittering gilt coffered ceiling until he came to Greene's designated seat.

He entered the pew, unhooked a hanging velvet hassock, and knelt as if in prayer. He covered his eyes with his left hand and began the furtive search with the right hand. His eyes darted up to the surrounding arched balconies to make sure there was no surveillance, deliberate or innocent. There was nobody. He dug deeper into the gap between the seat and the armrest, and then he felt a piece of flimsy paper. He curled his hand around it and kept it in his clenched right fist.

Before he got up to go, he told himself that while he was there, he might as well make a prayer—even though he was an agnostic if only by inclination. Besides, if he was being covertly observed by some curious ecclesiastic, it would look better. A bit of tradecraft never hurt anyone. He prayed for Anne, whom he missed more than he had ever thought he could.

When he emerged from the cool cathedral into the bright afternoon sun, he made for the Starbucks he'd noticed on the busy Place d'Etoile.

He found a booth, sat with his back to the wall, sipped his Americana, and smoothed the crinkled note out on the surface of the plastic table. It read: *Usual place 5:00 p.m.*

* * *

Greene had told him where he could touch base with Mahmoud Gaber, once he had an appointed time. It was in a hot and steamy hammam in the central area of Beirut.

Vaux returned to the safe house and gave the Glock back to Sergeant Pitt. Then he asked him to procure a handgun for him when he reported to the embassy.

"You'll have to personally sign for it, sir. I know them at the armory. They're sticklers for protocol. But you can borrow mine again. I could ask for something more suitable to guard the premises—the Enfield L25 would be my first choice, sir."

"I'm going somewhere where I have to take off my clothes, so any weapon is out of the question. See you later."

Pitt looked confused, scratched his head, and put the 9mm pistol in the kitchen drawer. Greene, on the low camp bed, sweating profusely and hardly conscious, had murmured that he had told Mahmoud that in the unlikely event that he couldn't meet him personally, he would send a colleague who would identify himself by conspicuously reading or holding a copy of *Time*.

Vaux, wrapped in a copious white cotton towel, sat in the anteroom of the big oval communal bath where naked men splashed and cavorted as they cooled their bodies after rough massages and super- hot saunas. His companions, as far as he could see, relaxed or slept as they lay along the wide stone slabs or sat upright to indulge in some form of meditation. He held the magazine up high so that it was clearly visible as he scanned the columns.

A young man suddenly slid down beside him. He crossed his legs and readjusted his big towel. "No Mr. Menzies?"

Vaux quickly recalled Greene's code name. "He's sick. Just a cold. What's new?"

Mahmoud Gaber looked perplexed. But then he seemed to gather his thoughts. In a hardly audible voice, he said, "I've made what I think you call in English a breakthrough. There's someone you must meet, *inshallah*. He is well -connected, and he offers valuable information on some new plans his side is preparing."

Then Mahmoud stood up, gave a quick, beckoning nod to Vaux who followed him out of the anteroom into the big locker hall where men were lazily dressing for the world outside. He shook himself into a pair of blue jeans and fished in his pocket for a piece of paper. "That's where he lives. He will be waiting for you."

"And you're not coming?"

"*Na'am*, yes, if you wish. Follow me."

Now Vaux wished he'd brought the handgun. He could have stashed it in his locker, and nobody would have been any the wiser. But Mahmoud acted as if there was no time to lose.

They walked south for forty minutes to a district named Snoubra. The narrow streets were clogged with old taxis, big trucks and anarchic cyclists.

"Snoubra is Arabic for *cedar tree*. Legend has it that here once grew a giant cedar tree that shaded the whole village for one hundred years," said Mahmoud.

Vaux thought it sounded like another Arabian tale. He was too hot and exhausted to reply with anything more than an interested grunt. They came upon a grocery store whose vegetables and fruits were displayed on crates that took up half the sidewalk. Mahmoud led the way to the wide-open entrance. They went up a narrow staircase and onto a gloomy landing. He knocked on a brown varnished door. There was no reply. But after a long minute, the door opened slowly and the man greeted Mahmoud with a laugh and a hug.

Then a long discussion in Arabic. The man was stocky but muscular and in his forties, with short grizzled hair and a Saddam Hussein moustache. Vaux looked around the room. There was a single bed covered with a thick brown blanket, a stained washbasin in a corner, and a table with two upright chairs next to a small window.

Mahmoud said, "He asks for your forgiveness. He doesn't speak *ingliz*. But he says his people, the Hezbollah, are planning to resume attacks on Israel very soon. The first time in two years. They will fire rockets from Zar'it and Shetula, just north of our border with Israel."

Then the conversation became animated. The informer put out his hand, and Vaux guessed why. "Tell him I can't pay him today. *Bukra*, tomorrow, I'll see you're all right."

The man shook his head, shrugged and ushered his guests to the door.

Vaux looked for a taxi and asked Mahmoud if he wanted a lift back to the downtown area.

"No, is all right. But if you don't pay him tomorrow, I'll be dead."

Vaux knew he wasn't joking. "I'll be at the baths tomorrow at midday. You'll show me your locker, and I'll put the money there."

"Thank you, sir."

Chapter 12

Mansfield decided to nip in the bud what he saw as Vaux's efforts to encroach on his turf. "You're out of bounds, Vaux. It's not your job to rendezvous with contacts and procure intelligence. That's our bloody remit, and you know it. You're supposed to chase down the big leak. Somebody in our midst is betraying us and thwarting our efforts to prevent further disasters in this benighted country.

"You were sent here to do a job we could have done ourselves. But the D-G has other ideas, and I can't do much about it. So we're stuck with you and your small team. But I want you people to keep to your own bailiwick. We'll run this Hezbo fellow ourselves. So tell your Mr. Greene what's going on. That'll free him up to help you—which is as it should be."

Mansfield delivered his rebuke in the wake of Vaux's report on Hezbollah's plan to restart hostilities against Israel in south

Lebanon. Mansfield had just approved a one-thousand-dollar payment to the Hezbollah contact in Snoubra, and he wasn't in a good mood.

To lighten the atmosphere, Vaux decided to address the veteran MI6 case officer by his first name: "Look, Anthony——"

"Tony, please."

"Very well—Tony. Our task is not easy, as I'm sure you know. Your earlier efforts came to naught. We still haven't solved the problem. The trouble is that we have seen no alternative to recruiting various informers or developing cutouts as necessary first steps. A few agents—and by the way, there are only two of us until Sir Nigel sees fit to augment the team—can't do much without an indigenous group of subagents.

"The leaker or traitor has to contact his own team about the identity of the undercover agents who work for you or your station's personnel. So who are his people, the players who will act on the leaked info? They are the soldiers of our enemy, surely. And we think they have to be citizens, natives or whatever, of this country. God knows there are enough sects, factions, tribes to choose from.

"So to get close to the killers, we figured we had to cultivate our own team of Lebanese who probably mix in the same circles— revolutionaries, fanatics, religious nuts—or just ordinary, perhaps radical, students. We as Englishmen or Americans can't do that job without our native sub-agents. Now do you see why we have to have contacts within the Beirut community?"

"I suppose," said Mansfield reluctantly. "We have parallel needs. But this guy your contact led you to, the Hezbollah man, looks like he could be a fount of critical information, and I'm going to pump the son of a bitch dry. He'll be recruited to our reinvigorated M network—whether he's a Sunni or a Shiite is of little importance to me. They all go to mosques, hence what we call the M network."

"So are we calling a truce in the turf war?" asked Vaux in a weak attempt at a little humor.

"Oh, damn the bloody turf war. There never was one." Mansfield then leaned over to a cadenza, picked up a stack of type-written A4s, and slid them into a stout leather briefcase.

"This is Eccles' homework. Likes to go through the briefs after dinner. Your report on the new informer will be the first the ambassador reads. Kudos for you, but don't forget the new man's under our wing from now on.

"And by the way, our gendarmerie contacts duly informed us about your roommate's unfortunate death. In the wake of their investigations, they say that this character Ahmed Hussein never had any uncle, and he wasn't a student at the American University. The flat where you stayed was in the name of some old Maronite widow. The murder, of course, remains a mystery for the local plodders to solve."

Vaux tried to digest this offhand nugget of information. In a final tribute to the dead young man, he had to give him top marks for his talent for deception. Then Vaux remembered the prime purpose for the morning's call on Mansfield. "The cash, old boy."

"Oh God, yes." Mansfield opened a desk side drawer and brought out a sealed manila envelope. "Ten one-hundred-dollar bills. Sign the chit. And tell your newfound sub-agent we'll be in touch."

Vaux grabbed the envelope and started to leave. When he got to the door, he heard Mansfield talking to him. "Sorry, what was that?"

"I simply asked how your interrogations were going, old man. Are you anywhere near winding up the whole damn exercise?"

Vaux decided not to give a serious answer. "I'm going through the process methodically—first the first secretaries, then the second secretaries, and so on. I think the third commercial attaché will be my final interview."

Mansfield couldn't tell whether Vaux was being facetious or serious, so his considered retort was similarly ambiguous. "There can't be many left—we're not that big an establishment here. But I hope you're carefully vetting all the EBSes as well as the more obvious TSes."

Mansfield anticipated Vaux's next question but waited patiently as Vaux, leaning on the brass door handle, composed a suitable reply.

"What sort of alphabet soup is that meant to convey to a sentient being?"

Mansfield shook his head with undisguised satisfaction. "My dear Michael, these are certain categories laid out in our national security clearance codes. An EBS designation signals to the likes of me and you that the person who has been awarded this classification may, for myriad reasons, be particularly vulnerable to espionage activities. A TS designation simply signifies that the person has passed top security vetting. These things matter—at least Vauxhall Cross thinks they do."

"Of course. But I go by old and tested instincts."

"Ah, well, can't argue with that."

Vaux closed the door gently.

* * *

Two thousand miles northwest of the Lebanese coast, Sir Nigel Adair, deputy director- general of MI6 and head of Department B3, a subgroup of Vauxhall's Mideast and North Africa desk, had called for his official black armored Jaguar XJ Sentinel to take him to his weekend retreat in Buckinghamshire. It was an old Victorian pile that Lady Adair had fallen in love with after visiting several possible homes where they would spend their golden years. His retirement, postponed for some five years now, was imminent. But before he left his Gower Street offices, he knew he should touch base with Alan Craw, his deputy.

"Anne!" He preferred to shout rather than fiddle with the desk intercom.

Anne Armitage-Hallard, Sir Nigel's gatekeeper and secretary, jumped up, smoothed her blue linen skirt, and entered what everybody at B3 called the chief's inner sanctum. "Yes, sir," said Anne. "The car's downstairs waiting."

"Oh, splendid. But I thought I'd have a word with Craw before I leave. Is he around anywhere?"

Anne knew where to find him. Earlier, he had asked her if he could buy her a drink later at the nearby Fitzroy pub where he usually spent the early part of a Friday evening.

"I can call him on the mobile phone if you wish, sir."

"Please do so." Sir Nigel looked pained. He knew very well where Craw was. He hadn't been a spymaster all his life without cultivating certain instincts about other people's habits and lifestyles.

Craw appeared ten minutes later. His face was slightly flushed and Sir Nigel could smell the beer on his breath. Anne retreated to her desk.

"You've been back a few days now," said Sir Nigel. "And I haven't received a report on your Beirut visit. I was hoping for a bit of week-end reading. Gets boring in the country, you know."

"Yes, sir, I understand. But certain late developments have taken place there. I need to dig a little further to see how they fit in with my overall appreciation of the situation. I shall give you a fully comprehensive update next week, sir."

Sir Nigel knew an evasive delaying tactic when he heard one. "You've been back five days now, Alan. You could have given me a foretaste. How's Vaux getting on?"

"He and Greene have come up against a lot of dead ends, sir. I endeavored to put them back on the right track in various ways. They have to contend with an awkward man named Mansfield—"

"Mansfield? I know that name. Isn't he Vauxhall's station chief in Beirut?"

"Yes, indeed, sir. But he's very protective of his own turf. Resents our intrusion, if you like."

"But that was C's decision. Sir Percy requested our help out there. Thought we'd do a better job at the sharp end because our set-up was small and efficient, not as cumbersome as the usually overmanned MI6 operations."

"Quite, sir."

Sir Nigel now wished again that Whitehall's austerity cuts hadn't included Her Majesty's secret intelligence service in general and his small and mobile department in particular. What a great help another deputy would have been in the circumstances. Craw was getting lax, too sure of his status, overconfident in his dealings with his chief. "Oh, very well. Give me something by Tuesday evening. I have a lunch appointment with the DG on Wednesday. It's of the utmost importance. And classify it top secret—for my eyes only."

Sir Nigel was aware of Anne's relationship with Michael Vaux, and he did not wish Craw's delayed report to be compromised in any way.

"Will do, sir. Tuesday, five p.m. will be my deadline."

Sir Nigel grunted, went over to the mahogany hat tree, grabbed his tweed flat cap, and left without saying good night to anyone.

Chapter 13

Vaux hailed a taxi outside the tall embassy gates and headed for the downtown hammam. The receptionist recognized him; nodded with a smile; and handed him a locker key, a thick white towel, and a brick of unscented soap. As he did so, Vaux realized he was also surreptitiously passing a damp piece of paper into the palm of his hand. Vaux headed for the locker rooms. There were only a few men in various stages of undress, so he quickly stole a glance at the note. It was handwritten, brief, and obviously from Mahmoud, although there was no signature.

> *Monsieur Westropp: Sorry cannot*
> *make it. Out of town today.*
> *The grocery is at the cross section*
> *of Rue Madame Curie and Rue Alfred*
> *Nobel. Good luck!*

Vaux turned on his heels, went back to the reception area, dumped the locker key, the towel, and the soap on the high desk and left without a word. The young receptionist shrugged and quickly gave the towel and soap to a newcomer.

Within ten minutes Vaux had arrived at the intersection. A crowd milled around the fruit and vegetable stalls that spilled over onto the sidewalk. He checked the cash-stuffed envelope that he had double folded and stashed in his back pocket. He made his way slowly through the clusters of women and old men whose excited haggling and cocky repartee transformed the chore of daily shopping into a social occasion.

Vaux climbed the narrow staircase to the first landing. The brown varnished door was ajar. He listened for any sound. Perhaps the man was sleeping or sitting in silence while waiting for the cash delivery. Now he wished he had brought Sergeant Pitt's handy Glock. He pushed the door gently.

Face down on the single bed in the corner of the room lay Mahmoud's new contact. Blood dripped down from the brown woolen blanket that covered the body up to the neck. Vaux looked around quickly. The room was too small to offer concealment and there was no bathroom or kitchen. He moved toward the body: throat slashed, mode of killing similar to that of both Azimi and Ahmed Hussein. The man's yellowed, bulging eyes looked at him as if in reproach. "Poor bastard," murmured Vaux as he moved back to the unsecured door. He avoided touching the handle and pulled the door open slowly. Nobody about. He heard the shouts, jeers, and laughing from down below—great cover for whoever did this.

On his way through the noisy crowd, Vaux picked up a Jaffa orange, put several Lebanese pounds into the hands of the hijabbed woman at the cash desk. Less conspicuous than if he had bought nothing. Then he walked briskly toward the Rue Alfred Nobel.

* * *

Chris Greene was sitting on Sergeant Pitt's shabby sofa with a large cup of chicken noodle soup in his hands. He was on the mend. Vaux had told him what had happened.

"And you are now suspecting my sole surviving cutout of betraying us? Killing the Hezbollah man and trying to frame you for the murder?"

"You were framed for Azimi's death—or have you forgotten already? Doesn't it seem strange to you that whenever one of our key contacts is killed, somehow it looks as if we did it? You were lured to the scene; today, I was lured to the scene. I loitered for a bit in a narrow alley, and then I heard the wail of the police sirens, so I scarpered—they were on their way, and someone in the crowd of lively customers probably would confirm that a western-type male had arrived and then disappeared up the stairs to the man's room."

Green looked shocked. "I don't know what to think. But whoever is identifying Mansfield's network of informers—what he calls his M network—is now informing on our people."

Vaux took the envelope out of his pocket. "We won't need this anymore."

Greene said, "But the info this guy gave us is still valid—the Hezbollah plan to make trouble on the southern border."

Sergeant Pitt appeared at the door. He carried a walkie-talkie, and they could hear far-off voices making indecipherable conversations punctuated by jangling bursts of static electricity. "Message from the embassy, sir. Ambassador Eccles wants to meet up with you at five p.m. Shall I confirm?"

Vaux looked at Green. "Any idea what it's about, Sergeant?"

"No, sir. But he sometimes has cocktails at that time to meet his staff. He's quite a social chap. I've got an embassy Jeep outside. I'll take you over there if you like."

Vaux climbed the stairs to his big, sparsely furnished bedroom. He felt now his mission had failed. Dead agents and dead bodies seemed to be piling up. Something or someone was bent on sabotaging his efforts to find the mole. Had he missed something? Was it, after all, somebody within the embassy who had access to top secret files on cutouts, informers, and the army of helpers who tag along with any intelligence outfit in a foreign country? Who could have tipped off Hezbollah about the defector in their midst—if it was Hezbollah agents who had killed him?

He knew he'd get no answers from the ambassador.

* * *

Mansfield had told reception to send Mr. Westropp to his office before they both left for the big conference room that now served for all the embassy's social occasions.

"Welcome, old boy. Urgent call from London. Here's the number—don't worry, it's our encrypted secure line." Mansfield handed Vaux a slip of paper. He recognized the final eight numbers. He looked at his Accurist—it was 3:00 p.m. London time.

"Darling! You got my message."

"Anne, darling—of course."

"I've been so worried. Why haven't you phoned? I'm always at the house in the evenings."

Vaux knew he should have phoned earlier, but he also knew that he just hadn't found the time to go through the elaborate mechanics of organizing a secure telephone call.

"I haven't exactly been static enough to get down to it, darling. I've been moving from pillar to post since I've been here, and I'm still not settled in a place where I can organize things like long-distance telephone calls."

Vaux could see that Mansfield, who sat opposite him, was enjoying the conversation. A cynical grin spread over his face while he changed the position of various office accoutrements; staplers, china mugs full of rubber bands, and paper clip boxes changed positions like pieces in a game of chess.

"Yes, all right, Anne. I promise. Yes, of course. I love you and miss you terribly. I'll try and arrange a long weekend. It's only a four-hour flight, after all."

"And did Alan give you the CD?"

Was that the first time Anne had called Craw by his first name? "Yes, it was a splendid gift. I'm enjoying it. And your father. How is he?"

"Lingering," said Anne, sadly. "It could be a week, a month, or tomorrow. But the day nurse is very good, and she cheers him up when I can't be with him."

"That's good. I have to say au revoir now. We're using up time on a much-used diplomatic line. Good-bye, darling."

"Good-bye, Michael."

Vaux observed Mansfield's efforts to look uninterested as he frantically opened one desk drawer after another in search of something. "By the way, did the cipher people get anything from the typewriter ribbon I filched from Azimi's place?"

"Azimi?" asked Mansfield, apparently puzzled.

"Greene's late informer."

"Ah, yes, indeed. I remember now. They say it's more than twenty years old—the tape, I mean. Useless."

Then Mansfield stood up and put his large hand around Vaux's shoulders as he escorted him to the conference room with the long rosewood table. The wide french windows were open, and the air conditioners were rattling at full power in an unsuccessful effort to keep the room comfortably cool. There were only a few guests, small groups of men whose sober attire and restrained voices suggested membership in the diplomatic corps. Most of them Vaux recognized from his face-to-face vetting interviews. Seward was notably absent.

On the long rosewood table, large incongruous Japanese Tsing-pattern dishes offered finger sandwiches stuffed with smoked salmon, egg salad and watercress. There was a small cocktail bar installed in front of the long windows.

Vaux made for the bar and asked for a Cutty Sark. But a white-coated English barman with an Essex accent and an attitude of hauteur smiled indulgently. "We've only got the malts, sir. Glenfiddich or Glenmorangie Seventeen." Vaux resigned himself to a bout of indigestion and asked for Glenmorangie with lots of ice.

He walked over to the open french windows and looked out to the parched lawn and the fast-spinning gooseneck sprinklers. Vaux saw that the garden was protected from inquisitive eyes by a wall of tall cypress trees and low-lying cedar pines. He felt a tap on his shoulder.

It was Mansfield again. "Vaux, old chap. This is Ambassador Eccles. John, meet Mr. Michael Vaux, a.k.a. Derek Westropp." Vaux thought that Mansfield's use of his cover name was a weak attempt at some inside joke. But Eccles, shorter than Vaux had imagined, smiled, shook his hand vigorously, and led Vaux down the few steps to the terrace. Mansfield made a diplomatic exit.

"I know you've been here a few weeks, and I apologize for not making contact sooner," said Eccles. "But you know how it is. Never seems to be a spare moment or a slow day. Anyway, nice to make your acquaintance. Heard a lot about you."

After a slow circular walk in the garden, the ambassador maneuvered Vaux back into a far corner of the big room where two upholstered Georgian chairs stood beside an antique table. Vaux sensed the ambassador was anxious to talk about any progress he had made in rooting out the unidentified mole.

"I know you've gone through everyone here. All the men who matter, anyway. Have you any serious reservations about any of them, Vaux? I want to know before we consider some other way of going about this damn problem."

"No. They've all been positively vetted. Face-to-face interviews, social lives examined, personal interests sifted, family connections. We have to look elsewhere. But where exactly? That's what I'm trying to figure out. I've got a feeling that our enemies are playing with us. Even my own newly -minted contacts have been ruthlessly eliminated, and no one, including the local police, has any idea who the perpetrators could be."

"Ha! You do understand, I hope, that they're all in it together. By that I mean that Hezbollah has infiltrated all the security forces from the local gendarmerie to the ISF. They are slowly becoming the virtual government, step by step. They are getting their money from Iran while their opponents, the Sunni factions, are being financed by the Saudis. Meanwhile, the Christians, as far as I can see, are playing both ends against the middle."

"A confusing picture, to be sure," said Vaux.

"And meanwhile, as you know, every operation we launch, based on intelligence received, blows up in our faces before the get-go. Did Mansfield tell you of the latest disaster?"

"I don't think so."

"Two of his M network agents were kidnapped by some faction. We don't know who. But a double agent contacted us and pinpointed where our two helpers were held. By the time we launched Operation Release along with elements of the Internal Security Forces, our plan were blown and so were our men—literally, blown to smithereens as they detonated some explosive device they had attached to them."

"Kidnapping is Hezbollah's main source of finance, I understand."

"I wouldn't say their principal source. As I said, the Iranians look after them, too. Then there's the Palestinians; they haven't got much money, but they make up for it in logistical and moral support.

"By the way, I passed on your invaluable information about Hezbollah's plans to stir up trouble in the south to the appropriate ISF people as well as to our friends at the General Security Directorate, the GSD—their intelligence outfit. They didn't seem too surprised; they told me it's a reaction to Israel's constant incursions into Lebanese territory. So that's the sort of mentality we're up against, Vaux."

At that moment both men stood up as a woman approached them, smiling and shaking her head. "I was looking for you in the garden, darling." She was tall and slim and wore a low-cut pale-blue sheaf dress that accentuated her high breasts and slender waist.

"My wife," smiled Eccles. "Miranda, this is Michael Vaux, seconded for a temporary assignment from London. Very hush-hush, so don't ask him any leading questions."

Vaux felt an instant physical attraction. Now he knew what was meant by missing a breathless heartbeat. Miranda Eccles was what in his university days he would have described as a knockout. Taller than her husband, there was something exotic about her dark olive skin and long black hair. Her petite feet, a particular soft spot for Vaux, were exquisitely clad in minimal strappy sandals.

Miranda Eccles broke the stunned silence. "I've heard all about you despite all the hugger-mugger stuff we all have to suffer." She laughed innocently at her own joke while looking at her husband to see if she had upset him. His only response was a mild lift of the eyebrows.

ROGER CROFT

Vaux saw Mansfield striding over to them. Miranda's eyes had fixed on his, and the signal could not have been clearer. She was available any time he chose.

"I'm sure we'll meet again, Michael." Again, the lingering eyes told him everything.

"I hope so. Great to meet you."

Chapter 14

Chris Greene was slightly miffed at not having received an invitation to the ambassador's cocktail party. To invite only Vaux seemed to him to be a slight, either deliberate or negligent. But then again (and Greene was the fair-minded type who could always see both sides of an argument) news of his battle with flu or food poisoning had probably percolated through the diplomatic channels and could explain his non-invitation.

But he felt a lot better now and was grateful for Sergeant Pitt's ministrations at his time of need. He decided to go into town and see if Mahmoud Gaber was back in action. Vaux had muttered something about having met Mahmoud but then quickly disappeared, claiming that something urgent had come up. Greene was still curious to learn why Mahmoud had so suddenly left the city. He also wondered whether he should tell Mahmoud of poor Azimi's fate but decided that the need-to-know principle, inculcated without mercy at the Portsmouth training school, should apply.

The cathedral was as quiet as a tomb. No one about except a black-cloaked woman who languidly dusted around the tall gold candlesticks on the altar. He knelt at the pew, shaded his eyes with his left hand, and scratched for the hoped-for message. He detected a flimsy piece of tissue paper and screwed it up in the palm of his right hand while glancing up at the pillared galleries and their iconic frescoes.

It seemed he had just missed meeting Mahmoud face to face. But he now knew where to find him: in a small kebab shop off Rue de Damas and close to the Corniche.

Mahmoud sat at the back of the smoke-filled restaurant facing the door. "Glad you're back safe and sound," said Greene.

"Yes. I think you will like the results of my journey."

"That sounds promising."

"I have lined up a meeting for you to meet Dr. Salim Kasem. He is well connected and a Druze."

"Does that make him particularly useful to me?"

Mahmoud feigned bewilderment. "Yes. Of course! He is often chosen as an arbitrator for various disputes. Disputes between Sunni militias and Shias as well as between the Phalanges gangs and the Muslims. He is also a champion of the Palestinians, and the government often calls on him to resolve disputes in the refugee camps. The Druze are a small minority, but they can be useful when problems arise over land claims and inheritances. Not to mention territorial disputes among the militias."

"And you think he could know something to help in my quest? May I remind you, Mahmoud, I'm here to uncover a traitor in our midst—not a Lebanese traitor, but England's." Greene considered he was at this moment at his thespian best.

"Kasem keeps his ear to the ground. He mixes in diplomatic and academic circles, I promise you. And he said he thought he could probably help you. I didn't tell him what you are doing here—just that you were a sort of visiting official. But I told him you are also my friend."

Greene knew this was Mahmoud's bottom line. To the Arabs, friendship and loyalty between two male friends is everything. It means love, truthfulness, and steadfastness until God/Allah calls on us to return to his side.

To put the conversation on a less emotional plane, Greene asked him what Dr. Kasem was a doctor of.

"Philosophy. He teaches at the Lebanese University, and I believe years ago he studied at Princeton, the same place as your Mister Scott Fitzgerald."

"Not *my* Fitzgerald, Mahmoud," said Greene. "He was an American."

"Whatever." Mahmoud laughed.

Greene felt his appetite had returned with a vengeance. He ordered two lamb kebabs with okra and tomato salad.

* * *

Dr. Kasem, short with a big paunch, grizzled cropped hair, and a neat beard, invited Greene and Mahmoud to sit on a long sofa over which a thick blue blanket had been thrown to hide the original leather's motley stains and cigarette burns.

After their meal at the small restaurant, Greene had climbed into a cab with Mahmoud, who suggested they act quickly on the doctor's invitation. Between 6:00 p.m. and 8:00 p.m., Kasem apparently held court with a broad swath of Beirutis from young students to old friends and colleagues. Mahmoud had earlier established the format: the confidential discussion between the doctor and Greene would take place after the last guest had left.

Now the last straggler shook hands with the doctor, picked up the two borrowed leather-bound volumes on Sophocles and Pindar, nodded to Greene and Kasem, and left.

Dr. Kasem sat down heavily in a low armchair and put his leather babouche-clad feet up on a studded footstool.

"Well, Mr. Menzies, Mahmoud tells me he is trying to help you in your various enquiries. I don't know if I can be of any help. I am very well connected, of course. I go to most of the diplomatic parties here in Beirut, and my American education at Princeton has helped me get quite close to the American mission here. As a matter of fact, they are currently in a tizzy regarding a big blowup in their spy network. I understand that Hezbollah has been quite successful in their counterespionage efforts and has unmasked a score of CIA agents."

"Really?" said Greene. He hoped he sounded surprised. Weren't MI6's problems here pretty much the same?

"Yes, indeed." Dr. Kasem got up and went through to a small kitchen. He glided back with a metal tray loaded with three small cups of thick black coffee and some small Lebanese cookies called barazeks and goraybehs.

"Sometimes, Mr. Greene prefers beer at this time of the evening," said Mahmoud in an effort, perhaps, to show his close friendship with the Englishman.

Kasem laughed. "Not here. The last beer I had was in New York before flying back here. That was twenty years ago!"

Greene gulped down the bitter, grainy coffee. Kasem had embarked on a long anecdote about his early years in the United States when Greene suddenly felt an overpowering tiredness. He struggled to keep his eyes open. He pushed himself up from the low sofa in an effort to shake off the enervating fatigue, but his legs gave way and he could not summon the strength. He flopped back into the velour cushions as his heavy eyelids closed off the shimmering vision of a smiling and chattering Kasem whose words became muffled and distorted. Within three minutes he was in a deep coma.

* * *

Vaux left the embassy with a stride that could have been described by a Hollywood scriptwriter as walking on air. He felt like a young man again. It was ridiculous and pathetic. But the elation was there, the resurgent sensations of youth, the promise of sensual delights, the portrait of a very attractive lady whom he knew (thanks to his well-tested antennae) fully reciprocated his feelings. Perhaps not long lasting. But what did it matter?

Well, it did matter. What about Anne? Like all easy betrayers, he put that delicate question aside with some alacrity. That was then; this is now. And perhaps it was just an ephemeral now. He would overcome and soothe his guilt with the balm of time. It would be complicated and could take some careful planning. But nothing was impossible when two romantic people were determined on an outcome.

It was a long sinuous walk from the embassy compound to the safe house. But for the first time since arriving in Beirut, he enjoyed being a pedestrian and he savored the bizarre milieu that was this metropolis: the honking taxis, the hordes of bicycling students weaving in and out of fast and stalled traffic, old cloaked men and women on two-wheeled donkey carts, and elegant women on expensive shopping jaunts to the now-celebrated Beirut Souks, a contemporary American-style shopping mall with hyper-expensive outlets like Gucci, Prada, and Versace.

When he got to the safe house, he found Sergeant Pitt in the kitchen. He was busy slicing and dicing eggplants, zucchinis and tomatoes. He wore a linen tea towel around his waist as a makeshift apron.

"Good evening, sir. Good party at the embassy?"

"Yes, very good," said Vaux. Then to himself, "Very, very good."

"And did you procure a weapon, sir?"

Earlier, just as he was leaving the embassy, Mansfield had taken him to the armory, a small box room in the basement. Mansfield punched in a code at the barred doors and went over to a steel filing cabinet where he punched in more numbers. He slid the drawer open, grabbed a Walther P99 and handed it to Vaux along with a leather shoulder holster and a box of 9mm bullets.

"No names, no pack drill, old boy. Keep in touch," said Mansfield.

Back at the safe house, Vaux now felt for the holster. "Yes, a Walther."

"Standard equipment," said Pitt, who went on chopping the vegetables.

"Where's Greene?" asked Vaux.

"He went out, sir. Didn't say where. But he's back on his feet, fully recovered."

Chapter 15

Chris Greene emerged from the black depths of oblivion very gradually. He would assure himself he was still alive only to slip away again into an abyss of a deathlike coma. But the moments of light started to come more rapidly now, and he began to realize that he would regain full consciousness and that physically, he was intact. He moved his legs slightly and managed to wiggle his toes, he clenched and unclenched his fists, his tongue smoothed his dry lips, and finally he dared to test his eyesight.

First he saw the dark, tobacco-stained ceiling. An unlit naked light bulb hung from its center. The room was dim; a heavy brown blanket had been draped over a high narrow barred window. He tried to haul himself up, but his elbows failed to take the load. So he surveyed his new habitat with darting eyes—the four blank roughly plastered walls, the solid wooden cedar door, a chamber pot in one corner. On the floor, his jeans and what looked like cotton bandages, probably used as blindfolds or perhaps to tie his wrists and ankles for the trip here. But where was he?

He listened for sounds that would give him a clue: the hum of vehicle engines, bleating car horns, screeching tires, shouts, whistles, laughter, cursing, radio voices, canned music—the usual susurrations of a vibrant city. But he heard nothing except the hushed chirping of small birds, presumably Lebanese sparrows and finches.

He looked for water to quench a raging thirst. But there was no water, no bottle. Not even a bedside table or chair. He fell back into oblivion.

Somebody was gently pummeling his dangling arm. He awoke to the deep brown eyes of a bearded man whom he had never seen before. He wore an olive safari jacket and a white surgical mask that hid the lower part of his face. But Greene could see that he was young—probably in his midthirties—with short black hair and a copious physician's bag at his side.

"I am a medical doctor, and I speak English," said the man without a smile. "I have been asked to check you over—to give you a checkup, as I think they say in English. I am Doctor Abdallah." By the slant of his eyes, Greene could tell now that he was smiling.

Greene nodded some sort of acknowledgement. He figured that whoever had whisked him away to this hellhole at least seemed to be aware of some vague Geneva convention that requires captives be given adequate health care. The doctor leaned toward him and tried to haul him up so that he could put a stethoscope to his chest.

Then in perfect English, he asked if Greene could please stand up. Greene stood unsteadily and naked below the barred window as Dr. Abdallah put the cold stethoscope to several parts of his back, checked his testicles from behind him and turned him around to put a small wooden spatula down his throat.

"You'll live, *inshallah*." God willing.

Greene slowly dressed, his anger mounting as the good doctor scribbled Arabic on a small white pad. Greene then pounced: "I demand to know why I am being held against my will. And I wish to be released immediately. You as a member of an honorable profession surely can understand that."

The doctor smiled at his patient. "That's for other people to decide. I have done my Hippocratic duty. I will ask for you to be sent water and some food."

With that, Dr. Abdallah zipped up his bag and left. Greene looked toward the heavy door and saw a white-robed figure emerge from the gloom. The man had bowed to the doctor and was bending over to relock the door as he walked away. Two loud shots then rang out as the guard slammed home the heavy bolts.

Greene flopped down on the hard narrow mattress. For the first time since gaining consciousness, he tried to recollect what had happened. Yes, he was at this small apartment of a Dr. Kasem, supposedly a college professor. He had been taken there by Mahmoud, whom he had known for nearly two months now and whom he had trusted with his life. He had thought that some delicate but firm bond had developed between them. Mahmoud had been his most trusted and reliable sub-agent, the core of his own private network. Without him, who was left? Azimi, the latest recruit to his planned network, had been ruthlessly killed, presumably by one of the factions who were lined up against his home team.

* * *

Vaux had gone to bed dreaming fitfully of the sensual episodes that could now punctuate his life in a town he knew offered as many earthly delights as a martyred Muslim's after-life paradise, but which in his own restricted activities had offered only a circumscribed private existence. In short, he was in love with being in love—or at least infatuated. He planned a short fling that would end inevitably with the successful termination of his assignment.

But he didn't sleep well. He heard movements from downstairs and presumed Sergeant Pitt was finding himself something to do in the kitchen. Then he heard him slowly climb the stairs to the big room with the balcony where he knew he liked to sleep and keep sporadic watch on the entrance from the dimly lit street. He looked at the faded face of his old Accurist. It was 3:00 a.m., and he hadn't heard Greene's usually loud and clamorous return.

He got up, slid into a pair of khaki pants, and skipped down the broad marble staircase. He tapped at Greene's door, turned the china doorknob and peered into the small room. No one. His bed in the corner still made up, army-style, with folded blanket at the foot and green sheets neatly tucked in under the mattress.

He found Pitt on the big balcony, lolling on a newly acquired canvas deck chair, smoking his beloved Player's.

"Hello, sir. Couldn't sleep?" he said as he quickly stubbed out the half-finished cigarette in a large overflowing ceramic ashtray.

"Greene's not in his bed. Have you seen him tonight?"

"No, sir. Thought he'd got in earlier, like. Never actually checked."

"Well, he's not there."

"Probably doing a bit of the light fantastic. Young guy like that, checking the fleshpots out, if you ask me."

"Greene's not really like that, Sergeant. For one thing he got engaged just before he came out here."

Pitt chuckled, half-heartedly derisive. "Exactly, sir. One of the last opportunities of a free man. Making hay while the sun shines."

"OK. What should we do? Do you have any standing orders to deal with a disappearance like this?"

"Whoa, whoa! Let's not jump to conclusions, sir. He's not exactly AWOL, is he? I suggest you go back to get some kip, and we'll deal with it in the morning. By then Mr. Greene will have come back or sent a message. We'll go from there, sir. I'll bring a cup of tea at dawn. I brought in some Peek Frean biscuits today. I'll bring some of them, too."

Vaux walked slowly up the winding marble stairs. For the first time, he noticed several long, silky cobwebs hanging from the vaulted ceiling.

* * *

Chris Greene felt a little better. The white-robed guard accompanied by two men who wore black uniforms and whose faces were covered by black masks, had led him to a narrow mildewed shower stall where he washed his hair and body with a heavy brick of

English carbolic soap. The white-robed man disappeared and the two militants sat on stools as they watched his ablutions and nursed their AK-47s between their legs.

Greene rubbed himself with a coarse cotton towel that had been given him. Then he was led—one guard in front, one behind—to a small room with a desk and two chairs. A tall bottle of Tannourine mineral water sat on the desk, and he made for the upright chair opposite the presumed interviewer's high-backed leather armchair. He was about to sit down when one of the guards gripped his arm and shook his head.

"*Non, non. Qam!*" Stand.

Greene checked for the time but remembered that his black-faced Shark Army dual-display watch, an engagement gift from his fiancée, had been missing since he regained consciousness. He was not surprised that his handy Sig Sauer had also vanished. His two guards remained standing and as still as statues. At last, an older man appeared through the open door. He was short with a stomach that hung over his leather belt. He was dressed in a sort of nondescript olive-green shirt and baggy cargo pants and sported a Vandyke beard. He gestured for Greene to sit down. The guards remained standing.

"English?" asked the presumed officer.

"Yes," said Greene quickly. "And I demand to know on what authority I am being detained."

The officer smiled and stroked his salt-and-pepper Vandyke. "Everything will be explained in due course. Meanwhile, I will enjoy improving my English, even though I shall sometimes lapse into French, the language of our old colonial masters and the first language I was taught at school." One of the guards behind Greene shuffled his feet and sighed.

"First of all, my name is Moulay Ali. We have no ranks in our organization, so you can address me as you wish. You have to understand we know all about you and what you are doing in Beirut. Or perhaps I should say what you *hope* to do here and in the greater Lebanon."

Moulay paused, perhaps waiting for Greene to respond. Greene's instinct was to cite his name, rank, and number as he knew members of the armed forces were told to do if captured by the enemy. But he wasn't in the army and he didn't know if he could call this a capture. He had been abducted, pure and simple, and he was at sea, metaphorically anyway. "I really have nothing to say. I am a British subject—your people presumably have my passport—and my name is Robert Menzies."

"But we understand your function here is that of a spy, Monsieur Menzies. We have a vast intelligence network, and there is very little that goes on that we don't know about. We keep our eyes on everybody—our friends and our enemies."

Greene had a sudden recall, a sensation of déjà vu. But unlike *Capitaine* Freige, this man was hardly a friendly Claude Rains–type gendarme. "First, I am not a spy. That's a ridiculous accusation. And I am certainly not your enemy."

"But you don't even know whom or what I represent."

"I think I can guess."

"Well, tell me."

"One of the militant groups whose power and influence continue to prevent the legitimate government of Lebanon from doing its proper job. Of course, I don't know which particular group you represent." Greene recalled the long briefings by the Arabists at Vauxhall Cross: black uniforms, red armbands, and combat boots signified Hezbollah.

"We are nationalists. We represent the majority of Lebanese. We are backed by the half million or so Palestinian refugees who have suffered in their miserable camps for nearly sixty years while the international community, let alone Israel from where they fled, fail to lift a finger to help them or Lebanon."

The Hezbollah officer (Greene looked in vain for any sign of rank) withdrew an unfiltered cigarette from a flimsy, crushed pack of Lucky Strikes. He paused while he lit it with a slim silver Colibri lighter.

He inhaled deeply, and two gray-blue plumes were exhaled through his nostrils. "But I am not here to argue with you or convert you to our cause. I suspect you are firmly ingrained in the western interpretation of the Middle East despite your collective failures in the post–World War Two era: the French withdrawal from Lebanon, the British-Israeli fiasco at Suez, the decline of Uncle Sam's influence everywhere.

"No. I am not going to waste my time. I have to inform you that we will be holding you incommunicado here or elsewhere in our country until and unless your government accedes to our ransom demands. This is how we have to finance ourselves. And you are just the latest victim of that unhappy situation.

"You will be treated well. And you can pray to your God that your employers value your services enough to accede to our demands. Thank you, Mr. Menzies—if that is your real name. You will have your passport handed back as soon as you gain your *liberation.*"

As a final gesture, perhaps toward international understanding, the officer emphasized the last word in French, as if he were General Charles de Gaulle addressing the Free French.

Chapter 16

It was a languorous Sunday morning at the British embassy compound. A skeleton staff performed a few daily rituals like checking the diplomatic bag from London and perusing news agency copy from Reuters, Bloomberg, and Associated Press. But Anthony Mansfield, MI6's station chief, had arrived for work at his usual hour of 7:00 a.m.

Any overnight classified material carried in the diplomatic bag would be hurriedly brought to him, sent if necessary to the encrypt-decrypt girls (only one was on weekend duty), and read to see if any immediate action was required. SIGINT material was sorted and routed to appropriate desks, including the ambassador's.

In recent weeks, Mansfield had observed that his assistant, the embassy's ostensible third secretary, apparently checked in as close to 7:00 a.m. as he could manage. This Sunday was no exception.

At 7:20 a slight tap on the door presaged the entry of a rather harried-looking Peter Browne. Mansfield decided to pull a little rank. "Good God, man, you're early. Doesn't look as if you had time to brush your long hair."

Browne quickly smoothed down his thick golden locks and checked to see if his college tie was hanging straight. "Sorry to barge in, sir. But a CIA contact phoned me twenty minutes ago. Their overnight intercepts indicate that Hezbollah are holding what they call a British asset. Celebrations all round, apparently, for a well-executed and carefully planned operation."

Mansfield took off his horn-rimmed glasses and placed them on his blotter. This was the sort of news he most dreaded. He looked at his nervous and excited underling with some scorn, for throughout his long career he had always admired and attempted to uphold British coolness, a lack of enthusiasm, what the sophisticated French would call sang-froid. "Calm down, Browne. Who do you think they're holding—and what makes you think it's the Hez?"

"Impossible to know. Could be a British tourist, I suppose, or one of our own. We'd better do a roll call. They are using Spring as code name for the captive."

Mansfield considered this as he watched Browne take out a handkerchief from the pocket of his gray flannel pants. He wiped the damp palms of his hands.

"Relax, Browne. This is par for the course. Our next step is to call old Alex Mailer who, you might recall, is the CIA's station chief. Did you ever meet him?"

"I know him—I've seen him here. But we were never formally introduced."

"OK. So now you can use this secure phone and get him for me. Code numbers are in the little red book." Mansfield shoved a small red diary toward Browne.

At that moment one of the embassy's floating part-time secretaries, a slim English redhead who had lived in Beirut with her veterinarian husband for thirty years, entered the office, made for Mansfield, and whispered in his ear that a Mr. Westropp was here to see him, and he said it was urgent. Mansfield, eavesdropping on Browne's conversation with CIA headquarters, nodded vigorously and signaled to let him in.

Vaux looked as if he hadn't slept all night. Before he closed the door behind him, he told Mansfield that Greene had disappeared.

Browne, all ears, overheard the message and put the phone down. "Hence the codename Spring."

Mansfield asked what he meant.

"Well, Greene...in the spring everything is green."

"Doesn't he operate here under an alias?" asked Mansfield.

"Yes. He's Robert Menzies," said Vaux.

Mansfield asked how long he'd been gone.

"Since early afternoon yesterday. He went to a dead-letter box to see if he could contact one of his agents. Haven't seen him since."

"No effort to contact you?"

"None."

The redhead put her head around the door and asked if she could bring any tea or coffee.

"Yes," said Mansfield. "And some of those sweet Lebanese cookies please."

"Mailer is coming right over," said Browne, eager to stay in the loop.

"Excellent. I've called in the cavalry, Vaux. The Yanks know more about abductions and kidnapping than anyone here, I can assure you."

Browne added, "They've had lots of experience."

Tea was poured, and a few goraybehs and walnut maamouls were munched in silence, then washed down with cups of strong Fortnum and Mason's breakfast blend.

Alex Mailer, in a navy-blue track suit and white sneakers, had not hovered at the door, waiting to be introduced. Mansfield later told Norbert Clark, head of the Mideast desk at Vauxhall Cross, that the CIA station chief had barged into his office without a say-so and immediately taken charge of the situation, which he spontaneously and unilaterally named Operation Retrieval.

"I've studied kidnappings carefully. I know the terrorists' modus operandi, OK? Langley, bless their hearts, are obsessed with the danger of abductions ever since the notorious kidnapping of our great operative William Buckley, one of my distinguished predecessors."

Vaux and his two SIS colleagues then listened to a fifteen-minute recapitulation of the Buckley case and how in 1984 Iran had financed what Mailer called Hezbollah's *coup de theatre*.

"How much did the Hez demand for his release?" asked Browne.

"Never revealed. Besides, Washington's policy is never to pay ransom to anyone. Benighted or enlightened? Who knows?"

"It's London's policy, too," said Vaux.

"Yep," agreed Mailer, as he quickly inserted a stick of Wrigley's between his lips.

"Unlike the French and West Germans, I understand," said Mansfield.

Vaux said, "Perhaps we're jumping the gun here. So far no ransom demand has been received by anyone. Greene is AWOL, but let's face it, he could have found a pretty girl or partied with some of the young Arabs he's got to know here."

Mailer snorted. "I know the signs; Langley taught me the signs. You have the option, you guys. You can sit on your collective arses and wait for the demands from one of the many groups who operate against western interests here, or you can act now and possibly save your guy before it's too fucking late. Just as we were too late for poor old Buckley."

Mansfield looked disapprovingly as Mailer, having wolfed down his last cookie, extracted a Camel from a gold cigarette case, vintage 1940. "Obviously, if Greene has been kidnapped—and we have no firm evidence yet—we'll have to call a war council to discuss strategy. Meanwhile, Browne, get on to Eccles. He should know what's going on."

"This time on a Sunday, he's with his wife at Saint Louis Capuchin, the only Roman Catholic church in Beirut. The Eccles are Catholics."

"But he must carry a cell phone, for God's sake!" exclaimed Mailer.

Vaux, who had done some research into how best to contact the Eccles household, had already punched in the numbers and was waiting for a reply.

* * *

Vaux had once read that improvisation was a key element in the game of espionage. That morning, he intended to test that assertion.

On arriving back at the safe house, eerily empty without the presence of Chris Greene, he looked for Sergeant Pitt. He found him in a small scullery off the kitchen, on his knees, his head inside an ancient and defunct dishwasher. Beside him were an array of screwdrivers, spanners and pliers. At the sight of Vaux, he withdrew quickly, stood up, brushed his hands together, and gave a half-hearted salute.

"When this bloody thing is put right, it will save me a lot of work, sir."

"Never mind about that, Sergeant. I've assigned you a much more heroic role," said Vaux.

Vaux had decided that his first task was to check out the dead-letter box. It was possible that Greene's informer had tried to contact him, and any message found there could give a clue about Greene's recent movements, even perhaps where his abductors were holding him. He had also decided to recruit Sergeant Pitt, of Diplomatic Protection Command, an offshoot of the UK's Special Branch, as a temporary secret agent attached to Department B3.

Vaux explained what could have happened to Greene, the strong possibility that he had been whisked away from a downtown street into the arms of one of the Beirut militias. And that he was likely being held until some big ransom was paid.

"That's terrible, sir. Poor old Mr. Greene, or should I say Mr. Menzies?"

He doesn't need sympathy Pitt. He needs *us*," said Vaux. "First I want you to commandeer one of those black Range Rovers I've seen at the embassy's car pool. Then we're good to go. Could you manage that?"

"I could try to, sir. I'll have to make up some story, though. This sort of thing in strictly verboten. Warrant Officer Haig of the Logistics Corps contingent is in charge of the transport unit. And he goes by the bloody book—a real martinet, I can tell you. Anyway, aren't your activities supposed to be very hush-hush, sir?"

"Yes, but you are on a safe house assignment. Nobody but the top brass knows the location of this decrepit mansion. You can say it's way out of town and that you need transport to do your job properly—get in supplies, food, bed linen—whatever."

Five minutes later, Pitt mounted the old Raleigh bicycle he had found in the gardener's shed at the embassy and threw away his earlier doubts about the possible consequences of Mr. Westropp's flouting of the rules.

* * *

At 10:00 a.m. the next morning, Vaux sat in the pew on the left of the sixth lateral aisle, casting his gaze around the quiet cathedral. There were a few early congregants who knelt in private and isolated prayer: old men in black suits, presumed widows in dark veils and flat shoes. A solitary priest knelt at the glinting gold altar of one of the dim side chapels.

Vaux also knelt as if in prayer. He searched the narrow gap and detected a piece of paper, not flimsy this time, and folded neatly. He clenched the message in his right hand and continued the theatrics of solitary prayer or perhaps meditation. After five minutes he raised his head and looked up to the ornate galleries but saw no one. As he passed through the vaulted vestibule, a pang of guilt prompted him to put a few tattered Lebanese pound notes into the collection box.

Sergeant Pitt and his newly acquired anonymous Range Rover were parked on a side street close to Saint George's Cathedral. He leaned over to open the passenger door for Vaux who unfolded the message as soon as he was seated. It was written by hand with a ballpoint pen.

We are holding Robert Menzies, a confessed English spy. For his safe release we wish you to contact our representative at Café Maurice, north (200 meters) of the statue of Rafiq Hariri in central Beirut. You are to sit at the small bar and you will carry a copy of TIME *for identification. Be there at 11 any night from the day you pick up this message. Any tricks and your spy will be dead.*
Allahu Akbar! God is Great!

Vaux read the note quickly and handed it to Pitt. "The bastards. Our worst fears."

"And no signature, neither," said Pitt as he pressed the ignition button.

Chapter 17

Alan Craw had moved out of his cramped basement pad in tony Kensington to a roomier, brighter penthouse in what he fondly called bohemian Hampstead. In Craw's socially conscious world, the new apartment qualified as a penthouse because it was on the fifth floor of a five-storey 1930s-style block of flats, and the living room opened up through french windows to a long non-descript asphalt roof on which he planned to place a few potted plants. His bedroom faced south and overlooked the lush greenery of Primrose Hill and historic Saint Paul's in the distance.

What drew Craw to this storied north-west borough of London was the proliferation of classic English pubs and, more important, the marked surplus of available single women. His targets included ex-wives with rich divorce settlements, single women who lived between pay-checks, and young secretaries looking for a partner or future husband. He had asked Anne Armitage-Hallard, Sir Nigel Adair's secretary and Michael Vaux's live-in lover, to come and see his new living space, but so far, she had declined.

On this particular weekday morning, Craw woke up to an excruciating headache. He was in his own bed, but he sensed the warmth of another body. He slowly opened his red-rimmed eyes and turned his head to the left. She was a big-breasted bottle blonde. And he remembered where and when he had met her: around closing time at the Flask, just south of Hampstead High Street, an ancient pub located in a narrow medieval alleyway and these days frequented by writers and journalists and anyone else vaguely connected to the arts. She was in a deep sleep, and he decided not to disturb her. But then the white, 1960s-style British Telecom telephone emitted its shrill ringtone. He fumbled through the bed sheets to pick up the receiver.

A very loud, irate and familiar voice came over the landline. "Craw!" shouted Sir Nigel Adair. "Get to the office immediately. We've lost Greene. Over there in bloody Beirut. C was just on the phone. I'm in the car now, and I shall be in the office within thirty minutes. Be there! And call Micklethwait. It's all hands on deck."

Craw knew there would be no time this morning for a delectable orgasmic encore. He jumped out of bed, went into the small bathroom, and turned on the taps. He missed not having a stand-up shower. But the commissionaire/janitor downstairs had told him the last renovations and plumbing works were back in 1961.

* * *

Chris Greene had been summoned to a windowless room some-where within the labyrinthine complex of the old crumbling building. He was ordered by a masked guard to sit. He waited patiently as he thought about his plight and his treatment by the kidnappers. On the plus side, he had been fed regular meals. Sometimes even with meat (usually chicken) and once with a plate of red mullet. There was never any shortage of Lebanon's ubiquitous flatbreads.

He had seen worse hovels than his cell, even though his narrow bed's mattress smelled of human sweat and the thick blankets were stained with liquids and human discharges he preferred not to think about. But they had given him a bedside lamp with no shade and had brought in various English-language magazines including *Time* and *Newsweek* and, mysteriously, a glossy *Tatler*.

Moulay Ali stood at the open door, nodding to the guard to leave. Ali moved around the desk to face Greene. He stroked his Vandyke, which looked better trimmed than earlier. The desk in front of him was bare of any of the usual office accoutrements except the cell phone that Ali had brought out of his olive-green shirt's breast pocket.

Greene waited. Ali seemed to be deliberately building up tension by saying nothing, looking straight at Greene and then around the room. He opened his hands and revealed a new red-and-white pack of unfiltered Lucky Strikes. He offered Greene a cigarette, and Greene, to his own surprise, accepted. It was his first cigarette in several years, and he wondered if this was a sign of the so-called Stockholm syndrome that Portsmouth's instructors had often warned their probationers about. He didn't know the answer.

But by accepting Ali's gesture, he felt he had established some tenuous link with his captors.

"*As-salama alaykum*," said Moulay Ali. May peace be upon you.

Greene had mastered the response to the Arabic greeting. "*Wa alaykum as-salaam*." And on you the peace.

The conventional salutations over and done with, Moulay Ali asked Greene how he was sleeping.

"Quite well, thank you."

"And the food?"

"Adequate."

"Good, good. You like Lebanese cuisine?"

"I like the cuisine of many countries. And, yes, I am fond of Mideast food."

"I have to inform you that we are still waiting to hear from your friends and allies. We have been in contact with your people, but we still haven't heard back from them. Perhaps they are wondering whether they can afford our reasonable demands," said Ali.

Greene thought his side's play for time was to be expected. "I'm sorry to hear that. But I don't know who you have contacted, do I? My mother in the UK, perhaps? As I have told you, I'm a visitor here, and I have no employers in Beirut who could come forward and answer what you call your 'reasonable demands.'"

Moulay Ali laughed and shook his head.

"Why don't you admit you are an employee of the British— probably the secret service, certainly you have had contacts with the embassy here. We have our methods, my dear man, and it's no use continuing to deny these facts. We just want to know what your function is. We know, for instance, you have been in contact with several male whores who have sold you information about our activities and our active personnel."

Greene wasn't going to take that. He thought of poor Azimi and guessed he was now looking at a key figure of the murderous gang who slit his throat in the drab squat. "I don't know what you are talking about. So I meet people, men my own age. We talk, and I learn about Lebanese politics. Is that a heinous crime? Does it prove I am an enemy of your people?"

Ali laughed again. He drew a deep drag on his cigarette and let the smoke out gently through his nostrils.

"Then why do you so often go to the British embassy compound? We have counted your visits over the last three months. And by the way, three months is a long time for a 'tourist' to be visiting our fair city. Wouldn't you agree?"

"I had some passport troubles I had to clean up, that's all. And as you may know, British tourists are advised to register with the consulate. Also, my mother has been pestering the embassy about me. She thinks I've sunk into some drug culture, and that's why I've never been in any hurry to rush back home. Now do you understand?"

"Only that the local gendarmerie arrested you on suspicion of murder some weeks back. The man they thought you had killed happened to be a turncoat, a double-dealer, a traitor to our cause. And he sold out for money—big money in the eyes of most Lebanese. And we know the source of that money was yourself, my friend. Don't keep on denying the truth. It won't help you. If you confess and tell us what you are doing here, then we will treat your case with some understanding and compassion. If you continue to stall, then things, conditions, could get worse for you so long as your English masters remain uncooperative."

Greene remained silent.

"Now I want to move on..."

Greene coughed as the unfiltered tobacco caught in his throat. He felt relaxed enough to ask what he hoped wouldn't be interpreted as a leading question. "Before you do so, may I ask where you learned your English?"

"Why?"

"Because it's near perfect. I feel you must have spent some time in the UK to speak so fluently."

Greene dimly recollected that a Portsmouth training tradition had it that in captivity, an agent should reach out to his inquisitors to test the waters. Friendliness and sociability could pay dividends: it could make day-to-day life more bearable and could even foster a more moderate and lenient attitude and thus enhance the chances of eventual escape.

"Yes, I did, as a matter of fact, Mr. Menzies. Very perceptive of you—just what I might expect from an intelligence officer. I studied modern languages at Royal Holloway, an obscure college affiliated with London University and not to be confused with Holloway Prison, the notorious women's prison where Englishmen lock up wayward girls."

A brief silence as Greene absorbed this idiosyncratic piece of information. But his ingrained tradecraft moved him to pursue this sudden and perhaps useful flow of seemingly irrelevant intelligence.

"So you must know London well." He remembered another Portsmouth mantra: common ground always opened up the possibilities of mutual interests and unguarded exchanges.

"London is a beautiful city if you are rich. I spent three years in a shabby one-room flat in Earl's Court. Life wasn't easy. I took your complicated tube network every day to get to the college. From Waterloo I took the conventional train to Egham in Surrey where the campus is. I think I had to change three times—at any rate it took nearly an hour to cross London. But I wanted that degree so much. Those were the days when I was aiming to be a teacher. I would return to my beloved Lebanon, help our children to learn their history and their culture and to strengthen their patriotism. In short, I was an idealist."

"Perhaps you still are," said Greene. "Perhaps we are both idealists."

"The difference, Mr. Menzies, is that my country has descended into chaos and near anarchy. Unlike you British, we have not been able to defeat our enemies. They are still there, plaguing us, stealing our wealth, our children, our ideals..."

Greene decided it would be diplomatic to deflect the impact of Moulay Ali's latest peroration. "It's true that we won the two World Wars and that I suppose you could say the West won the Cold War, but we still face many problems—"

"Problems? You compare your country's conditions with ours? We've had a devastating civil war, Mr. Menzies—fifteen years of fighting among ourselves, all sides backed by different nations whose interests are not the same as our own real national interests. So we rebuild, we do our best to recover from the ruins of the war, and then what? The Israelis bombard us with the latest US-made rocketry and firepower, invade our sovereign territory in the south, and do nothing to help the refugees they have expelled from Palestine."

Moulay Ali wiped his sweaty forehead and lit another Lucky Strike. "How much do you really understand the situation here in Lebanon, Mr. Menzies?"

"It's chaotic, of course. But given your recent history, the string of assassinations of prominent leaders, how could it be otherwise?"

"Umm. No doubt you have in mind Hariri, the most corrupt leader under whom we have ever had to suffer. His son is very much alive and well, as you probably know."

"But there's been a string of politically- motivated killings, a couple of presidents, leaders of the various parties and militias."

"And you think one particular militia group is responsible for all these crimes?"

"I'm sure there's enough guilt to go around. The subsequent official inquiries go on forever, and nothing seems to be resolved. Innuendos and accusations are about all that really come to the surface," said Greene, who hoped he was being adequately diplomatic.

Moulay Ali, now chain-smoking, then embarked on a punctilious review of Lebanon's recent history: the long civil war that cost 150,000 lives, the interminable rivalry between religions (which he called confessionals), the friction and enmity among different sects, clans and militias. Greene's eyes drooped occasionally, but he managed to keep alert with the help of a few more proffered Lucky Strikes.

* * *

A disheveled Craw was caged in the rickety narrow elevator that slowly took him to the third floor of the shabby Gower Street offices of Department B3. He glanced at the tarnished brass plate that proclaimed the small office suite as the head office of Acme Global Consultants Ltd. He resolved to get Sebastian Micklethwait, an underoccupied B3 operative, to get his hands dirty and give the gold plate the polish it deserved.

In the small reception area, Anne, looking radiant in a blue-striped silk blouse and denim skirt, sat facing the monitor of her computer and simply nodded toward Sir Nigel's door, a mute signal that the boss was waiting and in all likelihood in a rage. Craw braced himself for a rough ride and entered Sir Nigel Adair's inner sanctum. On seeing Craw, Sir Nigel forced himself to suppress his anger at the turn of events, which he now realized was probably beyond his deputy's control.

"As I told you on the phone, Craw, Greene's gone missing in Beirut, a kidnap situation in all likelihood."

"Sorry to hear that, sir."

Craw's response threatened to reignite his earlier rage. "Sorry to hear that? Is that all you have to say?"

"Well, sir, Greene is two thousand-plus miles away."

Sir Nigel took hold of an unused heavy cut-glass ashtray that for some reason had remained on his desk long after he gave up his pipe. He quickly hurled it toward a long-defunct iron radiator on the opposite side of his office. The explosion of shattered thick glass reverberated through the office suite, and Anne wondered if she should investigate.

"That's not the bloody point, is it! Our man is in danger, and you get in here at ten a.m.—bankers' hours as usual—and casually tell me he's too far away to do anything about it!"

Craw now assumed the demeanor of a cool, rational man. "Sir, if I may. We won't get to free him or solve the situation by wringing our hands and deploring the facts on the ground, however unpleasant they are."

"Bloody poppycock. I don't want soothing words, Craw. I want you to declare your own state of emergency and get out there and get Greene back!"

"If that is your wish, I certainly will. I'll ask Anne to find the earliest possible RAF Transport—it'll be quicker than British Airways."

A brief respite followed when Anne opened the door gently and asked if she could bring in some tea or coffee.

"Not just now," said Sir Nigel as he watched Craw kick the glass shards into a neat pile in the corner of the office.

"What bugs me is that I learned about this disastrous turn of events by way of Sir Percy, who in turn learned about it from Norbert Clark, whose contact over there is this chap Mansfield. I knew Mansfield in the old days when he was in Berlin. Somewhat erratic, but a good chap. I suspect he's serving time until he comes up for his pension."

"Yes, sir," said Craw, determined to be non-committal when discussing the D-G and Vauxhall Hall operatives.

"And what about Vaux? Where the hell is he? Is he working on Greene's case? If so, what do the kidnappers want? And talking of Vaux, how about Operation Cedar? What progress, if any, has Vaux made in tracking down the source of the leaks? You'll have to find out all these things, Craw. There's been a lapse in our game, a weakening of our resolve. At least that's what I feel in my bones."

"It's hard to foresee a kidnapping, sir. If that's what's happened. But I'll get right to it and leave tonight."

Chapter 18

In the small Café Maurice, within a stone's throw of the haunting statue of Rafiq Hariri, the former prime minister assassinated in 2005 by a massive car bomb outside the nearby Saint George's Hotel, Vaux sat at the small bar nursing a cool Almaza. Behind him, a few men sat together at scattered tables, smoking shisha pipes, talking loudly across to one another, and sipping from glasses of mint tea.

Vaux flipped through a tattered copy of *Time* magazine, whose cover featured a striking picture of Aisha, an eighteen-year old Afghan girl, her nose cruelly cut off by shrapnel. The banner read "What Happens If We Leave Afghanistan?"

Someone tapped his arm, quickly placed a manila envelope on the bar, and mumbled "*Al-hamdulillah*." Thanks be to God.

The messenger, in a long brown djellaba, his face hidden by a copious hood, turned and was gone as quickly as he had arrived. Vaux's cell phone vibrated in his inside pocket.

"We got lucky. I'm following a clapped-out Willys Jeep. Call you later."

Sergeant Pitt had found a narrow, cobbled parking space that faced the café. It was a perfect place to watch the comings and goings of its customers. He had seen the bearded old man walk circumspectly toward the coffee shop, looking now behind him, now to his left and right, and then gazing, with eyes shielded by his hands, through the large windows into the interior. He saw him enter and within a few seconds exit through the double glass doors. Then a Jeep pulled up with a screech of tires, and the agile old Arab jumped in beside the driver.

Vaux put the phone back in his pocket and ordered another beer. He opened the envelope. The short message was written in ink by hand in capital letters. The signature at the bottom was written in longhand with upper and lower cases.

MENZIES WILL BE FREED UPON
RECEIPT OF $5,000,000 IN
USED $100 NOTES.
PAYMENT TO BE MADE WITHIN 7
DAYS AT LOCATION TO BE CHOSEN
MORE DETAILS: ST. GEORGE
      (signed)   *Army of Peace*

Vaux looked around the room. It was getting noisier now. A group of about five men had entered and good-humored greetings and hand slapping were extended to each and every customer, even friendly nods toward Vaux himself. He put the envelope back in his pocket, drank up, and sauntered out.

There was nothing for him to do now. Pitt should be able to follow the Jeep to wherever the old man had come from—and there was a fifty-fifty chance that could lead to the militia cell where Greene was being held.

Along the dark and quiet avenues of the Achrafieh quarter, the fronds of the date palms rustled in the gentle night breeze as Vaux cautiously approached the safe house. As he turned the corner that faced the crumbling old Ottoman mansion, he suddenly halted: every light in every window was lit up, the big look-out balcony was ablaze with candles and oil lamps, and he saw ghostly shadows gliding past the uncovered windows.

He approached the wrought-iron gates cautiously but knew that when he pushed them open, they would produce their own particular whine of welcome. He now wished he had earlier asked Pitt to oil the rusted hinges. But it was too late for regrets. He pushed very gently and managed to suppress the jarring whine to a weak murmur. As he turned into the curve of the driveway, he saw three black-and-white Dodge Chargers, the local police vehicle of choice, lights dimmed and the doors left wide open as if the crew had made hasty exits.

He halted. Should he go in and ask what the problem was? Hardly. This was a safe house, violated by local police who knew nothing about British security interests, and in their eyes, he probably had less lawful right to be there than any squatter. So he turned about and left as quietly as he had come. He turned right along the dark avenue where the pine trees had formed a black backdrop to the moonless night. The nightly cicadas' chorus was at full pitch. Then he heard the muffled sound of a car engine, as a vehicle's headlights approached, and he recognized a black Range Rover from the embassy's car fleet. He guessed it was Pitt's return, and he got into the center of the road and in the glare of the headlights waved him down.

The Range Rover came to a quiet halt in the middle of the deserted road and Pitt's head popped out of the side window.

"What's up, guv?"

"Oh, Christ, Pitt, don't start calling me that. I'll think I'm back in Blighty fighting the class war all over again. Let me get in."

Pitt unlocked the passenger side door and Vaux climbed aboard.

"Put your parking lights on and move to the side of the road. Now tell me what happened."

"I followed the Jeep, and it was kind of tricky, really. They went through a lot of old neighborhoods with narrow streets and dim lighting. Lots of bloody potholes. But my trusty GPS helped me follow their direction. They drove south toward the airport, then turned east on Route 1 toward the Bekaa Valley. In the foothills of Mount Lebanon, I guess. Anyway, we passed a village called Qab Elias, if I recall correctly, and then a few miles farther on, he suddenly turned and entered a large compound that appeared to be an orchard or something. Down a narrow lane covered by overhanging cedars. I think they're called umbrella pines. They pulled up at a sort of bungalow or ranch house in the middle of all this, and I halted and turned around as soon as I see the old gaffer who met you get out and enter the building. The driver took the Jeep around the back of the house, and I took off pretty quickly. There could have been sensors or hidden surveillance cameras for all I know."

"You did well, Pitt. Could you retrace your steps?"

"What now?"

"No, no. I mean, can you remember how to get back there?"

"Yeah, of course."

"They're probably not holding Greene there anyway. They wouldn't have risked a tail."

"They never noticed me, of that I am quite sure," said Pitt emphatically.

"OK, now I've got some news for you. We can't go to the safe house. We'll do a quick drive-by, and you'll see why. Get going, Sergeant."

They slowly passed by the mansion. Lights were still blazing, candles guttering on the balcony.

Pitt, ever practical, said, "And where am I supposed to kip tonight?"

"We'll go to a nice hotel I know from my first days here. And we'll have a couple of stiff ones to celebrate."

"Celebrate? What's there to celebrate, sir?"

"Think, Pitt. You've gathered the greatest clue we've ever been given. It's a step toward finding Greene and the band of guerillas we're dealing with. It's a breakthrough, and you deserve a medal, old man."

"My missus would like that," said Pitt as he did a three-point turnaround, put the main headlights back on, and stepped hard on the gas.

* * *

Vaux had called Anthony Mansfield late that evening to tell him he needed to meet with him first thing in the morning.

At 7:00 a.m. Sergeant Pitt watched as Vaux got out of the Range Rover, nodded to the military guards who recognized him, and entered the rear staff door of the embassy complex. A sergeant of the Diplomatic Protection Command escorted him through the serpentine gray corridors to Mansfield's offices. Vaux tapped the door and entered.

Mansfield, who was finishing off the previous day's *Daily Telegraph* crossword puzzle, looked up and quickly feigned surprise at seeing Vaux so early in the morning. "And what has prompted Department B3's star secret agent to get up at the crack of dawn on this promisingly serene summer day?"

"Simply that I think an update's in order. Recent developments about which you should be apprised," said Vaux dryly.

"Sounds ominous. But first, here's one for you..." Mansfield looked down at the *Telegraph*'s crossword clues: "Loud sound in a storm...begins with *C*, four letters."

"Clap," said Vaux.

"Ye Gods, you're quick! That fits twenty-six across, which begins with an *S* and has seven letters. Clue: 'Crusader's foe.'"

"Saladin," said Vaux.

"You're not just a pretty face, then," said Mansfield as he folded the newspaper and stuffed it into his desk drawer.

Vaux was stunned by Mansfield's seemingly cool indifference to events swirling around him. He knew of Greene's abduction—Vaux had informed him only a few days ago—yet his first thought on seeing Vaux was to engage him in a crossword puzzle. He gave

Mansfield the two ransom notes and told him of Sergeant Pitt's successful pursuit of the messenger.

Mansfield took his time reading the kidnappers' messages. He read and reread the two notes. He compared the writing styles. Then he picked up the in-house phone and asked for a Mike Stevens.

"Stevens? Mansfield here. I've got something interesting for you. Could you come on over?"

Mansfield carefully replaced the old-fashioned receiver. "New man. Flown in to overhaul the cipher room operations. Those two wonderful girls we have for encryption etcetera are overwhelmed these days. He's from Bletchley Park, so he should know his onions."

"But the messages are in plain text," remonstrated Vaux.

"Even so, this Bletchley type is also a handwriting expert. He might even be able to see what kind of tribe the writer comes from."

Vaux wondered whether Mansfield was suffering from some memory loss or escape from reality. Perhaps in the distant past, he had served his masters at Vauxhall Cross in some small obscure African country or on an isolated Pacific island. "Tribe? You think we're dealing with tribes here?"

"Sects, subsects, Shi'ites, Sunnis, the Maronites, the Palestinian refugees—they all come from various desert tribes, Vaux. And sometimes these graphologists can detect what schools the writer went to and in what areas or locales."

Vaux felt he was in Alice's Wonderland.

Stevens was in his early- thirties with thinning brown hair and a slim build and was a few inches north of six feet. He wore wire-framed Coke-bottle glasses, which he cleaned carefully with a tissue before studying the flimsy notes.

"Written in both cases with a common or garden ballpoint pen."

"That much we already guessed," said Mansfield.

"I'll take them to my cubbyhole to see what more I can learn. Microscopic enlargement may produce something more interesting," said Stevens hopefully.

"Like fingerprints?" Mansfield was now his usual self.

To Vaux's observant eyes, Mansfield now seemed to shake himself out of the mystic trance to which he had succumbed just moments ago. "See what you can do, old boy. We've got nothing else to go on. This is a very urgent case—as you can see by the text."

Stevens nodded, got up, and walked out of the office with the two ransom notes.

Mansfield looked at Vaux expectantly. "Well, my friend, this calls for some special action. I will call a war council. Eccles will sit in. As will your Mr. Craw who, if I forgot to tell you, is flying over this very minute. Nobby Clark called me at his usual time of three o'clock in the morning local time. Though what good Craw can do here at this time of crisis is anyone's guess, what?"

Vaux thought he'd deal with that later. "What about the local intelligence forces? Can they be brought in to help?"

"Absolutely not. Whatever we tell them, they often use against us. The ISF has been infiltrated. According to which districts they come from, they're either loyal Hezbollah members or loyal unreconstructed Sunnis. Can't trust any of 'em."

"But the ISF is essentially for internal security. What about their intelligence outfits that work across borders?"

"That's the General Directorate of Security or GDS. Sometimes they can be of help, sometimes we draw a blank with them. They see us as their potential enemies—allies of the French and Uncle Sam—and supportive of their greatest enemy, Israel. They're very reluctant to share any critical intelligence with us. They suspect our motives but do involve themselves sometimes in things that can be damaging to themselves."

"Such as news that innocent people can be suddenly seized off the street and disappear. Bad for tourism or what's left of it," said Vaux.

Suddenly, the door opened, and they heard the tinkling of cups and saucers. A young Lebanese girl whom Vaux had never seen before came in balancing a tray laden with the necessities of an English midmorning tea break. Vaux noted the chocolate digestive biscuits which seemed de rigueur in any outfit supplied by Her Majesty's caterers.

Mansfield ignored the interruption by punching numbers into his encrypted cell phone.

"Mr. Ambassador, sir. Mansfield. I think we need a special meeting today. Vaux is here with me, and certain developments have transpired that you should know about. We have to agree on tactics, a way forward."

Vaux heard the suppressed but vigorous voice of John Eccles and wondered if he was having breakfast with beautiful Miranda.

"Yes, very well, sir. I'll arrange it. Noon tomorrow, you say? Very well."

Mansfield pressed the off button, looked at Vaux, and emptied the cup of Twining's English breakfast in one gulp.

"War council at noon tomorrow. Conference room where we'll probably have lunch. Be prepared, Vaux. We have to come up with solutions, priorities, tactics—the whole gamut. We've got to get young Greene back. Please come with a full brief: a game plan, if you like."

This was the first time Mansfield had referred directly to their incarcerated colleague, and Vaux now realized Mansfield himself had developed no strategy to rescue Greene.

* * *

Vaux told Sergeant Pitt to drive slowly past the safe house to check if there was any sign of life. But Vaux realized after three passes that he couldn't tell if the place was occupied unless he walked farther down the driveway. He got out and walked. At the curve of the driveway, he halted and looked up at the balcony. It looked abandoned. He listened. Silence.

Then he walked up to the big pillared portico where the old wooden steps creaked a warning to any occupants that a visitor had arrived. He walked through the big hall where some ancient landscapes, dusty and darkened by time and varnish, hung in faded gilt frames. Then up the stairs to the abandoned balcony. The large glass table was strewn with big ceramic ashtrays that overflowed with cigarette butts. Six empty coffee cups had been placed on a stained tin tray.

"This confirms what I was told, sir," said Pitt.

Vaux looked surprised. "What do you mean?"

"Well, perhaps I should have told you before. But a month or so ago, our little contingent did a sort of joint emergency exercise with the local police. Eccles—Mr. John Eccles, the ambassador, I should say—well, he said it was a sort of PR gesture for the locals. You know, British friendship and cooperation and all that bullshit, if you'll excuse the expression. It was a dress rehearsal, if you like. How both outfits would react and cooperate in the case of a big disaster. That sort of thing."

"Go on," urged Vaux.

"Well, I got friendly with one of the blokes, didn't I? Chap about my age—married and all that, kids. He invites me back to his humble home, and we become friends. Like all Arabs, as I've been told, they're great hosts. His missus' food—to die for.

"Cut a long story short, sir. I calls him yesterday and ask if he knows anything about a raid on a house on Baroudi Street. This street, as you may know. He checks and calls me back in a few hours. Yes, he says. The local station here got a call from some neighbor who thought squatters had settled in. They had been hearing noises and voices for several days, and they smelled cooking. So they calls the local cops and Bob's your uncle. They were here checking the place out, and they found no one. End of story."

"I'm completely astounded," said Vaux, amused and relieved.

Then Pitt set to in the kitchen where he prepared an omelet for Vaux and a cheese sandwich for himself. Vaux went upstairs to his big bedroom and found what he expected: his canvas travel bag, rifled through with eager thoroughness. Socks, folded jeans, and casual shirts thrown randomly to the floor. The false bottom had been detected and ripped open. But his little black book was safe and sound at Bletchley Park, and he wondered how much longer he would have to wait for Jack Sumner's decrypt of the enigmatic little diary.

Chapter 19

Sergeant Leonard Pitt of the Diplomatic Protection Command, an offshoot of the UK's Special Branch, tapped gently on Michael Vaux's shoulder in an effort to wake him. Vaux had slept for a couple of hours after eating his omelet and it was now around 4:00 p.m. It had been a deep sleep, and Vaux struggled to collect his thoughts.

"Thanks, Sergeant. This will never do. We have work to do."

Pitt raised his eyebrows. "Here, have a cuppa before you get up. I'll be on the balcony. Oh, and by the way, I got the shower head in that old bathroom working at last."

"Great. But wait a minute. I want to tell you what I'm thinking because time is of the essence."

"Oh blimey, I thought we could rest up till tomorrow when you're supposed to attend the big war council."

Vaux detected an element of sarcasm in the sergeant's attitude. "Don't get bolshie on me, Pitt. I was in the army once upon a time and I can smell treasonable thoughts as soon as they arise."

"Very well, sir."

"Listen carefully: I want you to contact your friend in the local gendarmerie. I've got a job for him for which, I promise, he will be handsomely compensated."

Vaux then told Pitt of his plan to free young Greene.

When the briefing was over and Pitt had got over the initial shock of his pending involvement in what Vaux decided to call Operation Rescue, they both started as they heard the familiar squeaky whine of the vestibule's double doors. Then they heard footsteps crunching on the broken tiles in the hallway. Vaux picked up his Walther P99 from the improvised bedside table; Pitt pulled out his Glock 17 from his shoulder holster. They pressed themselves against the wall on either side of the bedroom door as the heavy footsteps got closer.

The unlocked door was gently pushed open. The trespasser stepped into the room and turned his head to look toward the big windows when Pitt pounced. The man's eyes bulged as he stared up at the gray ceiling and choked and spluttered for life-giving air. Pitt had performed a perfect example of what his hand-to-hand combat trainers had called a rear naked choke. But when Pitt recognized the unarmed Alan Craw from his first days at the old mansion, he released him.

"For God's sake!" protested Craw as he coughed and shook himself free from Pitt's choke hold.

Pitt apologized and looked at Vaux for moral support. "Don't worry, Sergeant, you were just doing your job. Alan! Why didn't you let us know you were coming? There's a walkie-talkie system operating between the embassy and here. You should have used that."

"I didn't go to the embassy, old bean. Went straight to the Phoenicia and then thought I'd check in with you. Don't have your cell number either."

"Well, that's OK. I like to keep it as secure as is practical," said Vaux.

"Thanks very much. When can we get down to a briefing? Fill me in, Vaux. I hear you're in lots of trouble. Found Greene yet?"

"No, but I'm working on it."

Sergeant Pitt, white-faced and a little shaky, excused himself and descended to the kitchen.

Vaux took Craw to the balcony and brought him up to date.

"How's Anne faring?" asked Vaux, feeling guilty about his feeble efforts at communicating with her.

"She's bloody marvelous. But you should call her more often, Vaux. I think she's in a sort of limbo at present. Her dad's hanging in there, but he could go any moment. I think she'd just love to get back with you—"

"Get back with me? She's never left me. We are only parted geographically. This job won't last forever. At least I bloody well hope not." Vaux saw the flashing image of Miranda Eccles and wondered if it was all just a middle-aged fantasy.

Pitt brought up some cans of Bass Pale Ale. "Any munchies, gentlemen?"

"No, thanks," said Vaux. "But when you get back from that place I told you about, I want you to take me down to Greene's dead-letter drop. Word could have spread that this was the way he touched base with his contacts, and we could find some attempt by someone—friend or enemy—to communicate with us." Earlier, Vaux had asked Pitt to bring his Arab police friend to the safe house for a short but sweet face-to-face meeting.

Craw maintained a diplomatic silence. This was Vaux's responsibility. In his mind, his task, as deputy director of Department B3, was to contribute to the overall strategic plan which, he had just learned, would be discussed at tomorrow's war council. So Craw excused himself. He needed to catch up on some rest. Even though jet lag was a weak excuse for his fatigue—the flight time from London was only just over four hours by a Royal Air Force Boeing C-17—he said that at his age, the tiresome chore of traveling any significant distance took its toll.

Vaux was relieved to see him go. He settled down with another beer to wait for Sergeant Pitt's return from his visit to Sami Hakroush, Pitt's ISF contact. He needed to know whether the plan that he had hatched in his head before his siesta that afternoon could go ahead. If so, the first stage would take place after visiting Saint George's Cathedral.

* * *

Lieutenant Sami Hakroush of Lebanon's ISF was in his midthirties and married to a Palestinian refugee in her early twenties. They had two sons, aged two and five. The family lived in an austere military housing complex, north of the public park called the Pine Forest of Beirut and south of the major arterial Avenue de AbdallahYafi.

Hakroush was friendly and outgoing. He had learned English at his state school, and like most Arabs, he felt an affinity toward westerners and especially the English. So when his unit engaged in a joint emergency exercise with the British embassy's Special Forces protection outfit, he had no qualms about socializing in the off-duty hours with his foreign colleagues. Sergeant Pitt was a social animal, and the two law officers became close friends. Hakroush invited off-duty Pitt to dinner (zibdeh shrimp was Pitt's favorite), and the mutual friendship blossomed into one of the more encouraging examples of international cooperation.

So when Pitt asked him for help and at the same time offered the munificent sum of three thousand dollars as a preliminary fee for the potentially dangerous work involved, Hakroush quickly accepted—more, he said, because of their strong bonds of comradeship than for any sordid financial gains.

Pitt drove him to the safe house. Both Pitt and Hakroush had changed into practical civilian garb—blue jeans and black T-shirts. Vaux now wondered about the wisdom of revealing the location of the safe house to a member of the ISF. But he quickly decided that the end justified the means.

They set out for Saint George's Cathedral. Pitt found a parking space on the busy Place d'Etoile, and the two police officers waited for Vaux's return from the cathedral. Hakroush offered Pitt a dark tobacco Lebanese Forces cigarette. Pitt declined and pulled out a single Player's from his shirt pocket. Through the rearview mirror, he saw Vaux approaching.

"Nothing," said Vaux as he climbed back in the front seat beside Pitt. "So let's go."

Vaux's plan was to return to the small one-storey farmhouse nestled in an orchard where the old Jeep had ended its journey from the Café Maurice. There they would wait and watch. It was early evening, and his hunch was that the old man who had delivered the ransom note or the Jeep's driver would at some point make a move that could lead them to the terrorist cell they worked for. He thought it unlikely that they were holding Greene in the modest farmhouse if only because it was so vulnerable to detection and attack.

He had expounded his simple theory to Hakroush, who seemed skeptical. In his best English, he said, "I know these people, sir. It is too easy. They probably guessed they were being followed here. It could be, how you say? A red herring. I am saying that they're using typical evasive tactics. I don't think we have much chance of success here. Perhaps we should think again, yes?"

Pitt slowly nodded his agreement.

Vaux said, "I know it's a long shot. But it's the only lead we have. Let's wait and be patient."

They had parked up the road from the orchard in a small space that looked like a possible lovers' lane, a gap in the canebrake where the tall reeds had been crushed to the ground by drivers who wanted to get off the tarmac road.

Vaux was settling down to a long wait. He rolled down his window slightly to dissipate the thick clouds of tobacco smoke. He turned around to get a close look at Hakroush. He was about the same height as Vaux, around six feet, but he was probably fifty pounds lighter. He had the olive skin, deep brown eyes, a straight nose, and the very white teeth of a young Arab.

"Have you the necessary accoutrements for hand-to-hand combat, Lieutenant?"

Pitt laughed. "He won't understand that, sir. Ask him if he's got a handgun, a knife, and some rope. Plus a few rags for stuffing in noisy big mouths. And by the way, he passed his hand-to-hand combat class with honors."

Hakroush smiled and produced a long curved khanjar dagger from his pocket. Then he showed Vaux his snub-nosed Remington 380. When Vaux thought that was it, Hakroush rattled a pair of handcuffs before putting them back in his side pocket.

"And there's an M4 sniper rifle under the back seat—just in case we need reinforcements," said Pitt.

At that moment, they heard the revving of an engine, some guttural shouts, and the slamming of several doors. The sounds came from the direction of the house. From their hideout in the tall reedy canes, they could see the entrance to the driveway. The flat wide hood of the old Willys emerged cautiously into the road. The Jeep turned sharply right and headed south before it turned on to the Camille Chamoun Highway.

Pitt's black Range Rover edged out into the road and turned right. No words were spoken among the three men despite this lucky confirmation of Vaux's instinct. They tailed the Jeep southward for about an hour until they reached a small village called Ghazze. Pitt kept a safe distance from the Jeep until it suddenly swerved sharply right into the high open gates of a leafy driveway. The Range Rover sped past as Vaux tried to get a fix on the property with Pitt's army-issue night-vision binoculars.

"Looks like a rambling old brick building, a warehouse perhaps. The good news is that it's only one storey high. But a high brick wall surrounds it. Did you bring a grappling iron, Pitt?"

"Bloody right I did. I was a Boy Scout—always prepared, me. It's in the back, under the seat."

Hakroush looked baffled but reassured.

They followed the high brick wall and made a sharp right turn. The wall had long ago been painted white, but the patina had flaked and faded. As they drove past, Vaux could see that it still presented a sturdy barrier. The wall continued along the side of a narrow lane, and they now saw that the old brick barrier wrapped 360 degrees around the building. They turned right again and passed a smaller entrance with rusted but sturdy steel gates. The gates were secured by a large conventional padlock.

"The wall's about twelve feet high," said Vaux.

"I could vault that standing on Sami's shoulders," said Pitt.

"Let's just drive away from here and draw up a game plan," suggested Vaux.

Chapter 20

Vaux's plan had already formed in his mind. From what he had observed, the place was not heavily guarded. The kidnapping team must have thought their hideout was too obscure or too ordinary to raise suspicions. And they knew that an official search for the victim would be half-hearted. The lack of any real security around the building was a big plus.

Vaux also had the knack—by some sort of osmosis—of absorbing himself in other cultures: his instinct told him that evening mealtimes were approaching. The Arabs did not eat early like the primitive Brits. Nor did they eat, like the night owls in Spain, so late that evening merged seamlessly into the long night.

Now he was pretty certain that this was the hideout where the kidnappers were holding Greene. "I've checked for surveillance cameras and detection wires at the wall. Nothing. Not even glass shards on top of the wall. So we're placing an all-out bet here. We act on the assumption that Greene's in there somewhere, probably in a small cell or the basement, and that his keepers are relatively few. I figure they send out for take-out food, even though we saw an old woman leave about half an hour ago. She's probably the housekeeper. Who knows?"

Lieutenant Hakroush tapped Pitt's shoulder, an indication that he wanted to speak. "I sneak in first, very silently and gently. I listen carefully for any indications as to the whereabouts of Greene, yes? I have my sneakers on, and I will be quiet as a mouse."

"But we should wait a little," said Vaux. "I reckon the guards do very little cooking for themselves. But they have to eat. Once we see a delivery, that's our entry ticket. Agreed?"

Pitt and Hakroush nodded agreement, checked their guns, and gently opened the doors.

Pitt approached the unguarded back gate. It was heavily padlocked. Hakroush produced some wire cutters, but they were no use against the sturdy lock. Pitt then secured the climbing rope to a rusting piece of farm machinery that had been parked on the grass verge of the road. Then he bent over and let Hakroush step on his back so Hakroush could propel himself over the brick wall. He landed on a mound of dirt, which helped break his fall. He secured his end of the rope around the trunk of a sturdy eucalyptus tree.

Hakroush felt the impact of Pitt's body as he hit the ground beside him. On the other side of the wall, Vaux hauled himself up by the rope to the top and quickly slid down to the ground. The three men lay on their stomachs as they surveyed the one-storey building with their small night-vision binoculars. The evening dusk had given way to the pale luminescence of a gibbous moon.

"Looks eerily quiet," said Vaux.

"Probably getting near mealtime," said Pitt.

"OK, let's put the game plan into action. Lieutenant, off you go."

Hakroush jumped up and skirted the wall as he lowered his head and sprinted to the front of the building. He took advantage of the unruly clumps of prickly peach hedges and the trunks of tall pine trees to pause and reassess. Then he saw what Vaux had predicted. A pizza delivery.

The boy was in his early teens. He looked surprised when Hakroush ran up to him and told him that he would take care of everything. He handed the boy a fistful of Lebanese pounds. The boy smiled, bowed slightly, and returned to the waiting van.

Vaux and Pitt watched from behind a cluster of wild and unkempt bushes as Hakroush tried to push open a small entry hatch that was cut into the big double doors of the warehouse. It was locked. Hakroush knocked twice. The door opened, and a man's loud voice greeted his arrival with enthusiasm. He was beckoned inside.

The man who opened the door looked to be in his early twenties. He wore tight white pants and a knitted polo shirt. Hakroush waited to hand him the big square Pizza Hut box. But the man shook his head and pointed to a narrow staircase that spiraled down to a lower floor. Flickering candles in glass sconces lit the stairwell. Hakroush nodded. But as soon as the man turned his back, Hakroush seized him with a choke hold, whipped out his khanjar dagger and aimed for his carotid artery. Blood spouted from the young man's neck as he collapsed to the ground without a sound.

Hakroush looked quickly around the big hall. He saw a cedar armoire in the corner at the side of a pair of double doors. Some old robes hung from steel coat hangers. He pushed them aside and lifted the body gently onto the base of the armoire.

Hakroush gave himself no time to check on Pitt or Vaux. He closed the doors of the armoire, then turned and ran silently down the spiral staircase. There were only three rooms on the lower floor. Each door was firmly locked. Hakroush saw a tall, worm-eaten supervisor's desk in the corner. He pulled out all the drawers and found a bunch of keys. He scrambled to fit the right keys in the right doors. Then he rattled the bunch of keys to see if he could get any response. He was sorting through the jumble of keys when suddenly one key got home, and he turned it. The door clicked open and he was face to face with a man whom he had never seen before.

"Come quick," he said in his best English.

Pitt and Vaux had come quietly through the open front doors just in time to see Hakroush rush down the stairs. They both made toward the closed double doors to their left. They heard muffled conversation and laughter as the strong smell of cannabis drifted through the cracks in the doorframe.

Vaux signaled to Pitt to follow Hakroush down the staircase. His eyes fell on the puddle of blood, but there were more pressing things to worry about: again, he put his ear to the door. What sounded like an excited three-way conversation continued and he detected no sign of any physical movements.

* * *

Earlier, Chris Greene had lain in the hot stupor that overcame him at that time of day when he knew he would hear the light tap on his door that heralded his evening meal. A young man by the name of Mounir would enter his room, smile a silent greeting, and place a metal tray on a rickety table by the side of the bed. He wondered what today's one-choice menu would offer: sometimes it was a large meatless pizza, sometimes what suspiciously resembled Kentucky fried chicken, even the odd hamburger. All take-out food. But Greene knew it could be far worse.

He knew also he had been treated well. Apart from incarceration—in his mind an offense against nature—he had been allowed a daily shower, his underwear had been seized by a veiled old lady who had returned the washed garments within a few hours, and at night he had not been kept awake by continuous loud music or by any other cruel stratagems employed by professional torturers.

His black-faced Shark Army watch had been given back to him, so he never suffered from the cruel timelessness that he had been taught was another technique aimed at disorientation and despair. He remembered with some tenderness the evening that now seemed so long ago when Dana, his fiancée, had given him the watch and was surprised to see the time: Mounir was late this evening.

He was staring up at the peeling water-stained ceiling, his arms folded behind his head, when he heard keys rattling and the door click open. He looked up and saw a stranger dressed in black shirt and blue jeans. The man hurriedly gestured for him to get up and follow him. He put his forefinger to his lips to signal silence. Greene jumped up, slid into his loafers, and followed the man through the dim winding corridors of the basement.

Pitt saw Hakroush enter Greene's holding cell, turned around and ran up the spiral staircase. He gave the thumbs-up sign to Vaux and they both ran out of the building back to the rear wall.

"Did you bring a torch, Pitt?"

"No, sir. Why?"

"We should give Greene some sort of guiding signal. He'll be emerging into unknown territory."

"There's a lot of moonlight, sir. But how's this?" Pitt produced an ancient bronze Ronson cigarette lighter that instantly sprouted a tall yellow flame.

Greene found himself running across the moonlit graveled space in front of the warehouse. His Arab liberator was close behind. He pointed to a flickering light in front of some closed gates at the rear of the property between the high perimeter walls. Greene had no time to think and ran toward the rusting steel entrance. Hakroush then helped him with the rope, and he hauled himself up the twelve-foot wall. He fell heavily onto the road and came face to face with Sergeant Pitt. The sergeant pointed to a familiar black vehicle about thirty yards down the road. Vaux opened the rear door, pushed him in and told him to lie on the floor.

* * *

Within an hour Vaux and his team plus newly liberated Chris Greene were back at the safe house. Pitt opened an oval can of English ham, cut some slices, and stuffed them into portions of a long baguette. "Fresh from the embassy's 'pantry,' as they call that vast underused bloody kitchen."

They were sitting on the balcony finishing off a few beers when Vaux began his inquest.

"Sami. I saw blood spots on your jeans. What happened exactly?"

Hakroush drank the last of his coffee. He had peeled the ham away from his sandwich and seemed to be enjoying the hard, un-buttered crust. "I had to kill the guard. There was no other way. A fight would have made much noise, *non?* It would alert the men in the main room there. Either more killings and us endangered or a quick kill of the guard. That's what I was thinking. I hid the body in that old armoire by the side of the doors to the room where the other men were having their pot party."

Vaux now wished he had given Operation Rescue more thought. "Didn't you think of striking him, putting him out? You had the butt of your handgun or you could have taken a cosh with you. One hit and he would have been out like a light."

Pitt could see the way Vaux was thinking. "Look, sir, this was a combat situation, not a police action. I must defend my friend here. He did what was necessary. A quick resolution to a horrendous— what's the word? Dilemma. I think that's what you'd call it, sir."

Greene, whose feelings of gratitude and relief had no bounds, leaped to Hakroush's defense. "Sami here did what he had to do. It's no good second-guessing this type of action. The bottom line is that I am free again, that the British government won't have to find the few million that they demanded, and that it's one up for the Brits—thanks, by the way, to a true and praiseworthy ally in the person here of Lieutenant Hakroush of Lebanon's honorable Internal Security Forces."

"Quite a speech," said Vaux. "But it's me who will have to answer for our actions tomorrow at the so-called war council."

Greene said, "Should I notify Mansfield now about my situation?"

"No, leave it for tomorrow," said Vaux. "I think we'll stage a little bit of drama."

Chapter 21

Anthony Mansfield had been told by Ambassador Eccles to inform all interested parties that the war council would be held at noon in the main conference room.

Miranda Eccles, in a polka dot cotton dressing gown, her silky jet-black hair hanging over her shoulders, watched intently as her husband ate his customary second boiled egg. The glistening sterling silver egg cup and delicate spoon were part of a set his mother had given them as a wedding present. Yesterday's *Times* was propped up against a tall glass that had just contained a brimful of fresh orange juice.

The iconoclastic UK ambassador to Lebanon always enjoyed the ritual of breakfast with his beautiful and elegant wife on the terraced balcony of the unofficial residence—uncharacteristically, an apartment atop a modern post-war high-rise development that overlooked the Horsh pine forest, known among the ex-pat communities as Beirut's embassy row.

"Do you want me to attend the meeting?" she asked. He had told her that the war council session could go on through the afternoon.

"No, that's not necessary, my dear. Anyway, I thought you said you had something to do at the British Council."

"That won't take long. I promised I would help them catalogue a batch of books that some old English teacher in Tripoli left us in his will—there's fiction and non-fiction, and I don't trust the staff to know the difference."

"Why ever not?"

"Because they're mainly Lebanese, darling, and I don't have much faith in their ability to distinguish fiction from truth," said Miranda, finishing off her cup of tea.

Eccles raised his eyebrows and couldn't quite grasp whether Miranda was speaking plainly or trying to convey a more subtle message about the character of the Lebanese.

Eccles didn't pursue the question. As with his colleague Mansfield, one of his daily routines was to turn to the obituary columns to see if anyone he knew had recently met his or her maker.

But Miranda persisted. "What's it all about anyway?"

"What?" asked Eccles, as his eyes swept the columns for any familiar names.

"This war council thing. Do not tell me you are all expecting another civil war."

Eccles looked up. She was more beautiful when she was anxious. And her Brazilian accent became more pronounced, as did her pedantic text- book English. It took him back to when they first met. She had been a little unsure of herself then. But when the baby came, all that changed. She blossomed and matured as a woman and a mother, and he loved her more as the years went by. But then their child was brutally killed within months of his posting to this turbulent nation. It was the summit of his career, marred and scarred by the sudden death of Yasmin at the hands of unknown terrorists.

"No darling, nothing like that. But as you know, an undeclared war of sorts is still going on, and at this moment, we're facing a crisis."

"What sort of crisis?"

"Darling, you know I can't discuss classified stuff. Don't worry about it. It will all blow over. Whoever conjured up the term *war council* must be some sort of alarmist. Don't let it concern you."

But Miranda did look concerned. She got up quickly and went into the kitchen. Eccles stuffed his newspaper and briefing papers back into his attaché case and knew he wouldn't see her again until cocktail hour.

* * *

"Where's Vaux for heaven's sake?"

Mansfield had shepherded the cast to the conference room. Alan Craw had got to the embassy by 8:00 a.m. and was placed in a small stuffy room with newspapers and magazines. He was relieved now that the war council appeared to be getting underway.

"I'm sure he'll be here shortly," said Craw curtly. It was one of the rare occasions he found it expedient to defend his colleague.

The early arrivals sat at the long rosewood table. Three sets of french doors were wide open to the lush tropical garden whose beauty was only marred by the soggy grass lawn that was constantly overwatered by wobbly gooseneck brass sprinklers.

Peter Browne, the embassy's fictional third secretary and MI6 station chief Anthony Mansfield's deputy, offered to call Vaux at the safe house.

"That won't be necessary," said Mansfield. "Any news re Greene?" The question was not addressed to anyone in particular, and the response was silence.

There were several operatives Craw didn't recognize. But he assumed the diplomatic strength of a key embassy had to be kept up to the establishment levels laid down by the Foreign and Commonwealth Office. He only wished the same could be said for his own outfit. Craw resorted to his usual practice of killing time by drawing stick figures on the blotter that had been placed before him.

Sergeant Pitt, in casual jeans and open-necked dress shirt, suddenly stood at the door, and Mansfield told him to take any seat. "Left Vaux at the safe house, did you?"

"Yes, sir. He's on his way. Just a little business to attend to. He told me to tell you that you should proceed without him."

Mansfield did not try to hide his impatience. "Proceed without him? How the hell can we do that when he's our key man in this Operation—whatever we named it at the outset."

"Operation Retrieval!" boomed Alexander Mailer. The CIA's Beirut station chief had just entered the room unobserved. "At least that's the name I suggested. I don't know whether you adopted it yet."

Mansfield, who had a warm spot for Mailer even if he was slightly overbearing, coolly asked him to take a seat.

Silence descended on the group, an unconscious prelude to the entry of the ambassador.

"Morning, gentlemen." Eccles nodded to Craw, who he thought had left Beirut a week or so ago. "Are we ready to proceed?" Eccles sat in his usual Chippendale armchair at the head of the long table.

Mansfield addressed the ambassador respectfully. "Excellency... we are waiting for the arrival of the key man who is heading up Operation Retrieval—Michael Vaux of Department B3, our sub-group of independent operatives devoted to special missions."

Craw objected to this description of Department B3's mission. "Hang on, old chap. I'm hardly an independent operative...Put in nearly as many years as you with the old FCO, I should imagine."

Eccles hated this sort of time-wasting in-house bickering. "Very well. Browne, can you order up some coffee and biscuits? I'm sure none of us have had lunch yet, so I'm confident we could all do with some nourishment."

Browne got up and left the room.

As he was about to close the double doors after him, he saw Vaux approaching, smoothing his hair down and wiping his forehead as if he had been running. But now Browne thought he was hallucinating. For close behind Vaux loomed a man he had written off as virtually dead, taken brutally by men who demanded an impossible ransom.

On seeing Greene in flesh and blood, everyone seated around the long table—even those who had only vaguely heard of the kidnapping crisis—rose quickly to surround him. They all recognized him from the marathon face-to-face interrogations he had conducted with them over the past weeks, and they rushed to shake both his hands and hug him with varying degrees of warmth. Hammond Seward, the legation's official second secretary and initially Greene's prime suspect in the leak probe, jumped up to join in the bear-hugging scrum.

Eccles, as he later put it, was gobsmacked at the sight of the liberated secret agent whom he had felt ultimately responsible for. It was the climax of a horrible nightmare that could have ended disastrously. Greene's fate, inevitably, would have been compared to that of the notorious mid-80s abduction and killing of the CIA's legendary Bill Buckley.

Which was why, perhaps, Alexander Mailer now approached Mansfield, maneuvered him with a nod and a wink to a far corner of the room, and asked him quietly what the hell was going on.

"What do you mean, Alex? I thought it was all pretty self-explanatory."

"But you promised me full liaison and cooperation. We are experts at this type of thing. Why didn't you ever follow up with me—call a meeting, coordinate our plans?"

Fond as he was of the old CIA operative, Mansfield was never going to tell him that the operation had been taken out of his own hands by the unilateral and unpredictable actions of a rump group of lone wolf operators who were the bane of his and any other station chief's existence.

"It all happened so quickly, Alex. Eccles has classified the whole episode as top secret—UK eyes only. So I'm not at liberty to talk about it. When it's all blown over, perhaps I'll fill you in."

"Bullshit," murmured Mailer as he turned and walked away toward the open french windows. A cheerful young constable in a white jacket offered to refill his cup from a silver coffee pot, but Mailer shook his head and stared out to the kinetic movements of the water sprinklers.

* * *

To the surprise of all those in attendance, John Eccles called the meeting to order before most of them had finished their coffees.

"Gentlemen. Please give a round of applause to Mr. Chris Greene for his fortitude and gallantry while under the unfathomable pressure of all the restraints and inhuman sufferings any kidnapping inevitably entails."

Then the few low but polite murmurings rose to a sudden crescendo: "Hear, hear! Right on, sir!" A loud burst of applause ensued until everything went suddenly quiet.

"Since there is now no need for a war council, I propose we adjourn and regather at six p.m. for a spontaneous celebration—well, practically spontaneous—that will include alcoholic libations and a cold buffet. This is a great day for us all, and I think it should be celebrated accordingly."

Vaux and Greene, along with Sergeant Pitt, were escorted to the ambassador's office by Mansfield, who had been told to organize a preliminary debriefing as soon as the war council was adjourned.

The ambassador sat at his big desk, flanked by two drooping Union Jacks. Vaux watched him quickly switch off a small tape recorder that he had left quietly playing a bluesy old Jimi Hendrix number. On the wall behind him, a young Queen Elizabeth looked down from her official portrait with benign approval.

"This will be just a precursory debriefing, gentlemen," said Eccles. "A full-dress session will have to take place over several days, probably, and I'll expect a comprehensive report from you, Anthony, within a few days of the conclusion of that inquiry."

Vaux looked at Greene who looked back at him, concern written over his face. Sergeant Pitt looked up to the queen's portrait for reassurance. He tried not to think of the agony of a deep probe into Operation Rescue, for the three men had agreed that the vital role played by Lieutenant Sami Hakroush could not be revealed.

There were several good reasons in Vaux's view: Hakroush himself had requested complete cover, since the ISF had no tolerance for individual freelancing. To have worked with British intelligence on any project would probably have been a court martial offense. Worse, the killing of one member of the kidnap team was probably a capital offense—depending on what sectarian-dominated military court the accused landed up in.

But Vaux had to convince himself that the cover-up would forever go undetected. What helped here was the almost certain likelihood that the kidnap cell, whether they were Shiites or Sunnis or Druze, were not about to report the murder of one of their own to any security outfit or local police force. The young victim would have been quietly buried with all the rites his religion demanded.

Vaux realized Ambassador Eccles had just asked him a question. "Sorry, Mr. Ambassador. Could you repeat the question?"

"I invited you to tell us more or less what happened over the several days that it must have taken to find Greene. Be as brief as possible—I've switched the recording mechanism on, so it will all be taped and go down on the record. Easier that way in case there are any future probes."

Vaux related the story with the skillful omission of any foreign participant or outside help. He praised Sergeant Leonard Pitt's indispensable role in the operation: he was Vaux's right-hand man and instrumental in knocking out the sole guard at the kidnap site.

"Strange that they only had one man guarding Greene, don't you think?" asked Craw, who had always believed a tone of skepticism was a sign of a higher intelligence.

Vaux had anticipated that one. "Yes. But there were several others elsewhere on the premises. It was late evening, and the smell of kif or hashish was very strong. I guess we caught them off-guard and got lucky."

Craw pressed on with what he regarded as his vital contribution to the recorded inquest. "Sergeant Pitt. May I ask you how you put out the guard?"

"An old-fashioned but always reliable cosh, sir. He was still out and unconscious when I grabbed Mr. Greene here, and we ran like hell to the perimeter of the grounds where Mr. Vaux was waiting on the other side of the wall with the getaway car."

Craw nodded and turned to Eccles. "You understand, Excellency, that I will have to make my own preliminary report later today to Sir Nigel Adair, my chief."

"Yes, yes," said the ambassador. "One last question, Vaux." The ambassador twirled a long eraser-topped pencil in his hands as he thought through how to best address the internal politics of the situation.

"I'm trying to put two and two together, you see. Let's put it this way. You were sent here to investigate the tragic sequence of security leaks that has resulted in the murder, killings, or assassinations—call them what you want—of many of our former prime informants."

Then Eccles turned to Craw, who was fiddling with an unlit, half-smoked Senior Service cigarette in the strictly nonsmoking zone of the ambassador's private office.

"Craw, you're Sir Nigel's deputy. I'll take you as the B3 spokesman, shall I? What I want to know is what progress, if any, your team has yet made in what Mansfield tells me B3 has named Operation Cedar."

Craw coughed slightly and stuffed the unlit half-smoked cigarette into his navy-blue blazer's side pocket. "I have only just arrived back, Ambassador. I haven't had time for any debriefings. This whole kidnapping debacle involving Greene, one of our own, has tended to take up all the oxygen."

Eccles continued: "And Chris. I know you must be pretty exhausted after all the action. But we'll have to have a full report on your experience, your treatment at the hands of these bandits, their demands—apart from cash. Their interrogation methods etcetera. Plus what, if anything, you had to divulge about us, our intelligence operations, and our overall political stance toward the rebel groups here.

"The other thing that we haven't yet talked about is the actual abduction itself. I have left this alone because I feel it could be too painful to relate. Give it some time. But we'll have to pursue the facts wherever they lead."

Craw suddenly felt the unfamiliar pang of compassion for his young colleague. "And Chris, what about torture? Did you ever feel physically threatened?"

"No. That's one thing I want to make perfectly clear," said Greene. "There was never any physical abuse. Yes, there were a few brainwashing sessions, long speeches about the evils of western imperialism, how we are deliberately stoking divisions in Lebanon by siding with the Sunnis and Saudi Arabia against the majority of Lebanese."

"Who they claim are Shia, I suppose," said Craw, now a seasoned expert on the Shia-Sunni divide.

Suddenly, Eccles stood up, grabbed an old auctioneer's gavel from one of his drawers, banged it loudly, and declared the meeting at an end.

"See you all at six p.m. sharp. Greene—do get some rest, but please be here for the celebrations. You are the star of the show. Vaux, please make sure he rests up. See you all later."

With that clear dismissal, the men filed out quietly.

But Mansfield was not done. He called Greene and Vaux over and, in a sort of shoulder-hugging, hardly audible rugby scrum, quietly delivered the confidential piece of news Browne had given him just before the ambassador's meeting. "This so-called professor you met that evening when you were given the Mickey Finn—chloral hydrate, I should imagine—doesn't exist.

"We've combed through the staff lists of all the half dozen universities in this town, and the name Salem Kasem doesn't show up anywhere, let alone on any academic staff list. So you would be wise to track down this Mahmoud Gaber who brought you up to his flat that evening."

"Easier said than done," said Vaux.

Chapter 22

TO: AMB. ECCLES
FM: ADAIR
21/9/10
REQUEST THAT GREENE BE REPATRIATED SOONEST
REPLACEMENT EN ROUTE.
INFORM WESTROPP/CRAW.
REGARDS
NA B3
+
M6B3

Vaux read the decrypted telex in the small confines of a room cramped with archaic office equipment, old telephones, and a still-functioning Puma teletype machine, circa 1980. He could hear the raised voices and clinking glasses of the celebrants in the party room on the second floor, mood music supplied by Ambassador Eccles, who was playing a Muddy Waters number on the white Stegler mini-grand, backed by Hammond Seward on electric guitar and Pete Browne on drums.

Earlier, he had been approached by a nervous Mike Stevens, the new encrypt-decrypt man from Bletchley who had volunteered to man the telex and fax systems while most of the embassy staff celebrated Chris Greene's liberation.

On seeing Stevens buttonhole Vaux, Miranda Eccles, in a short white Versace halter dress and blue stiletto pumps, strode over from the bar and a boring conversation with Anthony Mansfield to address the unforeseen situation.

"I'll take care of it, Mr. Stevens," she said in her low-pitched Brazilian drawl. Then she looked toward the minigrand and the blues trio, who had just embarked on an enthusiastic rendition of Waters's "Hoochie Coochie Man." She grabbed Vaux's hand. "I'll show you where the telex room is. It's rather complicated—practically on the roof!"

Stevens nodded to Vaux. Miranda quickly marshaled him out of the rowdy room, and they were suddenly climbing the curved staircase, his hand held tightly by an exotic beauty right out of a romance novel.

On the fifth floor, her warm hand still gripping his, she opened a narrow white door. Vaux began to compose the anodyne reply he would make to Sir Nigel's urgent telex when Miranda pulled him over to a sagging old couch that had been positioned against the Puma telex machine.

She had pulled her short dress up from her magnificently long slender legs, a movement that unwittingly triggered a strong erotic response from Vaux, who had been a self-confessed leg man since his adolescent obsession with Betty Grable. The absence of panties made Miranda totally irresistible, and within ten minutes of their arrival in the small, hot cubicle, Vaux had fired off his reply to Sir Nigel Adair, his boss at MI6's Department B3.

They decided to return to the party separately. Eccles was still working the ivories and apparently oblivious to anything else going on around him. Vaux walked to the bar, ordered a J&B and found Greene standing next to him.

"Speak of the devil," said Vaux.

"What have I done now?"

"I've just sent a telex to Sir Nigel. He wants you home. And I confirmed for Eccles that you'll be on the next plane."

There was a clinking of ice cubes as Greene finished off a large vodka and tonic. "Thanks a bunch, Mike. Why, for heaven's sake?"

"He probably thinks you're in too much danger. Think about it: you escaped the clutches of some militia group. One of their comrades was brutally killed. Do you think if you're spotted they won't take you out? You know too much. You can identify that political officer you told me you had a few brain-washing discussions with. You're a walking assassination target."

"I suppose so. But how will you cope? We've hardly concluded our mission yet."

"He says he's sending a replacement. Probably young Micklethwait."

"He's six years younger than me."

"So?"

"When should I start packing?"

"Now. We'll have a double celebration tonight: your freedom and your departure for greener pastures."

"Oh! England's green and pleasant land!" exclaimed Greene.

Miranda sidled up to the two secret agents. She had not spoken to Vaux since the incident in the telex room. But she had a wry smile on her thick, sensual lips. "We should do something later. My husband's playing at the Blue Note Café at around eleven this evening. Why don't we all meet there?"

"Kind of a long party. I think Chris had better just go back with me to the safe house and prepare to get on tomorrow's RAF Transport flight."

* * *

But they did end up at the Blue Note, a mecca for jazz and swing fans, international artists and local pop stars. The small, smoky cafe-bar on Makhoul Street was jam-packed with music fans and serious drinkers. The nearby AUB campus ensured a large student contingent.

"Next week, Pascale Sakr will be here. She's a wonderful singer. Have you ever heard of her?" asked Miranda. She had squeezed into a narrow booth next to Vaux, who was busy looking at the picture gallery of performers and bands that lined the walls. He had just arrived with Chris Greene and Sergeant Pitt, who had been appointed Greene's bodyguard for the twenty-four hours prior to his trip back to the UK.

Vaux said he hadn't heard of Pascale Sakr.

"That is because you have not been here very long," said Miranda, teasingly.

"I like your husband's music," said Vaux.

"He has talent, yes?"

"Very much."

"*Muito, muito*, much, much." Then in a low, almost husky tone: "Where shall we meet?"

Vaux knew the question had to come. "Next week. A hotel I know. I'll contact you."

Miranda sighed audibly. And then she smiled. Whether it was on hearing the diplomatic trio's soft opening chords of "I Feel Like Going Home," another Muddy Waters hit, or in anticipation of the planned tryst, Vaux did not speculate.

Chapter 23

Vaux breathed a sigh of relief. At last he had received a response from Jack Sumner, former drinking buddy and brilliant mathematician who now worked for GCHQ at Bletchley Park.

DEAR MIKE
First: Not quite the goldmine of intel you thought.
Whoever created the mess was chronically disorderly and chaotic.
The good news: there is a traceable consistency in location of a series of cell phone calls to the Black Book owner who for some reason (paranoid?) traced the calls and wrote down the caller's number: these we reverse-engineered via hand-off call towers to a location close to the UK, Japanese, and Australian embassies in the Serail district of Beirut. The rest of the data is a chaotic, illogical private code of numerals, characters, and memes to which only the creator would have the key.
The next round's on you.
Cheers, Jack

Vaux folded the message, stuffed it in the breast pocket of his shirt, and grunted. He was sitting on the balcony of the safe house, sipping a coffee with a depressed Alan Craw, who was about to leave for the airport to pick up Sebastian Micklethwait.

"We've got to come up with a new strategy, Vaux. Let's face it, we're not getting anywhere." Vaux could see that Craw was irritated by his reticence to reveal the contents of the classified message Sergeant Pitt had handed him earlier.

"My first priority is to track down our friend Greene's asset who finally got him to the apartment where he was drugged and then taken to the kidnapper's hideout. I know his name or at least his cover name: Mahmoud Gaber. I met him on the day after I arrived here."

"But I thought he was the contact you discovered dead in that awful doss-house."

"That was Azimi."

"Like looking for a needle in a haystack. And if you do find him, what the hell are you going to do with him? He's working for the other side, obviously."

"Maybe I can turn him. This is a country where deals can always be made. Money counts for an awful lot, too."

"Yes, but let's just go back to square one, shall we? We are here to do one thing: find the bloody leaker, find out who's betraying our informers and sabotaging our efforts to penetrate the supposed enemy."

"But the enemy's not monolithic, Alan. We're not fighting the last war or the Cold War. These various private armies, these different sects and clans can all be played against one another. At least that's my theory. Let's face it: we don't even know which sect the leaker is loyal to—which private army. It could even be a Mossad agent."

"How do you make that out?"

"Last year there was a massive roundup of Lebanese officials who had been working for the Israelis for years. Even one of the bigwigs at the GSD, the Lebanese intelligence outfit, was arrested."

"What did the Israelis say about it?"

"Nothing. They never comment on that sort of stuff."

Craw looked at his watch. "But why would the Israelis be interested in wiping out our sources?"

"Perhaps there's something they don't want us to know."

"And I'll tell you one other thing," said Craw, bending toward Vaux to guard against any eavesdroppers or hidden mikes. "Don't you find it very, very curious that our ambassador is totally opposed to our reporting the Greene episode to the Lebanese authorities? Surely to God they could go straight to the hideout and arrest the blighters, round up a revolutionary cell of some sort, hold the criminals to account?"

"That's just the point I'm trying to make, Alan. This country is riven with cliques, sects, and private armies. I think Eccles is right: don't trust anyone in the police forces and certainly not in their intelligence outfits. They all have conflicting loyalties. You can bet your bottom dollar that any move to arrest the culprits would be instantly signaled ahead of time so that they could flee before the boys in blue got there."

"So Eccles decided to do nothing. Not even report the incident."

"Afraid so. I bow to his judgment. He's been here a lot longer than either of us."

It was all mystifying to Craw. He shook his head in mock despair. "This bloody place is like the old Russia: 'An enigma, wrapped in a conundrum, inside a mystery'—or whatever Churchill said about the Ruskies."

" 'A riddle wrapped in a mystery inside an enigma,' " corrected Vaux.

But he spoke to himself. Craw had quickly skipped down the wide staircase to join Sergeant Pitt, who was to drive him to Rafic Hariri International Airport and pick up Sebastian Micklethwait.

* * *

Vaux had asked to meet Mansfield early the next morning. While waiting for Micklethwait to make his appearance, he had gone over his final plan to flush out the double agent in their midst. He expected Mansfield to react skeptically, but he knew that, in the total absence of any plan of his own, Mansfield would finally endorse the new strategy.

At 7:00 a.m. Mansfield sat at his desk. He called Browne in to take notes and listen to Vaux's proposition so that he could comment intelligently on it when Vaux had finished.

"Has your new man arrived safely?" asked Mansfield amicably.

"Yes, the Middle East Airlines flight from London was only six hours late, but I hear that's par for the course," said Vaux.

"Always better to take BA or our own Globemaster, I say."

"I don't think Sir Nigel gave him much choice."

Mansfield grunted. He sipped his fine bone china cup of English breakfast tea and watched as Browne sipped his coffee from a Styrofoam beaker. He didn't ask Vaux whether he'd care to join them in the early-morning ritual.

"Well, what's on your mind?" asked Mansfield curtly.

"First, how's your M network doing?" This was Vaux's premeditated ploy to soften up Mansfield.

Mansfield raised his eyebrows. "Ticking over at best. We've been decimated over the past twelve months. Now attempting to rebuild and streamline with fewer agents in place."

"So time for some fresh ideas," said Vaux. "Let's use a time-honored tactic that dates back to the Second World War."

Mansfield looked a little pained. Then he looked up to Browne, whose eyes were fixed on his open diary, his hands unsteady as he made notes.

"I've read all the books and all the postwar briefing papers, Vaux. What tactic in particular are you referring to?"

"Disinformation—turning the enemy's agents into our own agents so that they can spread chicken feed and phony intelligence up the line of command," said Vaux, who now quickly grabbed an upright chair by the far wall to sit directly opposite Mansfield and to the left of Browne.

Mansfield smoothed his roughly shaved chin, his eyes fixed on Vaux. He was caught off- guard and couldn't come up with an immediate comment. Instead, he said, "Go on, Vaux."

"You might say, 'All very well, but we're not fighting a land war here. Our enemy is not monolithic. Quite the opposite: our slippery enemy comprises all the various sects and militias, the legal security forces, the fissured army itself—all fighting one another.'

Yes, all that is true. But even so, I can think of a tactic that could lead to the goal we all want to achieve."

"Which is?"

"To expose our little spy, the thorn in our flesh—the bloody leaker who has a long list of victims to his credit and an impressive array of blown operations, which our finest brains worked on ultimately to no avail. Wasted time and wasted opportunities, wasted lives. The result: we have been unable to advance our national interests in terms of penetrating the machinations and plans of those whose goals, for one reason or another, we would rather hinder than help."

Mansfield pushed back his chair. "That was quite a speech, Vaux. But I do see your point."

"That's just one part of our new strategy," said Vaux, as he warmed to his new plan. On the second front, I'll want the full cooperation of your friend Mailer at the CIA."

"He's not really a friend, Vaux. Just a colleague I have to tolerate now and again. They share bloody little with us and I try to reciprocate. In principle, I prefer not to call them in on any of our operations."

"But you'd agree, I take it, that they are far ahead of us in matters related to telecommunications technology and that sort of thing."

"I don't know if even that is true these days. But what's your beef? Get to the point."

Vaux then laid out his wish list.

Chapter 24

Alexander Mailer, the CIA's chief of station in Beirut, never doubted the mission of the country he loved, which was to spread the cherished gifts of freedom and liberty throughout a benighted world. His faith was partly based on the Protestant religion of his missionary parents. But mainly on the ideological convictions of the political ruling classes to which he was conscripted when a panicky mid-century Washington embarked on an unprecedented drive to expand its secret intelligence networks to thwart the nightmarish global ambitions of its rival superpower, the Soviet Union.

He was fiercely competitive, and many of his colleagues who devoted at least part of their lives to family responsibilities charged that Mailer was "married to the service." But that was largely an evasive answer to those who marveled at the young bachelor's rapid promotion in the intelligence world. At the youthful age of thirty-five, he headed up the CIA station in Algiers, considered by fellow spooks as a stepping stone to bigger and better posts like Paris or London.

But those prizes had evaded Mailer. His superiors had come to regard him as a supreme warrior against the eventually arthritic Soviet Union. But now their focus turned to a new world of terrorism and Middle East turmoil. And Beirut was considered to be the center of the new militant universe. The eventual non-military defeat of the Soviet Union only buttressed Mailer's stalwart faith in his country's mission. His task, as he saw it now, was to wipe out the evil unofficial militias of the terrorist nations and, as part of that eventual goal, to protect a beleaguered Israel which, like most devout Americans, he believed had a biblical right to be left in peace to prosper and propagate.

Mailer's great hero was a predecessor named William Buckley, the CIA's Beirut station chief in the 1980s whose legendary career ended when he was kidnapped and later died at the hands of the Hezbollah faction that had abducted him. Mailer had led the CIA's search for Buckley's suspected killer Imad Mughniyeh, a top lieutenant of Hezbollah. The quest for Mughniyeh went on for several years. And in 2008 Mughniyeh was assassinated by a sophisticated car bomb in downtown Beirut.

Like Buckley, Mailer was unmarried and preferred to live outside the confines of the US embassy complex in his own luxury apartment. On this particular sunny morning in August, nothing was unusual. He had his shower, shaved, checked his closely cropped graying hair, made some coffee, and tore apart a croissant as he perused the *Daily Star*, Beirut's major English-language newspaper. He sat on a tall stool at the marble counter that separated his modern white-tiled kitchen from the big living room whose tall windows looked out to the sea. Unusually, the Mediterranean looked ruffled this morning, white horses bopping up and down the choppy blue-green surface. He heard his windows rattle against the strong inland breeze.

Then he remembered: he had arranged to meet a newly- arrived member of Mansfield's staff at his place rather than at the British embassy for some reason he couldn't remember. He was expected within half an hour, at 9:00 a.m. So he whipped around the living room, cleared ashtrays, scooped up opened magazines, and collected last night's dirty bourbon whiskey glasses.

He heard the entrance signal and buzzed the visitor into the building. This, he knew, was against all the rules of tradecraft, and he sometimes wondered whether he subconsciously wanted to follow his hero Buckley's fateful footsteps. To be so careless and mindless of the ever-present dangers of living here in Beirut was criminally negligent. He had scant confidence in his cover as cultural attaché, and perhaps he was tempting fate, which was why he grabbed his suppressed Smith and Wesson MK-22 from a kitchen drawer before he answered the knock on the door.

He looked through the peephole to the elevator doors to confirm that the man was unaccompanied. He opened the door slowly, firmly gripping the handgun in the pocket of his house gown.

"Sebastian Micklethwait," said the visitor. But the name hardly registered with Mailer, who had expected a clean-cut young man in a gray Brooks Brothers suit, sober tie, and a solid pair of polished oxford brogues. Instead, he faced what he regarded as a semi-hippie, with long auburn hair that covered his ears and the back of his long neck wearing a leather bomber jacket, narrow blue jeans, sweatshirt, and striped brown sneakers.

Mailer said nothing as he motioned his guest into the entry hall. "Take a seat. Can I get you some coffee?"

"No, thanks," said Micklethwait as he headed straight for the big windows. "Great view," he said.

"Yes," said Mailer. "Please take a seat. This won't take long, I presume."

They sat opposite each other in low leather armchairs. Micklethwait took out a gold pack of Benson and Hedges 100s. "Mind if I smoke?"

"Yes. Verboten, I'm afraid."

Micklethwait smiled and put the cigarette pack back in his pocket.

"Thanks for seeing me, Mr. Mailer. As Tony Mansfield probably told you I work for Department B3, an offshoot of MI6. So I have to report directly to Michael Vaux, who heads up our operation here."

Mailer had heard Mansfield make the odd remark about what he called a "rump outfit" within the greater British intelligence network, and he had gathered that its operations often disrupted Mansfield's own valiant efforts in the secret world.

"Yes, of course. I have met Vaux, and I congratulated him on his successful liberation of one of your agents from the hands of some guerrilla group. Have you found out who or what outfit exactly abducted your man Greene?"

"Not yet. But Vaux seems to think he's on the verge of discovering the source of the persistent leaks out of our embassy. I'm here to help him now. Greene's gone home for obvious reasons."

"Yes, go on."

"Very briefly, we want to borrow the electronic talents of your communications people."

"You'll have to elaborate."

Micklethwait then attempted to summarize Vaux's plan to monitor all cell phone activity in close proximity to the triangular area of the British, Japanese, and Australian embassies in the Serail district. "We don't have the capability of doing that. We understand the CIA does. We are therefore requesting your cooperation."

Mailer needed a little time to compose an answer. He got up, walked to the kitchen, opened the fridge and grabbed a can of Coke. He carried it back to his chair, ripped off the seal, and poured the tangy cool liquid down his throat. "Our communications boys are top notch. No question about it. We're miles ahead of anyone else in this field. I understand we can intercept and trace calls down to the GPS position of any party, friend or foe."

Micklethwait's instinct told him that this grandiose claim would be followed by a big qualification.

Mailer continued: "But this is all very top-secret stuff. Our enemies are catching up with us. The Hez are getting technical assistance from the Iranians right now, and one result is that they recently rounded up a network of our field agents thanks mainly to monitoring cell phone conversations and uncovering cell phone numbers.

"But we're one step or even two steps ahead. I understand we now have the capability to install devices that can masquerade as cell communications towers and hijack the caller's IMSI. Are you with me?"

"IMSI?"

Mailer sighed. "International Mobile Subscriber Identity—IMSI."

"Ah, yes," said Micklethwait.

"It's upsetting the hell out of the civil liberties people, but who cares? Our priority is to wipe out the terrorists."

Mailer got up and placed the Coke can on a glass side table. "I have an appointment. Tell Vaux that, under the circumstances, we'll do everything to help. I have good contacts at Alfa, Lebanon's major telecommunications outfit—without whose cooperation... well, let's just say we need their full cooperation in such an operation. I know these leaks of information from your set-up have been persistent and tragic. We view your troubles as our own. After all, we are allies in these goddamned unfriendly waters, eh?"

"Yes, sir," said Micklethwait, who was elated that his mission had been accomplished.

"But before you go, I want to stress that what I have told you is very hush-hush, top secret. Tell Vaux I'll arrange an appointment with one of our communications geniuses within the next few days. We may have to fly him in from Cairo where we have a big StingRay set-up."

"StingRay?"

"That's what we've named the wonder device we've developed back at Langley. It's the enabler, if you like, for us to trace every phone call anyone makes and from where, all over this conspiratorial world," said Mailer as he led Micklethwait to the door.

* * *

At about the same time Micklethwait left Alex Mailer, Michael Vaux was climbing out of a king-size bed in room 501 at the five-star Radisson hotel. This was late for him, but he knew why: Miranda had stayed until well past 3:00 a.m.

Now he felt guilty because he had no regrets: she fulfilled all the fantasies he had conjured since he met her. Her uninhibited love-making only matched her sexy Latin looks. What was bound to happen after that first brief but climactic encounter in the embassy's confined telex room had indeed come to fruition. It is written, as his Arab friends often told Vaux when they tried to explain a good or a regrettable happening.

He was smiling to himself as he shook off the terrycloth robe and entered the over-size shower stall. Between the orgasmic heights had come longer and longer intervals of intense talk about their lives and their earlier loves. She was fascinated to hear of Vaux's escapades in the Middle East, especially his rebellious but romantic affair with a Palestinian who later turned out to be a PLO mole working at MI6's Department B3 in London.

"Well, I'm not a mole or a spy, I can assure you of that!" she laughed. "But I've had my moments." Then she paused as though she was composing her next piece of intelligence. "You must understand, Michael, that I love my husband, and I love the life we have. The one big mar to my happiness is of course what happened to my daughter, Yasmin. Killed in the south, close to the Israeli border. Some bastard fired a rocket at the small school bus, and twelve kids, including my daughter, were killed along with their teacher. It changed me forever. And perhaps that is why we are both here together. If she were alive today, I would not be doing this."

Vaux was momentarily shaken. It had been a cautionary tale, likely to put a damper on the escapade. But he wanted to change the subject to a more pressing question. "What do you see in me, anyway? I'm an over-the-hill, worn-out ex-journalist."

"I see a ruggedly handsome Englishman—I've always loved Englishmen—who's lived through and survived all sorts of tribulations and trials. In fact, you remind me of Martin Shaw, the actor."

"Who's he?"

"Oh, he's been in all sorts of BBC television series. Also, perhaps a bit over the hill, as you put it, but the sort of time-worn look some women like."

"You, especially."

She sighed. "Yes, me especially."

Then she raised her arms again and brought him toward her, and the sexual cycle replayed itself.

Chapter 25

When Vaux got back to the safe house, he found an immaculately dressed Alan Craw on the vine-strewn pillared balcony that overlooked the unkempt gardens. He was smoking a small Dutch cigarillo. Micklethwait had obligingly bought a few duty-free tins at Heathrow before his departure. In his lightweight navy-blue Savile Row suit and monogrammed white cotton shirt, Craw looked overdressed for this decrepit old mansion. When Vaux appeared, Craw was struggling to loosen the knot in his dark-blue crested Worcester College silk tie.

"Out on the tiles last night, were we?" said Craw when Vaux loomed from the open french windows. "Or were we hunting down the mole?"

Vaux knew Craw's brand of humor too well to take the questions seriously. Ignoring them, he asked where Micklethwait had got to.

"According to Sergeant Pitt, he was sent by you on an errand to liaise with the cousins—one in particular, I understand, their Mr. Mailer."

"I'll have to caution Pitt to be more discreet about the where-abouts of our agents."

Craw sighed. "Look Vaux, I know you're the blue-eyed boy since we found Greene, but let's maintain the discipline we all need to do the job. I don't have to remind you that Operation Cedar is still ongoing and unresolved. That's why I've had to come back to this godforsaken country."

Sergeant Pitt appeared with two bottles of Heineken but no glasses. He opened each with the deft movement of one hand and plonked them on the round glass table.

They waited for Pitt to leave them. Vaux said, "Mickle had an appointment with the CIA's station chief. I'll be needing their cooperation in a high technology area where they are far ahead of anything our people can provide. That's all, Alan."

Vaux's use of his first name had the desired effect of soothing Craw's worst fears. To resort to the cousins in any field associated with intelligence was to him tantamount to bad faith and lack of confidence in the home team's abilities to wage the clandestine war on all fronts.

"Well, you must do what you think is best," said Craw in a conciliatory tone.

Vaux then outlined the high-tech operation that he hoped could prove a big step forward in finding the treacherous mole.

They heard doors slam, and the two secret agents looked down to the curved stony driveway. They saw Micklethwait pay off the driver and walk toward the porticoed entrance.

"Don't tell me he went to the CIA chief in bloody jeans," said an alarmed Craw.

Vaux once again ignored his question and waited for Micklethwait's report.

* * *

Mansfield walked through the crowded, narrow twisting alleyways of the Dahiyeh district in east Beirut, past busy shawarma restaurants, small coffee house, and loud shisha bars. It was a 'catholic' quarter, in the real sense that Palestinian refugees, mainly Sunnis, mixed nonchalantly with Lebanese Shias and even Maronite Christians. Members of Hezbollah factions mingled with Hamas sympathizers. He had asked his trusted contact Citron a.k.a. Kamal Moussa to meet him at the usual place: Cafe Yet, a busy Internet cafe, just south of Shatila, where customers were too preoccupied with Google searches to bother to eavesdrop.

Citron sat in a corner of the bar close to a beaded curtain that covered an exit to two toilets and a side street. Mansfield put up with the odd whiffs of urinal odor in exchange for the advantage of a quick escape. Citron looked up from his thick computer science text book and smiled a greeting.

As always when vastly outnumbered by Arab men, Mansfield lowered his voice almost to a murmur. "I have a very delicate job for you."

Then Mansfield outlined the tasks he wanted Citron to undertake within the next twenty-four hours.

"You'll have to meet up with one of our technical men. He'll give you what you need in terms of gadgets and a transmitter. I can arrange a meeting for tomorrow. Your job is to thoroughly wire the place. Don't forget the balcony and the areas where Vaux and his team eat and maybe socialize. You've surveilled the house enough times, so you know the address."

An old, grizzled waiter with a long white apron that reached down to his sandals came over with today's special—habashi with mozzarella cheese. He handed the two plates to his two regular customers. Mansfield gave the old man a fistful of Lebanese pounds, and the two men then ate quickly and in silence. Without further ceremony Mansfield then left by the back door.

If he had seen Mouli Aly, a ranking member of a local Hezbollah cell, quickly approach Citron as soon as he had left, it would have made little difference. Only Chris Greene, now two thousand miles away in London, would have recognized the Vandyke beard, the paunch, and the short legs.

* * *

Two days after Citron's rendezvous with Mansfield, Michael Vaux was about to start his morning shave. He turned on the tarnished old brass hot tap and heard a gurgling sound as a few warm drops of water trickled into the palm of his hand. He called out to Sergeant Pitt, who was down in the kitchen preparing breakfast.

"I'll get on to the embassy. They've got all sorts of handymen on call. They'll get a plumber. Meanwhile I think a beard would suit you, sir."

Vaux had never liked the feel of whiskers, let alone a nascent beard. So he swore under his breath, put his shirt back on and made for the balcony where Pitt usually put out coffee and croissants.

Two hours later, the embassy's plumber arrived. Clearly a local, he carried a hefty bag of tools and was left alone to repair the boiler and check the serpentine piping that served the old house. To guarantee Citron's unfettered and unobserved access to the villa, Vaux and Micklethwait had been summoned to the embassy for a meeting with Mansfield. Sergeant Pitt drove them in the Range Rover.

* * *

It was a busy and harrowing morning for Anthony Mansfield. His first meeting at 7:00 a.m. was with his deputy Peter Browne, who he decided would bear the brunt of the day's logistical maneuvers.

"I want you to help my man Kamal, a.k.a. Citron, set up his communications equipment on the top floor. You know—that small room in the attic with the dormer windows. We've wired B3's safe house with several miniature UHF voice transmitters, and from today we'll know just about everything that those bright boys at Department B3 are cooking up. I expect he'll be here around midday."

Browne looked more harassed than usual. "Yes, sir. But may I ask a simple but hopefully not insolent question?"

"Go on," said Mansfield, an impatient frown suffusing his flushed face.

"Why are we bugging our own side?"

Mansfield leaned back in his leather swivel chair. His eyes looked up to the white popcorn stucco ceiling as if reading the gospel according to veteran spymasters everywhere. He took some time to compose an answer that he hoped would placate a young ingénue and set him on a path to the healthy departmental rivalry on which he had thrived his entire professional career.

"Listen to me, Browne. These B3 people are interlopers, non-professional freelance agents who tend to muddy our waters—with apologies to the ambassador. We all know he loves Muddy Waters—"

Browne managed a sympathetic snicker.

"I sent one of our plumbers to the old house this morning. Like it?"

"Another Le Carre nickname?" Browne thought it better to humor his boss when tensions were running high.

"No! We called them plumbers before Le Carre came on the scene. Anyone tracking down a double agent was called a plumber since way back. Anyway, as I was saying, we have to keep tabs on what they're getting up to. For instance, had I done so earlier, we might have been able to prevent the abduction of their man Greene. I could have got one of our contacts to tail Greene and save him from the danger he walked into—blithely walked into, I might add. It's the name of our game, Browne. The more we know, the more effective we are."

At that moment Mansfield was relieved to see Nancy Sheridan make an unusual appearance. He hadn't heard her gentle knock on the door. "My assistant is away today, so I thought I'd bring you both some elevenses, even though we've got a couple of hours to go."

Mansfield had never seen Ms. Sheridan so cheerful and welcoming. But he had noticed before that when young men were around him, her interest in his well-being tended to increase.

"Thank you, my dear. Has Mr. Eccles arrived yet?"

"No. He won't be in till noon." She put the tin tray down on his mahogany desk, smiled at Browne, and left.

Both men opened their individually wrapped digestive biscuits and sipped their coffees.

Mansfield decided that there would be no more discussion. He would no longer attempt to justify his actions to a junior.

"So let's drop this inquisition, Browne. I'll need you to monitor the conversations at the safe house, summarize them each evening, and bring the results to me. Also, I'll want some information about their movements. That's why we've put a miniature GPS tracker under the chassis of Sergeant Pitt's black Range Rover. I might add that if we had done that earlier, we might have been able to provide an overwhelming firing force to back up their undermanned, under-gunned battle plan to free Greene. But that's in the past. We learn by our mistakes and omissions, eh, my boy?"

"Yes, sir," said Browne, thankful that the confrontation was over.

As he approached the door, Mansfield gave him one more instruction. "Look out for Vaux and this new chap Mickle-something, will you? They're supposed to be here by now. Show them in as soon as they arrive."

"Yes, sir," said Browne, now even more bewildered.

Chapter 26

Two knights of the realm sat at a strategic corner table of the just-renovated, sycamore-paneled River Room restaurant at London's plush Savoy Hotel. Sir Percival Bolton, head of the Secret Intelligence Service (MI6) had suggested lunch to Sir Nigel Adair, a deputy- general of MI6 and chief of Department B3, an offshoot of MI6's Mideast and North Africa desk. Sir Percy wanted an update on B3's intense probe into the persistent security leaks at the SIS station in Beirut, and what he expected to be mixed news at best could be digested better with the restaurant's classic sole meuniere and a bottle of his favorite Chateau Puy Lacoste.

Sir Percy, as he was known affectionately by MI6 operatives, made an effort to sweep the lengthy tendrils of his steel gray hair around the tops of his long ears as he listened intently to Sir Nigel's brief summary of the situation.

The conversation was halted while the diminutive Italian waiter put down two large long-stemmed glasses on the starched linen tablecloth before pouring the vodka martinis. Two silver-plated salt and pepper shakers were quickly shifted to make space for a bowl of green olives along with a sheaf of silver toothpicks.

"I gather from your quick appreciation of the situation that progress is being made, but a definitive resolution of the problem is still out of reach," said Sir Percy, whose long pre-spying career in the prestigious Royal Horse Guards had instilled the habit of employing military phraseology in most human situations.

Sir Nigel countered Sir Percy's pessimistic assertion. "I've sent my deputy Craw over there to expedite a solution to this problem, Percy. He's a good man, and I anticipate he'll bring a bit of much-needed discipline to the exercise. We should never have lost Greene in the first place. It was shameful the way he stumbled into that abduction trap. The basics of tradecraft were completely ignored, and the inevitable happened. The whole damned team were derelict in their duty. Fortunately, we got Greene back. He's here in London for obvious reasons."

"The only good thing about the outcome is that no ransom had to be paid. Give me the results of your interrogation as they become available, will you? Maybe we can learn something about his abductors," said Sir Percy hopefully.

"Vaux says he's certain they were a Hezbollah cell; that's all we know so far."

"Anybody injured or killed in the rescue operation?" Sir Percy poured himself a refill from the martini pitcher the waiter had left on the table.

"Not as far as I know. We'll learn more after I talk to Greene. Meanwhile, we've sent young Micklethwait over there to replace Greene. What have you heard from your man Mansfield?"

"I don't talk to him for security reasons. But Nobby Clark, head of the Mideast desk, tells me he's at last cooperating with Michael Vaux and is optimistic about the eventual solution to this bloody leak problem."

"We'll have to wait and see. I have the feeling that with Craw over there to oversee Operation Cedar, we should soon be seeing at least a glimmer of light at the end of the tunnel," said Sir Nigel with more hope than faith, as he eyed the waiter's deft filleting of the Dover sole.

Before both men started on the food, they raised and then touched each other's martini glasses for a mutually reassuring tinkle of collegiality.

Suddenly, Sir Percy, his jaws still masticating a small hairlike fish bone, said, "What about this fellow Micklethwait? You say you've sent him over there already?"

"Yes, indeed. He's our only spare body at the moment. I'm sure you don't want me to bring up the subject of our manpower problems at B3. Where's the deputy I've been told is on the way—for two or more years now?"

Sir Nigel smiled, a signal that he wasn't about to spoil the pleasant atmosphere of the luncheon.

"Yes, I know all about that," said Sir Percy with a sigh of helplessness. "It's out of my hands now. Whitehall's on one of its economy kicks, and until the belt-tightening ends, you'll be whistling Dixie for any staff increments. But to get back to the young man you have just sent over there, wasn't he mixed up in another kidnapping drama a few years back—in Morocco, wasn't it?"

"Yes, indeed. Bundled into a limo outside a nightclub where he should never have been. Completely unprotected and unguarded and unarmed. Silly blighter. Learned his lesson the hard way. Hope so anyway."

"Who took 'im?"

"AQIM, Al-Qaeda in the Islamic Maghreb. Completely different crowd."

"Don't hear much from them anymore, what?"

"No. They seem to be very quiet. Let's pray it stays that way."

* * *

Sebastian Micklethwait had got back to the safe house in time to see the embassy's plumber leave. The water was back on. He climbed the dusty white marble stairs to the second floor's ancient bathroom. But despite several twists and turns of the faucets, the shower still didn't work. So he turned on the bath's tarnished hot and cold taps, which, after a protesting groan, gushed murky brown water. He looked around for some soap and found the big brick of highly scented Crabtree and Evelyn that Vaux had bought at Heathrow.

He lay in the warm water and listened to the creaks and moans of an old house and wondered how this foreign assignment, the first since the Morocco fiasco five years ago, would end. In 2005, he had been on his first foreign job, only to be summarily kidnapped by AQIM operatives and eventually exchanged for one of their top men. The prisoner swap, organized jointly with the CIA, who had held the terrorist, and Department B3, went tragically wrong. He was freed, but the prisoner was killed in the sudden, unplanned shoot-out, and Vaux had been badly injured.

He guessed old Sir Nigel had been reluctant to send him on a foreign mission ever since his lack of caution on a carefree Saturday night in Tangier had led to the disaster. But now he had the opportunity to prove himself again. He had just marked his thirtieth birthday, and he wanted nothing more than to succeed in this clandestine career, if only to honor his beloved grandmother, who had worked with Alan Turing's code-breaking team at Bletchley during the Second World War. It was her influence that had helped him get the MI6 job in the first place.

He heard the thud of someone climbing the wooden steps to the double front doors of the house. Then the familiar squeak of the doors and the clunky footsteps of Sergeant Pitt, who wore heavy British Army–issue assault boots in all climates. He stood up, dried himself with one of the copious white cotton towels sent over from the embassy, slipped on his jeans and went down for a friendly chat with Pitt.

* * *

Michael Vaux sat with Miranda Eccles in the lobby bar of the newly built Radisson Hotel in central Beirut. As usual, the bar was quiet, and the solitary barman busied himself by shining glasses and assorting bottles on the mirrored shelves behind him. He occasionally glanced over to their table to check if they needed refills or fresh bowls of peanuts and olives.

They had had what Vaux liked to call a matinee session—but only to himself in honor of her dignity. She had arrived at 3:00 p.m. after a formal lunch at the British Council, the semiofficial arm of the British government that promotes cultural and educational activities that sometimes coincide with the nation's raw political and international interests.

In Vaux's eyes she looked elegant and beautiful. Her white blazer and blue cotton T-shirt set off her light tanned skin; the skinny white chino trousers and tanned loafers emphasized her long, slender legs.

"It's very difficult to get away at night, darling. Last week was easy because John had to go south to Beaufort Castle, an old Crusader fort where we've offered to finance some reconstruction efforts or something.

"The old fort was almost destroyed when the Israelis blew it up in 2000. They said it had been used by the PLO to stage raids into northern Israel. Anyway, my husband stayed overnight with some local dignitary. Afternoons are my only option, dearest."

Vaux had mentioned that daytime trysts were not exactly his preference. "Particularly now that we're revving up for our second front," he said.

"Second front? What is it that you mean by 'second front'?"

"Just that we're in a final push to find the traitor who's sabotaging all our efforts in this theater of operations…"

"Oh, my goodness." She laughed. "You sound like a general or perhaps a field marshal."

"Let's leave it. No shop talk."

Vaux was tired. Two hours of lovemaking, he realized with some nostalgia, was not as easy as it used to be. But Miranda had given herself with abandon that afternoon, and he wondered whether he was being fair to her. He had never mentioned any relationship with another woman, and he asked himself whether this was because his conduct had been frivolous or an ominous sign that his affair with Anne had reached a threshold. Could they ever take up where they had left off?

The secretive side of his nature took charge, and he led the conversation to an unexpected and disconnected topic. "I rather like your husband. Down to earth sort of guy, none of the pretentiousness of some of his colleagues in the foreign service. You never told me how you two met up…"

"That's easy," said Miranda. "We were students. Sussex University—what they called one of the plate-glass universities that opened up around the country in the sixties and seventies. We were on different degree courses, but sometimes our subjects overlapped. I met him on the same day our economics lecturer told us to study Keynes and his *General Theory*. We all rushed to the bookshop, and John approached me for the first time. He suggested we go halves on the big, fat, expensive book—and that's how it all started."

"Fascinating," said Vaux, urging her on to complete the briefing. "But what did you have in common besides being at the same college—he a typical English undergraduate, you an exotic beauty from South America?"

She laughed with an innocence that touched him. "Thank you, darling. After the book-sharing deal, we saw more and more of each other. Then he invited me to a jazz club in Brighton where he was performing that night. He played the piano in a four-piece blues band, and it wasn't difficult to fall in love when you were both in your early twenties and living independently in miserable digs— even if you had a view of the sea across that bleak pebble beach."

"And what made you choose to study in England, all the cold and the damp after tropical Brazil?"

"My father was a diplomat at the Brazilian embassy in London. He's retired now back in Rio. I often think John's eventually joining the Foreign Office had something to do with my father's fascinating stories about diplomatic life. They liked each other and got along well."

Vaux looked into her almond-shaped eyes and saw a trace of a tear. He threw a handful of peanuts into his mouth. "We should go," he said.

* * *

Peter Browne, officially the embassy's third secretary, factually senior assistant to MI6's head of station and currently listener to and monitor of the goings on at Department B3's safe house, sat in the Windsor chair opposite his boss Anthony Mansfield. It was just past 8:00 a.m. on a Thursday, and he had reviewed the first twenty-four hours of what Mansfield had named "the B3 tapes."

"What do we know?" asked Mansfield sternly.

"So far, not much, sir. Just gossip and chatter between Craw, Vaux and Micklethwait. Sergeant Pitt tosses in his odd bolshie remark, and so far the scene appears to be essentially a social occasion for a few highly critical and opinionated ex-pats."

Mansfield did not appreciate Browne's observations about their colleagues' attitudes or opinions. He just wanted solid facts. "I don't need your commentary about their attitudes or their demeanors, Browne. Just the facts. What are they cooking up that we should know about?"

"Vaux told Micklethwait that he should think about a bit of freelancing. By which he meant that Mickle—the handy moniker that they all seem to have adopted for him—should get out onto the street, cruise around a bit in the night spots, and make contacts. In short, recruit his own informers and set up a new network. Vaux called it 'diversifying our efforts.'"

Mansfield grunted. "Anything else? And keep it short."

Browne scrutinized his notes. "Nothing significant, sir. Craw goes in and out, and of course he's staying at the Phoenicia. When he's at the safe house, he seems to find fault with a lot of things, and the friction between him and Vaux is palpable."

"Palpable?"

"Well, obvious. Craw calls his boss in London every day on an encrypted mobile phone. Our decrypt team here have got him covered."

Mansfield suddenly recalled that he had given Mike Stevens, a temporary emissary from Bletchley Park, the task of analyzing the ransom notes Vaux had given him, and he had not heard back from him. He picked up the internal phone and dialed three numbers.

"Stevens?"

"Yes."

"This is Mansfield. You never got back to me on those two notes we picked up from the kidnappers."

"I said I'd get back if there was anything significant to report. But there wasn't, sir. Just a few smudged finger prints, a few of which matched those of your Mr. Michael Vaux."

"*My* Michael Vaux?"

"He works for you, doesn't he?"

"No, no, no. But I haven't got time to explain. Thank you."

Browne looked through his notes for any morsel that might pique Mansfield's appetite for hard news.

Mansfield waited in silence. "All right, Browne. Continue the good work. Listen for any specific plans they are dreaming up. If we'd known about the harebrained scheme to rescue Greene, we could have provided a much bigger striking force to take out the kidnap cell. I hope you understand that."

"Yes, sir, absolutely."

"Oh, and before you leave—what's the latest on the so-called telecommunications/signals wallah we are borrowing from the CIA folks in Cairo?"

"He should be here later today. He'll report to Mailer first, I suppose, and then we'll call in Vaux for a full session on what exactly the B3 team wants him to do."

"Oomph," grunted Mansfield.

Chapter 27

It was a warm, dusky evening, and the three men placidly sipped their favorite drinks: Vaux had his Cutty Sark, thanks to Sergeant Pitt's endeavors to find an accessible supplier (the Radisson); Micklethwait nursed a pint from the embassy's purloined keg of Bass; and Sergeant Pitt of the Diplomatic Protection Command was enjoying a rare bottle of Guinness recently brought back from Northern Ireland by one of his chums in the diplomatic contingent.

"I'll leave you gents if you want to talk shop," said Pitt. He sensed that Vaux was about to launch into a pep talk with his junior, who had arrived on the scene just a few days earlier.

"No, we'll leave our strategic planning until after dinner, Pitt. What time did you say you expected Craw?"

"Give him another couple of hours, sir. By which time my couscous will be well and truly ready," said Pitt.

Vaux said, "Meanwhile, get yourself another drink while we chew the fat, as they used to say when I was in the army."

The conversation was desultory and aimless as if Vaux had decided that no major decisions about the way forward could really be made without Craw's presence. Besides, Browne had called him earlier to tell him that the CIA signals expert from Cairo had flown in and had scheduled a meeting for tomorrow at noon. His arrival, Vaux hoped, could well presage a quick resolution of the problem they had all come here to solve.

He looked closely at Micklethwait as the light from the oil lamp flickered momentarily over the young man's face. He was slightly tanned from a recent holiday in Lisbon, and his deep blue eyes glistened in the unsteady glow. He had a slightly retroussé nose, full sensual lips, and long auburn hair. His ears stuck out a little. Vaux had never realized before how strikingly handsome the young Englishman was.

He also seemed pensive tonight. "What do you think of Beirut, Michael? I find it a strange city, full of lost souls searching for their own private redemptions—"

"Yes, all the competing faiths—or confessionals, as they call their different religions here—all mixed up with multiple political ideologies, different national loyalties. Truly, a warehouse of souls."

Micklethwait stood up and looked down to the wild, overgrown garden, now eerily illuminated by the pale light of a half moon. He stretched his arms and declared that he had to go down to "the bog" to take a leak. Vaux sat on the balustrade, and as he looked at the young man, he saw him suddenly freeze in place as though stunned, his eyes locked in a vacuous sightlessness. A small red spot on his forehead grew larger as blood trickled down to the bridge of his nose. Micklethwait's legs finally buckled and he collapsed.

Vaux looked quickly toward the area from where he thought he may have heard a muffled, suppressed shot. There was no movement and no sign of anyone. He called out for Pitt, who was banging pans in the kitchen and whistling "It's a Long Way to Tipperary."

Then he saw three armed figures rush toward the front doors of the house. A loud crash as they bashed their way in. Pitt, who had grabbed his L85 assault rifle that always stood by the pantry door, ran up the stairs to the balcony, and without a word between them, both men scrambled up another flight of stairs to Vaux's bedroom.

Vaux grabbed his Walther P99 from his leather holdall. Pitt checked the thirty-round magazine of his assault rifle. The three intruders were loudly cursing in Arabic and randomly firing their weapons as they trudged through the house and up the stairs. Bullets ricocheted and whined off the peeling plaster walls and the solid oak banisters.

Vaux locked the door and told Pitt to join him under the base of the big four-poster where they would be covered by the long, floor-length quilt and could concentrate their aim toward the only possible entry to the room.

Boots and rifle butts hammered at the old oak door. Vaux, in prone position under the heavy mattress, waited for the inevitable. Pitt had crouched at the side of a tall antique chest of drawers, a vantage point where he figured he could target anyone who came through the door. Then a squat, heavy-set man with a Vandyke beard, stormed in, shouting and cursing his enemy. He was waving the AK-47 in a sweeping arc, shooting at random, looking for a target as he shouted, "You killed my son! My only son! May Allah have mercy upon you!"

A taller, slimmer man followed, but the third figure Vaux had seen running toward the house had not appeared. Pitt was a sudden and easy target as he fumbled with his assault rifle. One of Vandyke's random shots hit him. Vaux felt the thud as Pitt fell, raised the fringe of the quilt from the floor, and aimed directly at the gunman who had shot Pitt. The other man had decided that the battle was won, and Vaux heard him scuffle up the stairs and open doors in a frantic search for anybody else in the house.

Vaux's shot crushed Vandyke's chest. The furious man fell heavily to the ground. Vaux stayed under the cover of the solid thick mattress. Then he heard the second man run into the room.

He cried at the top of his voice, "*Ya ibn el Sharmouta!*" Son of a bitch! He turned around and skipped down the stairs and out of the house. The third man wavered at the front entrance, apparently confident that their mission had been a success. They both ran to what Vaux assumed was their getaway vehicle, just outside the old gates.

Vaux then rushed over to where Pitt lay, blood flowing fast from his shoulder. He was groaning but seemed to be conscious. Vaux ran to the bathroom and grabbed a damp cotton bath towel, rushed back to Pitt, and put pressure on the wound to stem the bleeding. Pitt opened his eyes and gave a wan smile.

"Keep pressing hard," said Vaux. He got up and checked the bearded terrorist. His dead eyes stared fixedly at the corniced ceiling. He was gone. Then Vaux quietly moved out of the room and skipped down the stairs to the balcony where he had left Micklethwait—and his cell phone.

* * *

Pete Browne had been finishing his day in the embassy's audio control room. Usually, he set the safe house's monitoring modem to record mode for nighttime. On this particular evening, he had been listening to Vaux's sporadic and aimless conversation with Micklethwait and was just about to switch from live to record when he noticed an abrupt and ominous silence between Vaux and Micklethwait, followed by a heavy clattering thump. He was just about to discard his headset when he decided to concentrate more on their conversation. Now he heard Vaux shout for Sergeant Pitt who, as the bugs in the kitchen had indicated, was busy preparing dinner.

Browne bent closer to the monitor and turned up the volume. Pitt seemed to have dropped everything instantly—literally, as saucepans or dishes clattered to the old flagstone floor. The obvious urgency in the men's voices muffled the actual words between them, and heavy breathing indicated they were in the process of climbing stairs. Then he heard a heavy crash—doors being forced open?—and several men calling out to one another in Arabic. Several gunshots followed, and he could hear the ping of bullets that ricocheted within the building. Then more shouts, the clump of men rushing down stairs, and then total silence.

He adjusted the position of his uncomfortable headset in a futile attempt to figure out what was now going on at the safe house. He heard the distorted, suppressed voice of Vaux telling someone to press hard. Then silence.

* * *

Alan Craw sat in his luxury suite at the Phoenicia looking at the big-screen television. He had tuned in to the hotel's classic movie channel and was enjoying *Casablanca*. Although his various foreign postings had taken him to many of the world's capitals, he had never visited the fabled port city. But he had had the unfortunate experience of both Alexandria and Tangier in recent years, and he told himself that he probably hadn't missed much.

"Damn!" he said to himself as his cell phone chimed the first six notes of Britain's national anthem. He searched for the mute button on the unfamiliar remote, his forefinger hovering uncertainly over several possible options. He found it. "Yes?" he demanded sternly.

It was Vaux, and he sounded unnaturally calm, given the information he now imparted. "There's been a raid on the safe house. Micklethwait's been killed, along with one of the raiding party. Both Pitt and I are sitting ducks. Do what you have to do, Craw. It's a full emergency."

Vaux disconnected immediately. Craw sat in his low white leather armchair looking at Humphrey Bogart embracing Ingrid Bergman in the now-silent film. The news had momentarily paralyzed him. He thought of Micklethwait: young, inexperienced, but keen as mustard. "Christ!" he shouted to the empty room.

He riffled through his flight bag for the official Beirut embassy phone and contact book. He hoped to hell somebody was on night duty and knew how to contact Tony Mansfield.

Chapter 28

Three weeks after the safe house ambush, Michael Vaux was invited by Mansfield to give what he called a presentation of his new plan to expose the source or sources of the leaks that had for too long sabotaged MI6's intelligence efforts in Lebanon.

Mansfield ordered his small team of case officers to attend the top secret parley and issued an invitation to Ambassador John Eccles. Alexander Mailer, the CIA's station chief, attended on the strength that the CIA's top secret electronic intercept technology would play the major role in Vaux's detection plan.

The meeting was held in the main conference room that Pete Browne, now anointed Mansfield's eavesdropping expert, had thoroughly scrubbed for any bugs or other sophisticated listening devices. The long rosewood table came in for especially careful examination, its ornate legs and the unpolished curlicued underbelly offering obvious potential sites for any miniature mikes that could be disguised as part of the antique table's sturdy structure.

Mansfield also demanded that the gilt-framed portraits of the queen at one end of the room and Lord Nelson at the other be closely examined and, if suspicions were raised, the pictures be carted away pro tempore to the small storage room next to Browne's audio control room in the attic.

He now noticed that both the portrait of a serene young queen and the large canvas of a defiant Nelson at the Battle of Cape Saint Vincent remained in place. A tall bookcase at the far end of the room that contained unread rows of thick leatherbound tomes had been covered with a heavy gray blanket that Browne assured Mansfield would muffle any voices picked up by some tiny undetected listening device hidden in the belly of one of the books.

Mansfield invited Vaux to address the meeting. Vaux got up and headed toward the open french windows before which a dais had been placed. He looked carefully under the lighted note stand as if searching for undetected bugs. The move produced an amused titter from his audience. Then Vaux launched into the details of what he called Operation Triple Cross.

Bill Brady, an MI6 case officer who ran several key agents within the Beirut area and in southern Lebanon, jumped up to ask the first question.

"Are you suggesting that we deliberately lie to our best contacts—that we give them totally fictional information so that whoever the final leaker is can be flushed out, as it were?"

"Yes," said Vaux. "I believe that our target will expose himself as soon as we disseminate the false intelligence. It's a game of disinformation and deception. We want to seduce the enemy into believing a big defection plan is underway between some high official of Hezbollah and the Brits. The defector wants money and sanctuary, and we let it be known that we consider what the operative knows about his own and perhaps other terrorist networks—personnel, military plans, bomb plots, arms purchases, admin locations, quasi-military bases—is worth us agreeing to his demands.

"This is what you can tell your agents in place: that the defector is expected to offer a mother lode of vital intelligence that will help us thwart their collective efforts to destabilize the region and, incidentally, help the legitimate government of Lebanon handle the threats from these quasi-government, paramilitary groups.

"Specifically," Vaux continued, "you should all make clear that our defector operates in the south, close to the Israeli border. He is a senior Hezbollah operative currently in charge of negotiating a big arms deal with Iran. In other words, it's a prize catch for us, and we plan to go through with the deal. Our fictional turncoat will land up in the UK with a big pension paid by Her Majesty's grateful government."

Again, a light titter around the table.

"Why are we using Hezbollah as the fall guys?" asked Brady, a tall man with a shiny bald head, who clearly liked to play the role of skeptic.

"We don't have to. It was a random choice. We could say the fictitious defector is from Hamas or even a Maronite, if you like. Perhaps even an adherent of the Druze. But the Hez are the biggest and strongest outfit, I believe, and an arms deal with Iran seemed to me to provide a more credible backdrop to the defection."

Brady stroked his chin but failed to look satisfied with Vaux's answer.

Mansfield had listened to Vaux's disinformation and deception plan. He, too, had decided not to show any enthusiasm, even though he had heard that C and Sir Nigel Adair had approved the new strategy. "Basically, you think this bombshell will flush out our mole within days, I presume. The exercise will need painstaking attention to intercepting the communications and signals among our antagonists. How do you plan to monitor this?"

Vaux realized that Mansfield hadn't grasped the core of his argument. "Tony, our aim is to launch a super- SIGINT exercise which, with the help of Alex Mailer's communications experts, we now have the technological know-how to carry out. There's been a tremendous breakthrough in intercept technology, and thanks to our American friends, we can now take advantage of it."

Alex Mailer scanned the rows of skeptical faces now turned toward him. "That's right, Vaux. I can guarantee our full cooperation in this exercise, gentlemen. I hope we will be able to forge a new era of cooperation and mutual assistance in this area. I also hope and expect it will mitigate our somewhat strained relationship in recent years, which, as you all probably know, has resulted in a steady reduction in inter-agency coordination and cooperation."

Silence fell on the group of agent runners. They were perplexed. Some looked and winked at each other (just another futile exercise imposed on them from on high); others looked down at their notepads and scribbled indecipherable letters and crazy patterns, reflecting, perhaps, an innate cynicism.

Ambassador Eccles chose this moment to adopt the mantle of chief diplomat. He rose to thank them for their attendance. "Now, gentlemen, you must go out and spread the message. I think Department B3 has come up with an intriguing and certainly a technologically brilliant solution to the problem that has plagued us for too long and cost too many lives in the process. Surely, we can all agree on that. So let's go. The sooner we catch our bloody mole, the sooner we will re-establish the sort of watertight security MI6 demands, and selfishly, I'll be able to concentrate one hundred percent on what I was sent out here to do—represent Her Majesty's government in our efforts to improve relations with Lebanon and surrounding areas and particularly, to promote peaceful cooperation with all the varied pieces of the Middle East mosaic."

As Vaux prepared to leave, Eccles came over and shook his hand. "Excellent presentation. I wish you every success in your endeavors. Where's Craw, by the way?"

"That's what I'm going to find out. He's had a touch of the flu, and I'd better see if he needs anything," said Vaux.

Mansfield, always quick to see the way the wind blew, then came over to Vaux. He clasped his left arm and shook his right hand. "Well done, old man. Don't understand all the high-tech stuff. But if it works, so much the better."

* * *

Miranda Eccles, in a white linen pantsuit and black steel-heeled pumps, waited for Michael Vaux's return to the hotel. The Radisson where he was registered as Michael Westropp, businessman, had once again become Vaux's virtual safe house and a discouraged Craw, with no alternative to suggest, had approved the inevitable move.

Miranda sat in the lobby, and she saw Vaux go through the metal-detecting barrier without any trouble. He had placed his Walther P99 in a tray, which was then carried to the front desk by one of the security guards. They did not embrace each other but shook hands lightly. A waiter came over, and Vaux ordered drinks.

"Was my husband there?" asked Miranda. She knew Vaux had attended some meeting at the embassy that morning, and she wondered whether her husband's earlier than usual departure after breakfast had any connection.

"Yes, as a matter of fact. But I can't really talk about it just now. I'm sure you understand, darling."

"Of course. But I only have a couple of hours. I've got to go to a board meeting, too—UNRWA, as a matter of fact. It's one of the chores expected from an ambassador's wife. Or at least a British ambassador's wife."

"They do a lot of good work. I know that much."

"Yes, especially for the Palestinian refugees. That's a cause I think we can all agree on."

"Yes," said Vaux. He recalled the tragic death of her daughter and wondered whom she blamed for the outrage.

Vaux knew she had booked a room for herself, a wise bit of tradecraft that aimed to prevent any front desk gossip about their relationship. Vaux thought it was probably a lost cause; the Arab grapevine was as efficient as any highly organized spy ring, and he knew instinctively that there was nothing private about their assignations. He just hoped that discretion, a byword of every respectable hotel in the world, had thrown a thick blanket of obscurity over their periodic trysts.

She knocked gently on his door. She walked over to the big windows that overlooked the scarred hinterland and beyond, the indigo blue Mediterranean. With a fixed gaze, she searched the far horizon as she slowly stripped off her clothes and threw her silk panties onto the small table by the window. Then she stood like a poised athlete, quickly ran to the king-size bed and jumped into Vaux's welcoming arms.

Vaux held her close. He cursed himself for now obsessing about where and how this affair would end. And at the very moment when he knew he should concentrate on the sexual act itself, a faded image of poor Micklethwait came into his mind. But Miranda's skillful ministrations aroused him, and he was suddenly able to focus on satisfying both their needs. Finally, in a magically simultaneous act of abandonment, they were able to forget their worldly worries in a cataclysm of ephemeral ecstasy.

Chapter 29

Anthony Mansfield, apprehensive about what he had decided to name F-Day (for flush out, the launch date for Operation Triple Cross and a historical salute to D-Day, the day that marked the beginning of the end for Adolf Hitler), was relieved to order its postponement.

Sir Percival Bolton, head of MI6, with Department B3's chief Sir Nigel Adair's full support, had ordered an internal inquiry into the death of former secret agent Sebastian Micklethwait and into the circumstances that had surrounded the young man's demise. Sir Percy ordered that the inquiry should take top priority, over and above all current projects or programs related to the activities and functions of MI6 in Beirut and Lebanon.

The inquiry was to be headed by John Perkins, a former lawyer who, five years earlier, had joined the Foreign and Commonwealth Office soon after passing his Bar examinations. He would be joined by two men who represented the interests of the FCO and the Secret Intelligence Service, respectively. The hearings would be strictly sub rosa. Witnesses would be required to swear under oath not to reveal either the contents of any statements made to the inquiry or the identity of the witnesses and officials involved.

Mansfield had called Vaux for an emergency meeting. "There's nothing I can do, Vaux. Orders from Vauxhall Cross. F-Day is postponed. The three men arrive tonight. The internal inquiry is scheduled to get underway the day after tomorrow. It will be held in the conference room."

Mansfield opened his desk drawer and brought out a wad of A4s. "You'll be the chief witness. Can't be helped—you were there when it happened. Pitt, too, of course. Can you think of anybody else who would fit the bill?"

"Only yourself. I've heard that you had the place wired, and Browne set off alarms and whistles as soon as he detected the mayhem and the gunshots."

"I see you have set up your own internal spy network. No surprise. But we did that to protect you. To protect the safe house. So yes, of course I'll be a witness, as will Browne, who reported to me as soon as this bloody tragic business got underway."

Both men sipped their Twining's English breakfast tea brought in earlier by the ambassador's secretary Nancy Sheridan. She wore a heavy brown tweed two-piece costume reminiscent of the Queen's country attire. With her tightly permed steel gray hair, she was a constant reminder of the titular head of state whom both men served. In a renewed spirit of goodwill, she had decided to add Mansfield to the short list of embassy staff to whom she would serve morning tea or coffee and biscuits. But Mansfield had noticed that Styrofoam beakers had been substituted for the delicate bone china cups used when he shared the morning break with Ambassador Eccles.

Vaux had heard the argument about protecting the safe house and its occupants before. But he didn't buy it. "I think the bugs were placed there so you could know what we were planning, to listen in on B3's strategy discussions, perhaps to get a head start on one of our projects—"

"No. No, no!" exclaimed Mansfield. "Not true, not true."

"You said yourself that if you had known about our plans to free Greene from the terrorist cell, you could have gathered up a few special forces personnel and galloped to our aid, all guns blazing, and possibly wiped out the cell responsible."

"But isn't that true, Vaux? Think about it."

"I have. And all I can say is that it would probably have resulted in a blood bath that we successfully avoided."

"On the other hand, is it not likely that poor Micklethwait's killer was a member of the very cell that took Greene off the street?"

To Vaux, this was a circular argument that got both men nowhere.

"We'll see what the internal inquiry comes up with."

"Meanwhile, here's to remembering young Mickle." Mansfield raised his beaker, lowered it again to spoon out the tea bag, and quickly gulped down the dregs.

* * *

Unpredictably, Alan Craw was called as the first witness in the official inquiry into the death of Sebastian Micklethwait. He suffered from post-flu sniffles, and Vaux thought he looked more forlorn and lost than usual. The inquiry was held in the conference room, the three sets of french windows open to the lush tropical, pine-shaded garden. The hiss of the gooseneck sprinklers could be heard over light birdsong.

The long rosewood table had been swung around 180 degrees from its traditional position so that the three inquisitors (so named, post-inquiry, by Alan Craw) had their backs to the earthly delights of the manicured garden and could concentrate on their witnesses.

John Perkins, tall and lean with, in Craw's words again, a head as bald as a billiard ball, wore a charcoal gray suit with a white shirt and a striped college tie that Craw could not identify. He had brought a gavel along and banged it on the highly polished surface of the table to signal that the first session of the internal inquiry was now underway.

Craw, notified that he was to be the first witness, had arrived some forty minutes before the session began and already sat facing the three men who would be his interrogators. The glare from the early-morning sun prompted him to shade his eyes with his hand and request that the ancient and faded venetian blinds be adjusted to block out the light. A seated white-coated member of the domestic staff sprung to life and adjusted the blinds. Perkins then asked him to leave the room. He had suddenly recalled the Vauxhall diktat that the proceedings were not to be witnessed by any personnel other than British citizens who represented embassy staff or members of the various branches of the secret services.

"Mr. Craw. These proceedings are to be recorded by audio mechanisms and by good old-fashioned short-hand." He nodded to Nancy Sheridan, who had volunteered her services and was very happy to be of some practical use besides making tea for the ambassador and a few privileged staff. She kept her eyes on the notepad she used, her ballpoint pen poised for action.

Craw nodded. His arms resting on the table, he held his long, thin hands together and presented a picture of serene calm and equanimity. As he had earlier commented to Vaux, he could not for the life of him imagine why the three inquisitors should call him as a witness in the first place.

"I understand," said Craw, his voice low and almost inaudible.

"Please speak up, Mr. Craw. The mikes may catch your voice, but I doubt if our notetaker could hear you," said Perkins.

"Sorry. Please continue," said Craw who was an avid tennis player and felt he had chalked up advantage with the first exchange. Suddenly, a missile approached him across the surface of the table, propelled from where the interrogators were sitting. It was a small leather-bound Bible, which he grabbed before it fell from the table's edge to the floor. He then repeated after Perkins the usual oath to tell nothing but the truth, so help him God.

"You are our first witness because, as the senior representative of MI6's Department B3, you took it upon yourself to rent a private villa, an opulent villa I might add, to provide a safe house for your colleagues under your charge. Is that correct?"

"Correct—except for your description of the villa." Craw looked around to see if Vaux was amused.

"Elaborate, please."

"It was a rundown old ruin that previously had been an opulent sort of place—a Byzantium mansion, if you like. But ideal for our purposes. When I arrived, our principal agents were making do at hotels or in grubby little one-room apartments they had rented from the locals." An audible titter, but Perkins's darting eyes failed to identify the source.

"What was the arrangement under which you procured this accommodation? With whom did you deal?" This from board member William (Bill) Pym of the Secret Intelligence Service.

Craw puffed up, proud to focus on his worldwide social connections. "I know a certain gentleman, a Beiruti, whom I met years ago at college. He's from a wealthy family and has connections with Solidere, the company here that has more or less monopoly power in the reconstruction effort. He is an executive director, I believe. And the house was due for demolition to make way for a high rise, but the plans got stalled in the courts, and he let me rent it for a song. End of story."

The three members of the inquiry looked at one another. Perkins gave a nod to the FCO's Andy Austen, a portly and grizzled long-time diplomat on the eve of retirement. "This company you refer to—was it not engaged in many controversies regarding the city's reconstruction plans? The opposition parties have not only claimed that, as you have said, it enjoys virtual monopoly power, but that it was also corrupt, bribing city planners and indulging in all the excesses of monopoly power. Its chief executive, Rafiq Hariri, in fact became Lebanon's prime minister, only to be assassinated soon thereafter."

"You are obviously a history buff," commented Craw drily.

Perkins got back into the fray. "Please give the board the name of the executive you say gave you the lease on this old house."

Craw hesitated. "That would be Nuri al-Hamid. I think he's a vice president. But who knows? He could have retired by now or even when we did the deal. I don't think he worked full time at the company."

"But does it or has it ever occurred to you that this man, a Lebanese citizen, very probably has or had political affiliations, some of which may be inimical to British interests?"

Craw had no answer to that. The ensuing silence was only mitigated by the happy chirps of small birds in the garden enjoying the puddles created by the water sprinklers. An air conditioner hummed from a distant windowed corner of the room.

Perkins, irritated by Craw's non-answer, asked, "Well Mr. Craw?"

Craw breathed in heavily. He threw the pencil down on his notepad. "We are friends, for heaven's sake. Our friendship goes back to Westminster where we went to school. Then Oxford, together. So what if he gets into the weeds of politics. What businessman doesn't?"

"But that's my point. If he's politically involved, then how would you know that trusting him implicitly, shall we say, was a non-starter? In other words, he could well be susceptible to anti-British sentiments or pressures and he could, perhaps just on some social occasion, have revealed that he had let this apparently unsalable and unrentable house to a member of the British secret service. It could have even been revealed as a joke: 'Who'd have thought we could unload that old ruin at such a hefty rent?'"

"The rent was not hefty. Quite reasonable, in my opinion."

"How much?"

Craw realized he was under oath. "The equivalent of fifteen thousand pounds sterling a month. But remember, there were twelve bedrooms in all."

"Some uninhabitable, I am told." With that, Perkins banged the gavel and called for a break.

The interrogators moved to one end of the room, the chief witnesses toward the french windows and out to the garden. Even though it was to be another hot day, the colors of the tropical flowers and the ample shade thrown by the sprawling low-branched cedars invited them to linger. But after just ten minutes, a small bell tinkled, and everyone moved back to take their seats.

Sergeant Leonard Pitt of the Diplomatic Protection Command was called as second witness. Pitt, dressed in a light-gray Burton suit, a dark-blue shirt and a black-and-white-polka-dot tie, looked uncomfortable and hot. In recent months he had worn only army fatigues and casual combat wear, and he was not feeling comfortable in civvies.

"You may take off your jacket," said Perkins.

"Thank you, sir," said Pitt, who then repeated the oath.

"We understand that you were appointed a sort of general factotum to the occupants of the safe house in the Achrafieh district of Beirut. Is that right?"

"Well, sir, I don't know quite what you mean by *factotum*. I was sent there to guard the gentlemen, to provide security. But, yes, I kept house a bit, tidying up, sometimes cooking the odd meal."

"Yes, quite. Mr. Austen?"

Andy Austen had been scribbling some notes with an ancient Waterman fountain pen with a glistening eighteen-carat gold nib. He looked up, apparently surprised at Perkins' sudden decision to turn over Pitt's questioning so quickly to him. In Austen's mind, such supporting characters in a cast of major witnesses often yielded, sometimes unconsciously, key facts that could throw a different light on the whole murky situation.

He looked up from his notes and adjusted his bifocal horn-rimmed glasses. Then he fished a small dictionary out of his jacket pocket. He flipped through the pages. "Here we are: *factotum* means simply 'a man of all work, servant managing his master's affairs.' That at any rate is *The Oxford English Dictionary*'s definition."

Pitt nodded. "My primary duty was that of protection, sir."

"A duty in which you woefully failed. Is that not so?"

Vaux interjected. "That's a completely unjustified remark. Pitt and I were outnumbered—and without his covering me during the incident, I wouldn't be alive today. Sergeant Pitt was badly injured in the exchange with the gunmen. That's why his arm is in a sling."

"Order, order!" exclaimed Perkins. "Mr. Vaux, please do not again interrupt the proceedings. You will have your chance to speak when called."

Austen looked sheepish and signaled to the chairman that he had nothing to add. Perkins then invited questions from Vauxhall's William Pym.

"Sergeant Pitt, you are to be commended for your brave stand against the terrorists. I think you performed your duties commendably. I want to move on. Did you at any time suspect that the safe house was, shall we say, loosely organized, badly conceived even, or that the old derelict mansion was basically very insecure from many points of view?"

"Well, I realized that I had quite a job, really. I could have done with some backup. Looking back, I do see that we were kind of sitting ducks if anyone caught on that a group of undercover British agents were using the old house as an HQ, like."

"And who would you hold responsible for your basic inability, given your 'establishment' strength of one valiant protector, to defend the safe house from an assault of the kind that eventually occurred?"

Pitt looked at Vaux, then Craw. "Well, sir, I can't blame anyone in particular. A safe house was needed for their special project here, and Mr. Craw found this place, which seemed ideal at the time."

"Yes, but I put it to you that it was a contradiction in terms: there was nothing safe about this safe house!"

With that quip, Andy Austen took off his spectacles and closed the pocket *Oxford Dictionary* with a clap that, despite the book's small size, resonated throughout the room.

Perkins announced an hour break for lunch—sandwiches and soft drinks would be served at the bar. Witnesses and staff gravitated to the garden. Ms. Sheridan was happy to sit at the far corner of the room where the air conditioner rattled loudly to produce weak waves of tepid air.

* * *

Anthony Mansfield, MI6's station chief in Beirut, was confident that the internal inquiry could only bolster his standing among his peers in the intelligence community. For one thing, he had known Bill Pym for more than a decade, and they had often been on the same side in turf battles within the power spheres of Vauxhall Cross. He had never met Andy Austen or John Perkins, but as professionals, he was confident that they would favor his views against those of Department B3's amateurs.

"Mr. Mansfield, you are station chief of MI6's operations in Beirut and in greater Lebanon. Is that correct?" asked Perkins.

"Yes, sir."

"Can you explain to us, as briefly as possible, your relationship with the personnel of Department B3— in reference to cooperation and the integration of your joint endeavors here in one of the principal espionage theaters of the Middle East?"

Mansfield blanched at what he considered a vague if apposite question. He stroked his chin and pushed the small Bible away from him. "These people were sent here by the DG because he assumed they would constitute a sort of striking force that could zero into the big problem we have had here—the presence of an undetected mole who, over the last eighteen months or so, has blown some of our most critical missions, not to mention caused the loss of life among several of our key subagents."

"Yes, but I asked about cooperation. My intuition tells me that perhaps your relationship with B3 personnel has not always been conducive to a successful outcome of your endeavors."

"Intuition?" Mansfield looked around the room in a silent protest for some adherence to hard facts. "I'm not sure I know what you are getting at, sir. The B3 team is very small. It's headed by Michael Vaux, a nonprofessional freelance who is hired sporadically by B3's chief Sir Nigel Adair to conduct certain operations that are farmed out by our people at Vauxhall Cross."

Vauxhall's Bill Pym took his cue. "I think what the chairman is getting at is this: Have your joint efforts been at all successful or at least satisfying to you who, after all, are station chief here?"

"Well, the bottom line is that our mole is still in operation. So from that point of view, we have not made much headway. Meanwhile, our efforts have been slowed by various untoward incidents—"

"Untoward incidents?" asked the FCO's Andy Austen.

"Well, yes. B3's man Greene was abducted off the street—just like that." Mansfield snapped his thumb and finger in midair. "We got him out of the presumed Hezbollah hideaway, however. But it was bad tradecraft that got him kidnapped in the first place."

"But wasn't it Vaux with Sergeant Pitt who tracked them down?" asked Pym.

"Yes, indeed. But we cooperated together, obviously."

Vaux and Pitt exchanged glances.

"So the rescue party, as it were, consisted solely of B3 personnel while your team monitored their efforts. Is that it?" asked the chairman.

"That's about it," said Mansfield.

"And how would you describe your relationship with the B3 people? One of our remits here, you see, is to find out whether these joint efforts or programs are working effectively," said Perkins.

"Yes. We all get along fine."

"Let's move on. Bill—you're up."

MI6's William Pym quickly put aside a sheet of typewritten paper he had been studying. "We understand that you decided to wire the safe house. Was that a precaution against the very thing that eventually occurred? The terrorist raid, I mean—the fracas that resulted in our late colleague Sebastian Micklethwait's unfortunate death?"

"Yes, indeed."

"It had nothing to do with Mr. Alan Craw's claim that you were eavesdropping on B3 personnel out of a megalomaniacal desire to know what was going on there in the safe house...what plans were being hatched etcetera?"

Mansfield's calm posture was somewhat shaken. "When did Craw allege that? I never heard such an allegation. It is totally false." He looked around the room, but Craw, his duty served, had left.

The chairman answered: "In view of his flu, we deposed him at his hotel on our first day here. It didn't come up this morning, but it's part of the record now. However, I want to pursue one more point before we break for tea. I am looking for potential security leaks, you see. May I ask who you ordered to wire the safe house?"

Mansfield knew this was his Achilles' heel. For several days now, he had wondered why Citron had not been in contact. The deal had always been that he should talk with him on a daily basis. "One of my most trusted agents, sir. A long-time senior member of our network here—the M network, M for *mosque*. My ace in the hole so far as HUMINT is concerned."

"Ah! In other words an Arab, a Muslim, eh?"

"Well, yes, sure. Our own people can't go into the souks or the mosques and mix with the variegated groups that constitute Lebanese society. For one thing, very few of us speak fluent or local Arabic, let alone the Levantine dialect of same."

"Yes, but the operation—your scheme to bug the old house, would have exposed the very function of the establishment to potential foes. Is that not possible?"

"If you are questioning the integrity of my chief sub-agent—an asset who has been in my service for several years—I would say that no, it's not possible that my bugging operation in any way endangered the security of our colleagues."

Andy Austin raised his finger and Perkins gave a permissive nod. "Did it ever occur to you that such a job affecting the security of a top-secret safe house would be better carried out by our own people? Special Forces have a small contingent here, for example, and then there's the Diplomatic Protection Group, of which witness Sergeant Pitt is a member.

"With all due respect, sir, I am in the secret service, emphasis on *secret*. It would never do to expose any safe house to the general military establishment or, for that matter, to the Protection Group. Their personnel have not been vetted to the extent required by us in the SIS. So I never even considered using such insecure outfits," said Mansfield in a tone of finality.

The chairman echoed Mansfield's impatience with the loud bang of his gavel. The meeting was adjourned for afternoon tea and rock cakes.

* * *

Michael Vaux was sworn in. John Perkins led the questions. "Mr. Vaux. I understand that Sir Nigel Adair has often in the past asked you to serve queen and country in what we could call 'Special Projects.' Is that not so?"

"Yes, that's right."

"And your remit here is to ferret out the mole, as it were?"

Vaux gave a nod.

"Please speak up. It's for the record."

"Yes, that's our goal: to find the cause of the many leaks that have plagued this particular MI6 station."

"So far, I understand, you haven't met with much success. Is that correct?"

"We are making progress, sir."

"Good, good. Now I want to cut straight to this disturbing business of the compromised safe house. Were you at any time aware that the residence had been wired by our own people?"

"Not until well after the fact—when I learned that Mr. Mansfield's assistant, Browne, had raised the alarm following the shoot-out—because, thanks to the taps, he had heard all the commotion within the house. Of course, it was too late to help us. By the time a bus load of armed Protection Group personnel showed up, the danger had passed."

"Yes, but they did help save Sergeant Pitt's life, did they not, by the rapid transfer to the hospital?"

"I had managed to stop the bleeding myself. But obviously, he needed special medical attention."

"Where was he taken for that medical attention?"

"To the Hotel Dieu de France, I was told."

"Of course, we must recall the tragedy of young Micklethwait. I understand he was shot in the head at point-blank range?"

"No, no. It was a sharpshooter who fired from the grounds. Micklethwait was standing on the balcony. I was seated on the balustrade, and he stood looking down to the front gardens and the gate. I didn't know what had happened until I saw him collapse suddenly. Although I did see a red blotch spread slowly on his forehead just before he fell."

"So you never actually heard the shot?"

"No, the sniper must have been using a suppressed rifle of some sort."

"A tragedy, indeed."

"Yes."

"Were there any fatalities or injuries on the enemy's side?"

"Yes. I shot and killed the presumed leader of the group as he came into the room firing his AK-47 indiscriminately and wounding Sergeant Pitt."

"Was he with the members of his team at that point in time?"

"There were three of them. As soon as the leader kicked down the door, his partner ran upstairs looking for other likely victims, I suppose. The third man I saw approach the house after Micklethwait was hit must have remained outside, probably as a look-out."

"And did the presumed leader say anything or shout any words, so to speak, while the battle was underway?"

"Yes. He cursed us for killing his son."

"Really? Did you know what he was talking about?"

"I had no idea," said Vaux coldly.

MI6's Bill Pym received a silent signal from Perkins to take over. "Mr. Vaux. Your reputation precedes you. You are held in high regard at Vauxhall even though you may not realize it."

The compliment was met with a murmur around the room, but Vaux found it difficult to analyze: Was it out of shock or approval?

"And you have no idea how the enemy discovered the nature of your work or the purpose of the residence where you stayed with your colleagues—Greene and our late colleague Sebastian Micklethwait—and of course Sergeant Pitt?"

"No idea."

"Did Alan Craw, your senior at B3 ever reside in the safe house?"

"He visited us often. But Mr. Craw stayed at the Phoenicia. That was his preference."

Bill Pym yielded to the FCO's Andrew Austen. "Mr. Vaux. I want you to answer yes or no to the following question: When you found out the whereabouts of the kidnappers' hideout, did you ask Mansfield and/or the embassy for armed back up?"

"No. I thought we could be on a wild goose chase, and I didn't think it would be helpful to show up with a conspicuous convoy of military trucks and personnel. I wanted a small, quiet team to do the job."

"Yes, but you could well have been overwhelmed by their defenses, and you could have got all three of you—Pitt, you, and Greene—killed in the process, or at the very least taken as hostages. Or in Greene's case, of course, *retaken* as hostage."

"Hindsight is twenty-twenty. Under the circumstances, my decision to go it alone worked out pretty well."

"And, for the record, it was just you and Pitt who freed Greene."

Vaux nodded.

"Speak up, please. We need this for the record."

"Yes, just the two of us."

"Were there any injuries sustained by the terrorists who guarded Greene?"

"We had to eliminate the young guard, of course. But we got lucky in that he was the sole sentry. Pitt was skillful with the cosh. We found Greene in a basement cell while his presumed captors were partying in a room on the main floor looking at television and smoking hashish."

A titter ambled around the big room. "What method did you employ to knock out the guard?"

"As I said, Sergeant Pitt used a simple cosh."

"So the guard is alive today—he could identify both of you."

"I don't think so. We were wearing hoodies."

Pym smiled indulgently and yielded back to the chairman.

"I declare this session closed. We shall gather again tomorrow morning at ten a.m. in the same place. My first witness will be Ambassador Eccles. But I advise all former witnesses to be in attendance for any supplementary questions the inquiry may have. Thanks, everybody."

Chapter 30

Four days after the conclusion of the internal inquiry, all the parties concerned in Operation Triple Cross agreed that the following Monday would be designated F-Day.

At a long session with case officers and senior MI6 operatives on the eve of the great day, Vaux chaired a meeting in the embassy's large conference room. The long rosewood table had been moved back to its historic position, and all traces of the inquiry had been cleaned away, including the audio systems, the board members' notepads and the chairman's gavel.

"Our task is to advertise as widely as we can the disinformation data I shall outline for you in the simplest terms. Please take notes and remember, the news has to spread like wildfire from here to all your contacts, all individual network assets, all informers, and where possible to the local police authorities including the ISF and our own protection group, CIA officials" (here Vaux acknowledged

Alex Mailer's presence with a nod) "even the Special Forces contingent at the US embassy. Plus our entire embassy staff, including domestics and humble clerks and gardeners. Have I left anyone out?"

Mike Stevens, the underemployed cryptologist from Bletchley Park, put his hand up. "What about the other embassies? I've noticed very heavy signals traffic from the French mission here. Also, the Saudi Arabian legation."

"You have a point. But I think the more we spread our efforts, the less likely we'll be able to pinpoint the source of our leaks. So let's just concentrate on the United States and the limeys," said Vaux.

The remark produced a snicker from the US representatives, prompting Vaux to address Mailer directly. "All your monitoring systems are ready to go, Alex?"

Mailer and Vaux knew that conventional monitoring—listening in on cell phone and radio conversations, tapping land lines, opening official and nonofficial mail, intercepts of telex messages and e-mails—was one, perhaps two legs of the stool. But the third—that was the secret weapon nobody else knew was about to be employed for the big hunt. The signals expert from Cairo, one of the CIA's privileged team who had pioneered the breakthrough StingRay technology, sat opposite Vaux, his bland face and indifferent attitude betraying no special or specific knowledge about the imminent field testing of the new GPS mobile phone tracing abilities.

Mailer replied with a curt "Yep."

"OK. So here's the story. Each of you will receive a typewritten précis of the false intelligence material. But I'll summarize it now as best I can. Here is the fiction that has to be spread far and wide: let it be known that the Brits have been approached by a high-ranking officer of the Hezbollah organization operating in the south of the country, close to the Israeli border.

"The man who uses the alias of Amneh Dagher is soon to be sent by Hezbollah command to Tehran to negotiate a new arms deal with Iran. Once there, he plans to defect to the US side via the auspices of the Canadian embassy because, as you surely know, there is no current US diplomatic presence in Tehran. He plans to bring all sorts of intelligence material with him. We're talking about Hezbollah's military strength—weapons inventories, manpower, arms caches, base camps, long-term strategic plans plus tactical programs like cross-border attacks and skirmishes into Israel.

"This is the short but sweet message we have to get out to the wide world outside these walls. It can be memorized—it's brief enough—and you all can be as loose lipped as you want—within the bounds of credibility, obviously. So whether it's to your 'joe' out there or to the ambassador himself, we want this disinformation to get out as fast as possible."

"When do we get the green light?" asked Pete Browne.

"Release date is midnight tonight."

"What is the defector's motivation, sir?" This from a young, rosy-cheeked case officer Vaux had never seen before.

"Freedom and money."

* * *

That evening Vaux made a courtesy call on Alan Craw at his big suite at the Phoenicia Hotel. He found him lying languidly on the silk chaise longue that faced the big-screen television, dressed in one of the hotel's complimentary navy-blue terrycloth bathrobes, his long feet clad in white cotton flip-flops.

Vaux quickly glanced at the big screen and saw two naked young men sharing a bathtub. It was Jude Law and Matt Damon, enjoying the delights of living in a grand baroque villa in Ischia. Craw promptly pressed the remote's off button. He seemed to think an explanation was required. "*The Talented Mr. Ripley*—terrific film. Did you ever see it?"

"I read the book."

"Sorry, couldn't make it to your briefing session, Vaux. Still recovering from the bloody flu. And besides, I couldn't face seeing that infernal internal inquiry team again. They really get on my wick—all words and no action. No sympathy or consideration for us at the sharp end."

Vaux wondered how exactly Craw defined the sharp end. "They have to do their job, I suppose. Anyway, here's the briefing notes. Short and sweet." Vaux handed Craw the outline of the disinformation plan. Craw stretched over to a side table where he had left his Gucci half-moon reading glasses. It seemed to Vaux that he read the notes twice, his lips moving slightly as he parsed the words.

"Excellent. I hope it works, that's all. It's our last desperate move, I suppose. If this doesn't work, what will?"

"I'm pinning everything on the new StingRay technology the CIA came up with. Mailer's been very cooperative, by the way."

"Yes, well, he should be. Who's going to monitor the signals traffic that this little billet-doux should spark?"

"We've set up a joint operation that will operate out of the CIA's complex at the US embassy. They'll be in direct contact with me and their own chase teams. As soon as we get the green light that indicates the source, we'll shoot hell for leather from every angle of the city. One advantage we have is that Beirut's a compact city."

"Yes, well, my next task is to call old Sir Nigel and brief him on what we're doing. You haven't spoken to him, I assume."

"No. I hope you're using the fully encrypted mobile."

"Don't teach your grandmother how to suck eggs, Vaux." Craw got up with a moan and walked unsteadily over to his briefcase. He fished out the replica of a conventional cell phone and punched in some numbers. He looked at his watch to check that the two-hour time difference should mean that Sir Nigel was still up and about.

Vaux moved to the small bar, took down a half-filled bottle of J&B, and poured himself a large one. He had one more task he promised himself he would complete before retiring to the Radisson.

Craw's conversation was short, and while Vaux hovered around him, prepared to answer any questions the chief could raise, Craw suddenly hung up. "Said he was in no mood to talk. Has to get up early tomorrow morning for poor young Micklewait's memorial service. Private affair. The old grandmother, who used to work on one of Turing's teams many moons ago, is to attend. Must be in her nineties. The old man's too emotional to talk, so we got nowhere, really. He says to say hello."

Vaux said, "This is going to be an emotional evening. Could I use the phone to contact Anne? I owe her a call and I should check up on the health of her old man."

"Be my guest," replied Craw, reluctant to be reminded of the rivalry with Vaux for the heart of Department B3's dashingly beautiful girl Friday.

Vaux listened closely as the phone rang only twice at Anne's home in Hatch End, a few miles north-west of central London.

"Oh, darling, I've been so worried—"

"Why?" asked Vaux, knowing the answer before he asked.

"You haven't called for well over ten days, Mike!"

"Sorry, Anne. I've been terribly busy and preoccupied. You can imagine."

"When are we going to see each other?"

"Very soon, I hope. I'm due for at least a long weekend, so just count the days. It won't be long. How's your father, by the way?"

"I saw the doctor yesterday. He says he could go any minute. He sleeps a lot, poor dear."

"You know I can't talk too much over the line. But I promise to speak to you before the end of the week. Love you, darling."

"Love you, too," said Anne, as always, frustrated by the brevity of the infrequent chats with the man in her life.

Vaux went through the usual routine: the Walther P99 was placed deftly in the tray while he passed through the metal detectors. A nod to the desk clerk who put the handgun into a bubble envelope and then up the five floors to room 501.

As the elevator doors closed silently behind him, he turned and saw a man sitting on the thick carpeted floor, his back to the wall and legs stretched out. Before he could think about any defensive action, he recognized the slim figure of Sergeant Pitt.

"Pitt! What are you doing here?"

"Just a brief visit, sir. Something on my mind, like."

"Come on in."

They entered a chilly room, and Vaux switched the air conditioning monitor to off. "What's up?" he asked as he made his way to the small minibar. He extracted two cans of Heineken.

"It's this business of the official inquiry, sir."

"Yes, what about it? It's over now, I hope."

"Yeah, but didn't we both commit perjury—I think it's called that when you tell a lie under oath, sir? I can go to jail for that."

"Oh Christ, Pitt. We lied to protect your Arab friend, Sami. If we had said that he was with us—an irregular, unofficial helper, paid for his efforts with embassy cash—and that he did the dirty work on someone who turned out to be the cell commander's son, he'd have been well and truly in the shit. Court martialed and probably shot at dawn if for no other reason than helping the enemy. You know as well as I do that the Lebanese forces don't regard us or the Americans as allies. No matter what we do to help them regroup and reconstruct after their bloody civil war and the Israeli bombardments, they'll never see us as friends."

"Yeah, but we were under oath, sir."

Vaux went over to Pitt who was looking out the big picture window at Beirut's sparkling nightscape. He put a hand gently on the shoulder that had been injured, and he could feel the gauze that still covered the cotton dressing. "Look, Pitt. There are times in this life when a white lie harms no one and probably saves a lot of pain and grief. Sami will be OK now. His family will not be broken asunder by legal maneuvers and shenanigans to get him punished and locked away, even shot, for killing a member of the Hez.

"Yeah, but—"

"No 'yeah, buts.' We did the right thing. Now go back and get some sleep."

Pitt took a long pull of the beer, shook Vaux's hand, and said he'd see him tomorrow.

Chapter 31

Around six o'clock the next morning, Sergeant Leonard Pitt parked his black Range Rover in the small courtyard outside Vaux's hotel. He had called from his cell phone, and Vaux said he would be down in five minutes. He knew it would be more like fifteen minutes by the time he had a quick shower and a shave and collected his Walther at the front desk.

"Let's go," said Vaux as Pitt pushed the starter. Pitt looked straight ahead and sighed with impatience as they waited to push into the solid flow of oncoming traffic.

"Morning rush hour in Beirut starts at dawn and is as chaotic as Athens and as noisy as Cairo," observed Vaux.

"I wouldn't know, sir, not having been to either place. But Limehouse and the docklands get pretty busy, too."

"Word is out, I presume," said Vaux.

"Sorry?"

"They should have given the green light to Operation Triple Cross, Pitt. Midnight was the embargo release date. That's what we are all about today."

"And maybe tomorrow. How long do you think this is going to take, sir? To flush the bastard out, I mean, if you'll excuse the language."

"I haven't a clue. But the whole idea is that the news should come as such a bombshell that the lines will start buzzing in no time. The spies and informers will be shouting from the roof tops, the cell phone lines will be inundated, and tongues will wag for hours. At least, that's the hope. That's why we'll be on the case, Pitt, from now until some malevolent mole bites the bait. I don't think it's going to take too long."

Sergeant Pitt would always remember those words in the early hours of the first day of Operation Triple Cross, for they turned out to be uncannily prophetic.

They drove south on the wide Rue Fakhr ed Dine freeway toward the British embassy complex. Vaux had decided that the area was as good a place as any to launch the listening operation. He would be in constant communication with the CIA's monitoring team and could only wait for the message that would pinpoint the location of the elusive double agent. He didn't know where the other patrol cars and their chase teams would be located, but his instinct told him the embassy area would be a good starting point.

Pitt parked close to a derelict bomb site only one hundred yards down the Rue de l'Armee. They sat and waited. Pitt opened a bar of Nestlé's KitKat and offered a stick to Vaux, who shook his head. He adjusted his headset while he listened to the chatter among the various CIA monitors as they listened in to private conversations: a mixture of banter and earnest messages in Arabic, English, and French, spoken, sometimes shouted, by anonymous Beirutis who thought their conversations were secure.

Then through the windshield something caught his eye. He grabbed Pitt's army-issue Steiner 1050 binoculars from the glove box and watched a familiar figure walking briskly toward the imposing National Conservatory of Music building. It was the handsome Hammond Seward, talking animatedly into his cell phone as he dodged traffic and skipped on and off various sidewalks and traffic islands.

"My God" said Vaux. "Perhaps I was wrong. It looks like Chris Greene's suspicions were right all along."

He passed the binoculars back to Pitt who studied the man whom Greene had suspected of being the double agent in their midst. He recalled Greene's arguments: the man was a potential loose cannon, susceptible to blackmail because of his barefaced gay lifestyle. But Vaux had always argued that Greene was living in the last century. Nobody cared anymore about sexual identity, and therefore, he wasn't a security risk. Pitt had kept quiet about his own feelings, though if he was asked to take sides, he had favored Greene's arguments.

"Well, blow me down. Anything from the listeners?"

"No. They're basing their monitoring on what they know about previous messages, locations, and patterns. It's complicated. But they obviously can't monitor every cell phone in the city."

"Let me go and grab his phone, sir. That will tell us everything we want to know. We have the right to do that."

"Not so fast, Pitt. But do me a favor: approach him and tell him you're on a routine surveillance job. Ask him to hand over the phone. See what his reaction is."

Pitt was at a loss to know what Vaux meant. But instinctively, he jumped out of the Range Rover, dodged a few horn-blaring cars, and strode toward Seward, who was still talking into the phone as he glanced around at the pedestrians and traffic. Pitt now confronted him, and Vaux saw Seward stop abruptly, put his phone back in the side pocket of his navy-blue blazer, and begin to look increasingly angry. Pitt had his hand out, presumably demanding that Seward produce the phone. Seward was shaking his head, and the two men had clearly reached a stalemate.

Vaux heard the radio crackle. "Suspect is calling from the Horsh area close to the National Museum. Recipient of the call located in the Serail district. Wait a second. Caller is traced to Rue du Musee at the junction with Taleb Hobeich. Informant confirms that's in a district called Badaro, otherwise known as ambassador's row—lots of diplomats live in the luxury high-rises there."

Vaux slammed his fist down on the horn. He saw Pitt look over the wide boulevard toward him, and he signaled him to return quickly. Pitt left Seward in midsentence, and Vaux saw Seward give an indifferent shrug as his eyes watched Pitt run back toward the Range Rover.

By now, the CIA monitor had given Vaux the coordinates. Pitt, settling himself in the driver's seat, fiddled with the GPS. Vaux told him the suspect was walking in the area of the National Museum. "We go south on Ahmad Beyham to Boulevard Saeb Salam, then east on Abdallah El Yafi. We pass the ancient Hippodrome and turn right, south to Rue du Musee. Our man is at the intersection with Taleb Hobeich."

Six of the CIA's cars, driven by co-opted US Special Forces, were fast converging on ground zero, the monitor's term for where the suspect was standing or walking as he talked on his cell phone. The CIA listeners had heard all they needed to know: the double agent had even spelled out the name of the alleged defector— Amneh Dagher.

Vaux saw the figure in the distance. Somebody was sitting on a park bench in a small belvedere that overlooked the large Lebanese cedar forest, known by locals as the Horsh. The tall and slight figure, clad in white, now stood and walked south while still talking into the cell phone.

The Range Rover skidded to a halt on the dusty surface of the road. Vaux jumped out and ran toward the solitary figure who was now walking briskly toward the Military Hospital complex just west of Rue du Musee. Pitt saw Vaux stop abruptly. He shouted something as he drew the Walther out of his side pocket. Then Pitt watched as a scene played out that he would remember for the rest of his long life: the suspect in white had turned to face Vaux defiantly. It was a woman. Her long black hair fell to her shoulders as she took off her blue beret. Pitt would have known that beautiful face anywhere. It was Miranda Eccles, the party-loving wife of the popular British ambassador, John Eccles.

They slowly walked up the Rue du Musee together like a pair of lovers. Pitt had opened the rear door to let her in. Vaux took the handcuffs from him, and they clicked as he secured her wrists. She said nothing as the Range Rover sped toward the British embassy.

Pitt had told the CIA listeners that everything was under control and that the suspect was about to be delivered to the MI6 investigating team.

Vaux was overwhelmed. "Why?" he asked as she looked out to the traffic and the buildings that flashed by.

But she said nothing. She turned to him, tears welling up in her eyes. He offered her a Kleenex from his breast pocket, and with an apologetic, wan smile, she tried to wipe the tears away.

Pitt now saw the fleet of six desert-tan Toyota Land Cruisers of the US Special Forces Command beetling toward them on the opposite side of the road. "Johnny-come-latelys," he muttered.

Vaux closed his eyes in an effort to come to grips with what had happened. Suddenly, they were passing the sentries at the embassy complex. A squad from the protection group waited to escort her to Anthony Mansfield's office.

Chapter 32

The veteran spymasters at Vauxhall Cross had never witnessed such a quick and blatant cover-up. Anthony Mansfield grabbed wads of kudos—a few said justifiably so—for his prompt handling of the immediate crisis and the lightning removal of the current ambassador to Lebanon. But the tongue-waggers knew very well that he could not have done it all himself.

Michael Vaux, who brought her in, was summarily dismissed as soon as he informed Mansfield of the undiluted success of Operation Triple Cross. Mansfield had questioned Miranda Eccles for two hours. Sandwiches and coffee were sent in. No recording devices were employed, and Peter Browne, his deputy, was kept out of the loop by Mansfield's insistence that he accompany Vaux back to the hotel and stay there—as a precautionary and defensive move. Sergeant Pitt was ordered to resume his day-to-day duties with the Diplomatic Protection Group.

When Mansfield had heard enough from Miranda Eccles, he called Ambassador Eccles on the encrypted cell phone. Eccles had apparently gone home early to sort through a number of briefs relating to intelligence updates, general security, and upcoming staff requirements. As usual, he had been handed the briefs in the late afternoon by Mansfield, who was fully aware that he took them home to study in the evenings.

Miranda had told him, "I went through his briefs every evening. That's how I knew what was going on. Naturally, I was completely taken in by the hoax. I was alarmed that their people could lose such a senior man to the Americans. It goaded me into very prompt action the following morning—this morning. It was very clever of you, Tony. Or was Vaux behind the ruse?"

"Never mind," replied Mansfield. "But why did your husband not lock the bloody briefs away as soon as he had read them? That's what he is meant to do."

"He kept them in his attaché case in the bedroom. I'm an insomniac, so he never bothered to wake up when I went to the bathroom to scan the material."

"All top secret, I suppose."

"Most, yes. But some were just stamped 'restricted.'"

She's as cool as a cucumber, thought Mansfield.

Eccles arrived, disheveled and worried. He rushed to her arms, and they hugged each other as if they never wanted to let go.

"Please sit," said Mansfield to both of them. "I want you both to go home—just like any other evening. I'm sure you haven't had dinner yet. Just act normally while I find out what my superiors want me to do. That's all I can say, John. And please don't do a runner. The Cold War is over, and neither of you has anywhere to go."

Mansfield then called Norbert (Nobby) Clark, his direct boss on the Middle East and North Africa desk. Clark then called Sir Percival Bolton, Director-General of MI6. The conversation was brief. Sir Percival promptly called Sir Nigel Adair, head of Department B3, who followed up with an unsatisfactory call to Alan Craw. It was 10:00 p.m. Beirut time, and he assumed he had caught Craw dozing after a gourmet dinner—if such a luxury was available in Beirut.

The immediate outcome was that on the day after Operation Triple Cross's successful conclusion, the Eccleses were rapidly de-fenestrated—which meant they, with all their family baggage and mementoes from former postings, were put on a London-bound Royal Air Force flight out of Rafiq Hariri International airport at 7:00 a.m. the next day.

Weeks later, the news was quietly but definitively broadcast that Eccles had been let go to pursue other interests and that his wife remained with him and supported his latest career move to set up a new blues band in Brighton, Sussex.

"But what was her motive?" asked Vaux over a beer with Tony Mansfield in the crepuscular depths of the Checkpoint Charlie bar.

"She told me that she held the Israelis responsible for her daughter's death in the south. The tragedy was close to the border, and for some weeks, there had been skirmishes and rocket attacks—Israelis firing on Hezbollah militants who reciprocated in kind. The school bus was blown up by an eighty-two-millimeter Israeli RPG-7 shoulder-launched missile. Of course, she didn't choose to believe the Israeli claim that many of their armaments were purloined by the terrorists. So her young daughter's death was the spark that triggered her treachery, old man. There's always a motive in these unfortunate betrayals."

"But how does that lead to helping and assisting the militias and the private sectarian armies?"

"She wanted to hit back at Israel. She thought that by helping these Muslim groups, whether the Hez or Hamas, she was helping the enemies of Israel."

"Well, I suppose she had a point."

"Yeah, but it's a great loss for us. Eccles was an excellent man, and she was very popular—what with her good looks and ebullient personality."

Vaux looked at Mansfield with surprise, never having heard such praise when the Eccles couple were enjoying their halcyon days. "So there's to be no prosecution or reverberations of any sort?" asked Vaux.

"How could there be? For one thing we never ask the wives of diplomats to sign the Official Secrets Act, so her only offense is disloyalty. And she never divulged any information to foreign governments or their agents—only to these guerilla-type groups. So no legal action is to be taken. Everything to be nicely swept under the carpet. Can't afford another spy scandal, can we?"

Vaux picked up his glass. "Here's to the happy couple, then."

Mansfield hesitated. He thought the toast inappropriate. But he nodded and raised his glass in silent homage to Eccles, a man he had grown to like.

But Vaux was still curious. "Who was she phoning when her call was detected? We finally dealt with the leaker, but what about her contact?"

"Who knows? A militant of some sort—Hezbollah, presumably. We didn't even bother to follow that angle up. What's the point? We never would have found him."

Vaux finally looked satisfied. But Mansfield now nursed an unanswered question. "So since we are tidying everything up, crossing the *T*s and dotting the *I*s, may I now ask you where that ex gratia payment of three thousand US dollars ended up? Not, I presume, in the safe house's general housekeeping account, now conveniently dissolved?"

Sami Hakroush, the happy recipient of the confidential helper's fee, now flashed in Vaux's fast-fading memories of Operation Cedar. "I know nothing about it. But Pitt assured me it went to a very good cause."

* * *

Ten days later Michael Vaux alighted from Sir Nigel Adair's official armored Jaguar XJ onto his long paved driveway. Sir Nigel had told his chauffeur to pick him up at Heathrow and drive him wherever he wanted to go. Vaux wanted nothing more than to go home.

Inside, the house smelled of dampness, and the early autumn staleness of decaying leaves and wet grass permeated the bungalow. He went through to the kitchen, and here a pungent dank odor rose from the drains. He turned on the taps and was relieved to see no dead insects in the kitchen sink. Then he opened the glass doors of the welsh dresser where he found a half-full bottle of Cutty Sark. He grabbed a crystal tumbler and poured himself a large one.

He went through to the lounge and could see the neglected lawn through the french windows. Crabgrass and denuded dandelions had invaded the green swath of early summer's neatly trimmed lawn, and he wondered why John, his part-time gardener, had neglected to keep things in shape. Perhaps he was ill? He sat down on the long leather couch and ripped open the manila envelope the official chauffeur had given him. It was marked "Private and Confidential" at the top of the envelope and rubber-stamped "Restricted" at the bottom.

The A4 typewritten note summarized the findings of the official internal inquiry into the death of Sebastian Micklethwait. The major findings were bulleted at the top of the main text:

* The inquiry finds that the death of Sebastian Micklethwait was directly caused by a 7.62 x 39 mm bullet fired by an AK-47 rifle from a range of about thirty yards (hospital records appended).

* The sharpshooter was a member of a three-man terrorist squad that embarked on a planned assault on the safe house and its occupants.

* Security at the safe house was problematic. Listening devices had been installed, linking the residence with MI6 monitoring locations. The purpose of the eavesdropping exercise remains unresolved. MI6 station chief Mansfield claims it was for security reasons. But the occupants (B3

operatives) were not informed that the residence had been wired.

* The gun battle that ensued in the wake of Micklethwait's shooting resulted in the death of the leading terrorist and a mild injury to a member of the Diplomatic Protection Group (hospital records appended). The marksman and the driver of the get-away vehicle escaped apprehension.

CONCLUSION: Basic security norms were ill-observed. No guard(s) or lookout had been appointed because the B3 operatives had not thought it necessary. The old abandoned mansion had been rented to Mr. Alan Craw, deputy director of Department B3, via a former college connection who is of Lebanese birth and citizenship and who was not vetted under basic security guidelines.

The fact that the listening devices/interception operation/ installation was organized by one of Mansfield's senior local subagents whose location is not now known (according to Mansfield) only adds to our conviction that a major security breach occurred when local operatives were employed in place of British personnel (see Recommended Practices Manual, 1980).

Vaux threw the document on the glass-topped side table. Then the phone rang.

"Michael! You got home all right?"

It was Anne. "I thought you might have called into the office on your way, darling."

"Sorry. I just wanted to get home. I was exhausted."

"Did the driver give you the internal inquiry doc?"

"Yes. I've just read the summary. Looks like Mansfield could be in for the high jump."

"I don't know. But what I do know is that I'm coming down to see you this weekend, darling. Is that all right?"

"What about your father?"

"He's fine. The nurse will stay over."

"Wonderful. Can't wait to see you."

"Did you like the CD I sent you?"

"Loved it," lied Vaux. "The Duke's my favorite."

He wondered now where he had stashed the unopened gift. Probably along with the little but treasured black book under the base of his leather holdall.

After Anne rang off, Vaux listened carefully for about thirty seconds. He heard the familiar click that Department B3's antiquated monitoring apparatus always produced. He smiled, finished off his whiskey, and fell asleep.

* * *

ABOUT THE
AUTHOR

Roger Croft is a former journalist whose reports and features have appeared in numerous publications including *The Economist, Sunday Telegraph* and *Toronto Star.* He also worked in Egypt where he freelanced and wrote editorials for Cairo's *Egyptian Gazette.*

Visit: www.rogercroft.com

Made in the USA
Lexington, KY
23 December 2017